The
FALLEN
SHIP

Rise of the Gia Rebellion

Mark Wayne McGinnis
and
Kim McGinnis

Other Books By MWM

Scrapyard Ship Series
Scrapyard Ship (Book 1)
HAB 12 (Book 2)
Space Vengeance (Book 3)
Realms of Time (Book 4)
Craing Dominion (Book 5)
The Great Space (Book 6)
Call To Battle (Book 7)

Tapped In Series
Mad Powers (Book 1)
Deadly Powers (Book 2)

Lone Star Renegades Series
Lone Star Renegades (also called
   'Jacked') (Book 1)

Star Watch Series
Star Watch (Book 1)
Ricket (Book 2)
Boomer (Book 3)
Glory for Space Sea and Space
   (Book 4)
Space Chase (Book 5)
Scrapyard LEGACY (Book 6)

The Simpleton Series
The Simpleton (Book 1)
The Simpleton Quest (Book 2)

Galaxy Man Series
Galaxy Man (Book 1)

Ship Wrecked Series
Ship Wrecked (Book 1)
Ship Wrecked II (Book 2)
Ship Wrecked III (Book 3)

Boy Gone Series
Boy Gone Book 1

Cloudwalkers
Cloudwalkers

The Hidden Ship
The Hidden Ship

Guardian Ship
Guardian Ship

Gun Ship
Gun Ship

Hover
Hover

USS Hamilton Series

USS Hamilton – Ironhold Station
(USS Hamilton Series Book 1)
USS Hamilton – Miasma Burn
(USS Hamilton Series Book 2)
USS Hamilton – Broadsides
(USS Hamilton Series Book 3)
USS Jefferson – Charge of the
Symbios (USS Hamilton Series
Book 4)
Starship Oblivion – Sanctuary
Outpost (USS Hamilton
Series Book 5)

**HEROES and
ZOMBIES Series**

HEROES and ZOMBIES —
Escape to Black Canyon
(Series Book 1)

The Test Pilot's Wife
The Test Pilot's Wife

Published by: Avenstar Productions
Paperback ISBN: 978-1-7372475-9-3

To join Mark's mailing list, jump to:
http://eepurl.com/bs7M9r

Visit Mark Wayne McGinnis at:
http://www.markwaynemcginnis.com

Chapter 1

B&B Café, Castle Rock, Colorado
Sam Dale

Sam Dale sat at his regular table, a still-steaming cup of black coffee warming his right hand. Dressed in blue jeans, a heavy red flannel shirt, and well-worn work boots, Sam could easily have been taken for a construction worker, or perhaps a hunter who'd just returned from a run up in the mountains but, oddly enough, had found time to shave and swipe a brush across his longish brown hair.

At just over six foot tall and one hundred and eighty-five pounds, there was nothing all that noticeable about him. That is until you took a second or third look. It was something akin to confidence, but it was more than that. Perhaps it was resoluteness of movement. Something that could not be practiced or taught. It was something that just arrived one day after years of one's body being pushed to its very limits of endurance, strength, and level of skill. A cohesion of too many different factors to put a name to—but when you saw it and sensed it, you knew enough to leave it be. To not poke the bear.

There are few that have had the honor of achieving what is

necessary to become a Green Beret. Even fewer that have been honored with both a Medal of Honor and a Purple Heart. Sam Dale just happened to be one of those few. Thus, small-town notoriety. A notoriety Sam neither wanted nor exploited. He'd just as soon leave all that back in Kabul, or Kandahar, or Lashkar Gah.

Sam took pride in his progress. The sessions had helped. Helped him to not be that proverbial bear. To know his *triggers*. To shed his warrior persona. And for the most part, Sam was that everyday, good-natured, likable kind of guy. The one you'd want as your neighbor or friend to grab a beer with down at the local watering hole.

So accustomed was he to the early morning noises within the B&B Café, he no longer noticed them—dishes being stacked, flatware tumbling into respective plastic bins, kitchen help prepping for the imminent morning rush.

This was Sam's favorite time of the day. Time when he wasn't required to directly interface with other people. A manila folder sat open on the oak-top table with a stack of printouts of last week's financials. After a year—approximately how long he'd been back here in Castle Rock—his businesses were doing better, but still not out of the woods yet. For the hundredth time, he asked himself why he had purchased them. *But I know why.*

As he was bringing his cup up for a sip, the overhead lights flickered—the cash register drawer suddenly dinged and flew open. A chorus of voices united, yelling out, "Solar flare!"

They'd been occurring somewhat regularly for three months now. And not just here in Castle Rock, but around the world. *Solar flares!* Had become the universally good-natured hail out to all humankind, the universe, or maybe God. They had been hypothesized as some kind of atmospheric electrical influences—anomalies that NASA had first attributed to solar events, while, of late, the scientific community was not so sure they could be explained so easily.

Two tables over, a group of five men, a little loud and rowdy for 6:20 a.m., were being seated by Harper. Sam's concentration was being tested as she tried to get through their drink orders.

"I like your Café T-shirt, sweetheart. The way the B&B letters line up with your…uh, attributes."

They all laughed at that, including Harper—although her laugh was obviously forced.

Sam felt their eyes settle on him. Notice him for the first time. But it was more than that—and it didn't let up. The notoriety seemed to follow him wherever he went. At least here in Castle Rock, people, on seeing him, would lean into one another, suddenly speaking in low tones. Sam was indifferent to it. He'd never been one to let others' opinions of him much matter. He wasn't here for them.

"Coffees all around, guys?" Harper asked. "Anyone want orange juice, grapefruit—"

Another of the Neanderthals blurted out, "Nah…those are most definitely not B's…C's…yeah, most definitely C-cups."

Sam let his eyes stray from his columned Excel printout over to the other table. He listened to their broken English. He tried to place their nationality. Five big, beefy guys. All were dressed in a similar fashion. Sure, a kind of uniform, but not one in which there was much consistency. They looked messy. Sloppy. They looked unkempt. For instance, a city employee, such as within the police department or fire department, had a well-defined dress code. You were representing your organization's established, time-honored practices. It was the simple things. Laundered trousers and shirt. No rips, no tears. Or army fatigues that you felt proud to put on each morning. If you were going to represent your department, your business, your country, whatever, you were the walking, talking proxy for that organization. But clearly, White's Plumbing and Electric wasn't concerned about such trivialities.

3

"Come on, guys…the sooner I get through your order, the quicker I can put the ticket into the kitchen."

"Oh, we are needing separate tickets. Leave menus, honey. Come back when we beckon you."

Sam looked up in time to see Harper's anything but gracious expression. They had pushed a button, and it was taking everything she had not to snap back at them. Sam inwardly shrugged. She was a big girl, and a certain amount of this bullshit came with the territory. The last thing she needed was to be further embarrassed by someone sticking his nose in where it didn't belong.

She hesitated at Sam's table. "Sorry, didn't mean to ignore you. You want your usual this morning, Sam?"

"I'm in no rush."

The White's Plumbing and Electric employees had moved on to talking about Harper's backside, which was in perfect view of their table. Sam averted his eyes, seeing her lightly freckled cheeks had gone pink. She said, "Ignore them, Sam," as if knowing what was going through his mind.

He smiled and raised his palms in mock defense. "Hey, I'm just here for coffee and an omelet."

She gave his shoulder a quick squeeze as she hurried off toward the kitchen. She'd never touched him before. It meant nothing—and maybe everything.

Sam ate while studying his reports. He thought about his responsibilities. More than a dozen people were counting on him. He liked them, and he thought they liked him too. They knew him as just Sam—the easy-going boss who never let much get to him. Little did they know. *Triggers.*

Chairs clamored and scraped on floorboards as the White's Plumbing and Electric guys stood and put on jackets and sweatshirts. With a glance over at their table, Sam saw that as messy as the tabletop was, the floor was a disaster. Someone's dropped fork, a spoon, three wadded-up paper napkins, and a saltshaker. A big glob of peasant potatoes was stuck to the table support. Someone, of course, would have to clean up after them. Clean up after these self-absorbed troglodytes whose expectation would be, *Hey…they pay people to clean up that shit.*

Sam checked his watch. He had a lot on his plate today; he needed to get moving. He paid the bill with cash and left a separate folded $20 bill under his empty coffee cup as a tip. He looked for Harper, heading for the door, but didn't spot her.

Outside in the crisp morning air, he breathed in the Colorado morning. The sun was just coming up. Golden light glistened off a row of nearby windshields. Around the side of the building, parked halfway down the block, was Sam's car. A car that just so happened to be parked next to a twenty-year-old, faded blue and white panel van. In oversized lettering, "White's Plumbing and Electric" was emblazoned across its side. And like the guys' rumpled uniforms or the dumpster of a mess left on the restaurant's floor, this van exemplified callousness and indifference. The taking of life's easy shortcuts.

Obviously, they were in no hurry to get to work or to their first job site. Laughing and kibitzing, they were huddled, smoking and talking with exaggerated arm gestures.

All that was fine with Sam. There were times he missed that kind of comradery. But then he saw one guy who was resting his ample left ass cheek on the front driver-side fender of Sam's one indulgence, a 1966 Mustang—the fastback model with the 289ci V8. Having been recently restored, it sported a pristine, sky-blue paint job with dual white racing stripes, along with an all new pony interior. The main problem with having a car like this, one so noticeable, was that everyone always knew where he was.

"Excuse me, man. You mind getting off my car?" Sam said with a chin gesture.

5

He was standing atop where curb met sidewalk. And, like virtually all curbs built across the country, perhaps the world, that meant he was standing an additional six inches above these five men. So, for the man seated on the fender of the Mustang to act as if Sam's presence wasn't noticed, or like he perhaps didn't have a good eyeline on him, well, that just wasn't a possibility. The laughing continued. There were more deep drags on their smokes. And while Sam knew his presence had obviously not gone unnoticed, not one of them ventured a glance his way. It was almost funny. Almost. But Sam had been putting up with this shit ever since his return. *Triggers.*

Green Berets are among the most highly trained and conditioned special forces operators in the world. The US Modern Army Combatives Program (MACP) teaches recruits how to handle themselves in combat situations using a variety of martial arts techniques such as Muay Thai, Brazilian jiu-jitsu, boxing, and others—all taught for one to become as lethal an adversary in hand-to-hand combat as you can imagine.

"I'm going to ask you one more time. Move your fat ass off my car." Sam tilted his head just enough—a kind of body language inflection. He was no longer simply asking.

The biggest of the crew was not the man sitting on the fender. It was the one to his left. The one that had *Manager—Ivan Dvorak* embroidered onto the upper left of his uniform, just above a smeared-in grape jelly stain. Ivan was easily two hundred and fifty pounds and maybe six three. Sam had read the guy's number the second he'd taken note of him back in the café. Loud and used to being in charge. Getting his own way. The kind of big, swinging dick that would just as easily mock and humiliate you as he would use violence. Sam wondered what his preference would be now. The man's accent had been distinct. Sam's guess…an Eastern Bloc country. Maybe Albanian or Czech.

"Relax, my friend," Ivan said. "You let us finish off last drags on smokes, eh? A beautiful morning. Birds are out and singing. What so important to do?"

Sam offered back his own smile. "I have responsibilities. Things I have to do—"

"And people to meet, yeah, yeah," another of the men offered up. They all laughed in unison.

Ivan said, "You know. I don't think I am ready to go to work. How about you boys? Another quick fag before we go?"

By the sounds of their adolescent cheers, it was as if they had all won the Pick 6. Ivan, now in the process of having his cigarette lit for him by the smallest of the quintet, clearly his bitch, had his eyes locked on Sam.

There comes a time, a moment, when reason, or being reasonable, no longer works or has any meaning. And this had gotten well beyond that moment in time. Sam moved fast, with well-practiced fluidity. Lifted by his elbows in a kind of weightlifter's barbell curling motion, up went the man who'd been sitting on the Mustang. Holding the guy with arms pinned but legs flailing, Sam shoved the man's bulk into Ivan's broad chest. Both went down onto the pavement in a cluster of tangled arms and legs. A haymaker came at Sam's head, which he easily blocked and parried with a jab to the man's face. He both heard and felt the crack of hyaline cartilage within the distal portion of the nose.

Sam cringed. *Maybe I should have pulled that punch a tad.*

The man to Sam's right, tall and lanky, with a silver spike through the bridge of his nose, kicked out with a modicum of skill. Maybe he had served in the armed forces or had taken classes as a kid at the neighborhood dojo, but whatever training it had been, at this moment in time, it was coming up lacking. Sam turned his hips, and instead of moving away from the kick, he moved into it, absorbing the blow while it was still more like a shove than a real kick. Sam drove an uppercut into the man's solar plexus, instantly bending the man over, hearing his gasp for breath. The only two still standing were mentally debating whether to get involved in this fight. He could see it in their eyes.

But this hadn't been a fight. More like a tussle. If it had been a fight, all five of them would already be on the ground, and not one of them would be getting up any time soon.

"Don't do it," Sam said, offering up a half smile he didn't feel. "I guarantee this morning can go a whole lot worse for you two."

They exchanged a quick glance, then both nodded.

Ivan and the other guy had gotten to their feet. The big one had a nasty gash on his cheek that would need a couple of stitches. A flurry of cuss words and spittle spewed from Ivan's mouth, of which not a word was in English. But he was keeping his distance just the same.

Sam unlocked his car door and eased himself in behind the steering wheel. He wound down the window and looked at each of them—making extended eye contact. "I see you here again, I'm going to say hi. No need for hard feelings…right? But I hear you talking shit to Harper again like you did today? I'm going to bring you back out here and pound you into the ground. Like a fucking pile-driver. It won't matter if it's one at a time or all five of you at once. The results will be the same. A lengthy stretch in a hospital bed. We understand each other?"

Reluctantly, four of the five nodded. Ivan, on the other hand, just stared. With that one, Sam had just made another enemy. *Whatever. He can get in line…*

Chapter 2

Oakleaf Medical Offices, Castle Rock, Colorado
Sam Dale

"Why are you here, Sam?" she asked.

He felt her stare. He opened his eyes and let out a slow breath.

"Sam? Are you listening to me?"

He didn't answer. He watched as she made another notation on her pad. This was their third, no, fourth session. They had already talked about his childhood and his military career.

"Sam, are you present here with me, or is your mind somewhere else right now?"

The air was stale, like someone needed to open a window. He allowed himself to take a breath, even though there didn't seem to be enough oxygen in the confined space. Filtered sunlight fell on a glass-covered print on the wall. The reflection made it difficult to see. A woman...no, that was a man. Or was it both? He hated this shit. Everything was a damn test.

"I'll just sit here until you feel ready to speak. We have twenty minutes left, and you haven't said anything yet."

Sam's frame was too big for the furniture. The modern, teal-colored couch was uncomfortable. Maybe that was on purpose. So why didn't he leave? Being here was his doing—no one else's. He sat with his elbows on his knees. His head was down, and he was staring at wisps of fuzz clinging to the top of the beige carpet.

"Why did you change out the artwork?" Sam asked, lifting his head to meet her gaze.

"I find it's good to change one's environment from time to time," Dr. Leslie Sikes answered.

Her tailored charcoal pants suit fit her like a peel on a banana, hugging her curves without being provocative. Her posture was perfectly straight, her bottom positioned near the edge of the seat, present, but ready to get up at a moment's notice. Her face was angular and soft at the same time, with high cheekbones and lips that other women would have envied. She had an unflinching stare, but at least she blinked from time to time.

"Does change make you feel uncomfortable, Sam?" Sikes asked, leaning a tad forward.

Sam leaned back into the sofa, his head grazing the bottom of the mirror above him. His arms stretched out, open palms down on the linen upholstery. It was rough and scratchy to the touch. All of his senses were telling him to get up and walk out.

"No, I don't like change. It pisses me off," Sam said.

"Why does it piss you off, Sam?" she asked.

"Because change in a war zone is bad. And that's where I am a lot of the time. Change is dangerous. Like crowds disappearing from an area. And if I miss that change in my environment, I'm being complacent. And complacency kills."

Sikes gave him a half smile and made a quick note on the steno resting on her lap. She attached the clasp of her Montblanc to the circular metal binder and put the pad down on the table next to her.

"How did you hurt your hand? Your knuckles?" she said, gesturing with her finger toward the small scab forming on his right-hand knuckles.

Sam kept some things to himself. A few years ago, out of anger, when he was alone, he would slam his fist into walls. Even to the point that he broke knuckles. Mainly to feel the pain, which was better than feeling numb all the time. He usually didn't act against others until yesterday.

"An oil change—car maintenance can be a dangerous business," Sam answered as if he had been coached, not missing a beat.

"Uh-huh," she said, not buying his bullshit. "Tell me about an event that sticks in your mind when you think of war."

"What do you want to know?"

"Let's start with something simple. Talk to me about your military career…in general terms. Just as a refresher."

"I graduated West Point as second lieutenant. I selected infantry. Completed Infantry Basic Officer Leader Course…that was seventeen weeks. Next came Airborne School, another three weeks, then I completed Ranger School; that was sixty-one days. At that point I'd earned and wore a Ranger Tab. But I wasn't actually a Ranger because I didn't serve in the 75th Ranger Regiment."

Sikes made more scratchings on her pad.

"I served as a lieutenant for four years, during which time I saw action in Afghanistan as part of Obama's surge and distinguished myself as a solid tactician and leader. I was promoted to captain. Then, in 2012, I was rotated home. That's when I decided to become a Green Beret…another way of saying Army Special Forces."

"What did that entail, Sam?"

"Attended Special Forces Preparation Course for six weeks. Went on to Special Forces Assessment and Selection; that was another three weeks. Uh, then on to completing the Special Forces Qualification Course. That took longer, another few months. And then—"

"And then you returned to Afghanistan in 2016," she said,

reading from her pad.

He nodded. "Uh-huh, as part of the new train, advise, assist mission. Commander of mostly special recon operations."

Dr. Sikes looked up from her pad. "How many people did you lead?"

"It was a standard twelve-man ODA there in Tagab."

"ODA?"

"Operational Detachment Alpha."

The overhead lights suddenly started to flicker. The doctor's iWatch began flashing. Her eyes went to the ceiling and then to her wrist. "Solar flare," she said with mock enthusiasm. Becoming serious, she said, "Do you want to talk about your triggers now, Sam?"

The room went quiet for close to a minute. Sam looked at the door to his left. There was a flickering candle on a table next to the door. The flame had captured his attention. He didn't recognize the scent…*Is that lavender? Jasmine?* He didn't know. It smelled like the outside, like spring, maybe. The flame crept up over the melted edges of the candle, casting shadows onto the wall behind.

"Where are you now, Sam?" Sikes asked, more softly this time.

"Afghanistan." Sam finally spoke in a monotone. He stared at the dancing shadows on the wall.

"Tell me what you see."

"Tagab." He cleared his throat. "I'm in Tagab."

She waited for Sam to continue.

"My ODA is traveling through Tagab to conduct a KLE— that's a Key Leader Engagement—with an ANDSF commander. Shit, sorry, that's Afghan National Defense and Security Forces. Military loves their acronyms." Sam's face went serious. "The weather had changed. A hailstorm…visibility was for crap. We were four and a half hours out from base, and that's when the Taliban attacked our convoy of three MATVs. I think maybe they thought we'd discovered what they were up to."

"What exactly did they do…how did they attack?"

"All these villages have scouts. They use Roshan cell phones. Cheap and easy to dump/change out SIM cards. But they'd initiated a relatively complex ambush. Set up IEDs and hit us with RPGs and small arms fire. I lost two men right away when the trailing vehicle got hit. We had no choice but to return fire and attempt to fight through the clusterfuck. We'd been on comms with base the whole time. Requested air support. We were in way over our head but were denied the support because of the shitty weather conditions. They'd be en route just as soon as the weather cleared."

"That must have been demoralizing."

He shrugged. "That's the way things worked out there. So, we held our own. We were trained for those kinds of scenarios. Our plan was to repel, since no other forces were in the area, to return to a friendly location, a forward operating base.

"But then I saw her through binoculars. She was no more than seven years old, skinny as a mop handle—crying and running, frantic. She was carrying something in her arms wrapped in a blanket… maybe a baby? There was blood on her dress. More than a little."

Sam swallowed and mentally regrouped. "I made the decision to proceed. Soon, we were taking the fight to them…making tactical advancement on their position. Before we knew it, we were upon their village…more Taliban insurgents, vehicles, tents, and mud-brick structures known as qal□ahs."

"What else did you see, Sam?"

It was a while before he answered. He knew what she was probing for.

"Cages. A whole lot of cages…"

"Go on."

"Once again, we were in over our heads, and I was ready to call it. Withdraw. Get us the hell out of there before I lost any more of my squad. But seeing that they had hostages…Well, at that point we—*I*—was committed. We had to fight. Fight and win."

"Can we get back to the hostages, Sam?"

He glared at her, irritated at her interruption. *I don't want to talk about the girls...*

He swallowed. "We could see the cages were jam-packed."

"With?"

"With young girls. Teens, mostly."

"And they were all alive?"

He clenched his jaw. "No. Outside of the cages, there were bodies scattered about the village's center square. There were pieces of clothing on the ground. I remember seeing a trampled and muddied flowered dress, a dress a child might wear to church. There were also bodies that must have been there for two or three days. Small bodies of children and some adults; they were decomposing, bloated and covered in flies and maggots. Even from a distance, the smell is something I will never forget. Putrid feces, spoiled meat, rotting eggs...to describe it does it no justice. Later, we'd discover they'd been tortured, raped, and ultimately killed. I think we'd interrupted their...festivities. The Taliban had molested and executed approximately 20 percent of the villagers."

She waited for Sam to continue.

"We engaged the enemy for another hour. That's when they began firing rounds into the cages. I don't know if it was to silence the hostages, or retribution for our presence there. Either way, dead is dead, right?"

"What happened then, Sam?"

"The weather cleared; air support dropped in from above. It was short work after that."

"Were there any..."

"Surviving villagers?" he said with a sneer. "Yeah, there were six. Five Afghani teen girls and one woman, a mother. Six out of forty-three. The young woman was wailing, holding a lifeless girl's body in her lap. She was holding the dead child tight to her chest, her face distorted with an otherworldly pain that was beyond description."

"How many of your team were lost?"

"Total of four."

A long silence hung in the air.

Sam shrugged. "Once we'd secured the area, we released the villagers…the girls and the woman—the ones that were still alive. Their bodies were emaciated. Clearly, they had been there for some time. What they had endured…We provided basic medical assistance. One of my men found blankets in a nearby tent."

"When you finally had a chance to decompress after returning to base, what were your thoughts about the day?"

He shook his head. "My thoughts were not for me…but for the four dead servicemen and the dozens of girls killed that day."

Dr. Sikes stayed still in her seat, seeming to be calculating her next words. "Thank you for sharing that, Sam. What are you feeling at this moment?"

"I don't feel anything, Doc," Sam said.

She studied his face. Maybe she felt he was hiding something.

"I'm sorry, but I just realized I have to be somewhere," he said, readying himself to stand. "Besides, we're almost out of time, right?" Sam asked.

"We have a few minutes…" Sikes said. "Are you sure you don't want to talk more about what you just shared?"

"No, I'm all good. Like I said, I have to be somewhere." Sam opened the door and then strode out with purpose—the candle flame danced, then blew out.

Chapter 3

In the skies above Castle Rock, Colorado
Junior Lieutenant Cypress Mag Nuel

It was hard to think around the multiple, increasingly loud and angry-sounding alarm beacons. How could so much go so wrong in such a short amount of time...

Junior Lieutenant Cypress Mag Nuel of the 234th Landa-Craft Squadron continued to pull back on the controls in an attempt to gain sufficient altitude, but nothing he did was making a difference. And of course, this had to happen now. His final stealth run over the only terrain yet to be surveyed by his ship's sensor collectors. Strange...These small, highly maneuverable Landa-Crafts didn't just stop working like this. Rigorous, constantly running diagnostics had made this kind of unexpected failure almost a thing of the past. But then again, the key word here would be *almost*.

For the umpteenth time, Cypress tapped the comms key on his primary controls array, only to chastise himself for his forgetfulness; he now remembered the other pilots, and their Landa-Crafts were gone. His vessel would have been the last one to disembark from this God-forsaken planet. The six others had been doing the same thing he had been doing these past few weeks—scanning, data collecting, cataloging the planet's surface and subsurfaces. You didn't invade an alien world without proper preparation.

He and the other pilots, with their stealth ships, had crisscrossed the globe hundreds of times. There was nothing their deep-penetrating scans had missed. Military fighter jet air bases, fortified infantry ground installations, and every subterranean missile silo. Also, the many naval bases had been located and scrutinized, as had every warship and submarine, many with nuclear-tipped-missiles. No, an invasion of this magnitude required adequate preparation, and Cypress was proud to have been a part of that effort. In a matter of days, these human primitives would have a hard time comprehending what was happening to them, and by the time they did—well, it would be too late.

His Landa-Craft shuddered, bringing Cypress back to his present predicament. Considering, by now, that all six of his fellow pilots had made it back to the jump gate—had left the quadrant—he truly was all alone.

The alarm beacons suddenly went quiet. The flashing warning lights and all the little indicators and readouts…blinked out. Cypress felt it. That ominous feeling in his gut of uncontrolled falling. His Landa-Craft was now little more than a falling rock. His fate was now in the hands of gravity, and gravity was seldom kind to those who were unprepared. Figuring he was about twenty thousand feet up…how long would he have? He did some quick mental calculations. The gravitational pull of this world was about 9.807 m/s². Almost identical to that of Naru. He was falling at about two Earth miles or ten thousand five hundred and sixty Earth feet per minute…Hmm…he had less than two minutes, so he needed to think of *something*. Some way out of this predicament.

Nothing came to mind. He had specific orders if such a situation should ever arise.

He was to self-destruct *immediately*. To blow up his craft and himself along with it. It would be fast and painless. A mere millisecond and he would be vaporized—atomized—his molecules quickly dispersed into the atmosphere.

So be it…

Cypress reached for the switch, flipped up the protective cap, but then hesitated. *Shouldn't I say something? This is a profound moment—undoubtedly the most impactful moment of my life. A quick prayer, maybe? Perhaps a blessing to Orlicon Tharsh.*

Then again, Cypress had never been all that religious. *No time to rethink that decision now…* He thought of Orlanda…beautiful, kind Orlanda. They were to be joined soon after his return home. Both of his hearts missed a beat. *She will never know what happened to me.* Why he had failed to keep his promise to come back to her.

He squeezed his eyes shut, flipped the switch up, and waited.

Now that's odd…

I'm not dead.

Another full minute ticked by, and his Landa-Craft was still falling fast.

It was in that split second or two that Cypress was able to see out through the vessel's canopy into the darkness. The Landa-Craft was not so much falling straight down but descending at an angle. The blur of dark treetops whizzed by. There were the sounds of snapping branches, then, all too soon, the ground was coming up fast.

Forward momentum made the impact somewhat less devastating than it would have been, say, if the craft had plummeted straight down like that proverbial falling rock analogy.

A splash, a jarring, abrupt deceleration, and immediate pain—much pain, then blackness.

Cypress awoke, not knowing how much time had passed. With a quick self-assessment, he was confronted by a stark reality. He was in bad shape.

Typically, he would have referred to his helmet's heads-up

display (HUD) for a comprehensive medical assessment. But his HUD had gone dark back when the ship's power had cut out. Considering the two systems functioned independently of each other, well, that was most odd. So, he'd do things the old-fashioned way. Through eye-watering pain and with gritted teeth, he began evaluating the condition of his body.

First off, all his limbs were still attached. Some good news there. But there were broken bones—maybe too many to count. He felt around on his abdomen and winced—as expected, there was, most likely, some internal hemorrhaging going on. Organ failure was imminent. Cypress glanced back to an aft area of the cockpit, where he knew there was a reservoir of nanites, in this case, lifesaving Hydrating-Medibots. He felt dizzy. Clearly, he'd sustained a severe concussion. He closed his eyes—in his condition, there'd be no way he'd be able to access that reservoir. And with the power out…what was the point?

I am dying.

Dying was more of a concept than a reality to most Silarians back home on Naru. It wasn't so much that Silarians didn't die. Sure they did; accidents happened, but it was rare. And it was mostly unnecessary. Those of his world lived full lives, probably not so different from those inhabitants here on this backwater planet. But with one big difference…at the end of one's life, say two, two hundred and fifty years or so, one simply *transferred*. No one really died of old age in these modern times. One passed one's consciousness onto, *into*, one's awaiting bio-form.

But there would be no awaiting bio-form here…no prospect of a consciousness transfer. His all-too-imminent demise was a reality—*is my reality*. Cypress sat back and stared out through the mud-splattered canopy. What to do with his remaining moments? There would be nothing he could do about the Landa-Craft. There was no way to destroy the thing. The simple fact it had survived this impact in one piece was evidence enough of the craft's durability. Its Carbone-graphene outer hull was nearly impervious to anything other than a direct missile strike, or the ship's own fusion-reaction self-destruct process—which he knew was no longer an option. It occurred to Cypress that, yes, this ship would be found. That was not good. Terrible, in fact. But the one thing that would be worse…would be finding an advanced alien life-form sitting within it. Dead or alive.

The simple act of breathing was becoming difficult, a kind of darkening tunnel vision becoming an all too obvious reminder of what was soon to come. Without thinking, Cypress moved as fast as his injured body would allow. His anatomy had three primary technology implants—two were easy enough to excise. Silarians pilot vests were outfitted with a tactical knife, among other things. He removed his helmet and went to work making a one-inch-long incision at his left temple. Using a kind of jabbing, crowbarring motion, Cypress removed his sensory comms implant. He placed that, bloodied and disgusting as it was, on the ship's dash. He opened his ship's go-bag, which contained medical supplies along with some other survival items whose function he no longer remembered or cared to remember. He sprayed organic patch skin over the incision area, and the bleeding stopped.

Next, he went to work on his left inside thigh. After a few agonizing moments, he sliced through his protective flight suit—not an easy task, considering the material was a blend of alien compounds created to withstand penetration. Holding his breath, he made an incision on his thigh, this one larger, three inches in length. Called his Geo-Mind, the implant had been an essential component of Cypress's life since being injected after birth—his secondary technological brain. Far more than just a computer, it was his connection to reality. To the stream. And like the ship, HUD, and his sensory comms, his connection to it was via wireless neural link.

Cypress's screams filled the cockpit as he began prying out the implant from deep within the muscle. The Geo-Mind, which looked much like the other implants, went up onto the dash with the sensory comms implant. He took a breath and felt woozy. Last but not least would be his essence implant. Cypress was reluctant to remove this last component from his anatomy. Everything that was *him* was stored within this one device. In fact, it was this technology that would have allowed for his transfer into an awaiting bio-form. Every thought, feeling, impulse, urge, memory, emotion, as well as his complete anatomical and genetic disposition up until this moment, was still being stored within its Silarian-prolimic storage cells.

Again, using his stubby knife, Cypress made one last incision laterally across his midsection. Blood spurted, then continued to ooze from the opening. Removing this last implant was less painful—and like the others, it utilized a neural link that was unique to his physiology. Like the others, no larger than an everyday supplement capsule, it came out with a little jabbing and crowbarring. Cypress tightened his fist around the small device as tears brimmed. Even now, he could feel the essence implant doing what it always did…chronicling his life—his very state of being for as long as his two hearts kept beating and his lungs continued to take in air.

He sprayed on more patch skin and leaned back to rest. He stared at the three bloodied devices on the dash where he'd left them. What to do with them now? He reached forward and took them into a tight fist. With his other hand, he opened a vest pocket. *I'll keep them close for now.* But he'd need to destroy them at some point.

With the Landa-Craft's power off-line, Cypress was required to mechanically unlatch the canopy—an agonizing process in his current condition. Once the twelve tension locks were unclasped, the canopy began to slowly pivot upward via its air compression hinges.

It was the swampy smell that first assaulted his senses. *How is it my last breaths will be on a world that smells so disgusting?* As he was looking up to the heavens, rain splattered down onto his exposed face while wind tousled his long black hair. He summoned what few energy reserves he had left to begin the arduous task of climbing up and out of the Landa-Craft's cockpit.

Although it had seemed like hours, it had probably been little more than a few minutes getting himself to where he was now—precariously balanced, one leg and arm dangling inside and one leg and arm dangling outside of the spacecraft's cockpit. Breathing hard, Cypress groaned. The pain was beyond anything he had ever experienced. *Keep going; soon there will be no pain at all.* Exhausted and feeling woozy again, Cypress lost consciousness.

He awoke in the dead of night. How he had managed to crawl here, onto this embankment within this soddy, muddy gulch, he had no clue. He thought about the brackish water, his incisions, and the raging infection he was sure to acquire. *No—I'm dying. An infection is the least of my problems right now.*

One minor consolation was that he still had his implants. Taking in his surroundings, there, off in the distance, he could just make out the dark silhouette of his Landa-Craft. With its still wide-open canopy, the ship looked to be screaming up to the heavens or perhaps offering a final blessing up to *Orlicon Tharsh*—one Cypress himself had chosen not to make.

Cypress was incapable of much in the way of physical movement. He tried to swallow but could not. *So, this is where it will happen. This shithole of a world that smells like an open latrine will be my final resting place. What did I do to deserve such a fate?*

When Cypress awoke again, which would be for the last time, he was only somewhat aware of the fact he was being physically accosted. Someone, *or something,* had found him. He tried to remember what the local species of this foul world looked like. He had visited so many star systems, so many worlds, these past few years…had made so many terrestrial scans. He considered accessing his Geo-Mind; he could feel its presence there within his vest pocket. *Why bother?* Something wet and slimy and, of course, disgusting, was pressing up against his face.

Managing to open one eye, Cypress croaked out a scream. A wild, mud covered, and hairy beast was upon him, literally straddling his legs. *And that smell—even worse than the surrounding foul gulch.* He saw a snout and teeth. So many teeth. But he was being licked, not eaten. Coming to terms with the fact that this monstrous creature was not dangerous, he looked into its big brown eyes. Cypress saw a kindness and vulnerability there that surprised him. He didn't want to think of these primitives in those terms. Not with what was planned for them.

Cypress watched with fascination as the creature, now on its back, was wiggling, gyrating its furry mass there within the sloshing wet muck. Contented snorts erupted from its long snout. He noticed the beast had a tail. Seeing its rhythmic wagging back and forth, Cypress, despite his pain, his all too imminent demise, couldn't help but smile. *What a strange and delightful being you are.*

It was at that very moment that Cypress came to a very serious and consequential realization. *I'm just not ready to die…not yet…*

Chapter 4

Off of Lake Gulch Road, Castle Rock, Colorado
Sam Dale

He started awake, hearing, "Pimp Daddy says wake up, motherfucker…Pimp Daddy says wake up, motherfucker…Pimp Daddy says wake up, motherfucker…"

Sam blindly reached over to his iPhone, where it was now illuminating the contents of his nightstand. He used his thumbnail to silence the damn thing. This was what happened when you worked with morons and you didn't password protect your phone. An employee, thinking he or she was funny, got into it and changed your ringtone.

Half asleep, he answered the call. "Dale…"

"Sam? Uh…sorry to wake you, man…Weird. I was calling the garage—"

Shit. Tony did it again.

"Expected to get Tony. We have a situation out here."

Only now did Sam place the voice on the other end of the line. It was Officer Eagan Pitt with the Castle Rock Police Department. And the Tony he was referring to was Tony DeLago, one of Sam's employees. He had a number of them. Too many of them, some

24

would say. Sam owned five Castle Rock business establishments—one of which was Garcia Tow, Repair, and Stow. Sam believed the Garcia moniker was that of the business's original owner, which was some time way back in the early 1940s.

His overpaid and underworked employee, Tony, was supposed to be on call tonight. He must have forwarded the garage line to Sam's personal cell phone. Sam remembered him mentioning something about having a hot date tonight. Sam glared at the digital clock on the nightstand—2:30 a.m. *Must have been some date.*

"What's the situation, Eagan? Can't this wait till morning? Tony's not—"

"Sorry, Sam, but the captain wants this tow to happen tonight, like ASAP."

He swung his legs over the side of the bed and raked fingers through his hair. He heard raindrops drumming down onto the rooftop overhead. Sam hated driving the tow truck. He was convinced it didn't like him. "Fine…it's all right. I'll need to get over to the garage to switch vehicles. Where am I headed?"

Within twenty-five minutes, Sam was turning onto Lake Gulch Road. It was late spring, and there were still remnants of plowed snow pushed off to the side shoulder. The vehicle started to shake and rumble; clearly, the big engine was contemplating a stall—and of course, it had to happen right here within the intersection.

Sam eased off the gas and tried to sweet-talk the truck. "Come on, big girl…don't give up the ghost yet…you've got plenty of life left in you." The truck shuddered again. There were all types and sizes of tow trucks: flatbed tow trucks, hook and chain tow trucks, wheel lift tow trucks, boom trucks; the list went on and on. But this was a small town, and Garcia's was a small outfit. Garcia's basically had this eight-year-old Ford F350 flatbed tow truck, and another, older-model hook and chain tow truck that had been sitting back at the lot in need of a valve job for close to a year now.

Sam downshifted into second. The mere thought that he might need to call a competitor like Jerry's Tow Service, or AAA Towing over in Parker, having to explain how Garcia Tow, Repair, and Stow's truck needed a tow…Well, that was a humiliation he just wasn't willing to put up with right now.

He let out a measured breath as the Ford began to accelerate. Ineffective wipers slapped back and forth on the bug-smeared windshield. Up ahead, perhaps a half mile in the distance, he saw the strobing of blue and red lights at the scene. Looked like three police Ford Interceptors, which was their name for a modified Ford Explorer. Sam had been eavesdropping in on the tow trucks' police band radio, and there hadn't been much reported about the accident.

He veered off the road and parked behind the last in the line of police units. Switching on the truck's rooftop emergency lightbar and leaving the engine running, he opened the driver-side door and hopped down into the pouring rain. Wearing a bright yellow plasticky rain slicker, red knee-high rubber boots, and a blue and orange Broncos baseball cap, he was well aware he looked ridiculous.

Flashlight beams swung left and right and crisscrossed down below where he knew the gulch snaked its way through several miles of open pastureland.

En route, sloughing through mud, he'd used the truck's Maglite to assess the terrain he'd no doubt soon be navigating the tow truck over. There were a few large rocks he'd need to watch out for, but if he drove slowly, it should be okay.

When Sam reached the gulch, Officer Eagan Pitt hurried over to him.

"Thought that was you. That's quite a getup you're wearing, Sam."

"Keeps me dry," Sam said, looking over the man's shoulder into the gulch, now turned to a small river. A semi-submerged dark shape caught his eye. "That's the situation you were referring to?"

Eagan turned, Sam's Maglite illuminating his consternation. "Uh…we got a call. Woman jogging…said a vehicle, maybe a minivan, went off the road and got stuck down there in the mud."

"That's no minivan, Eagan."

"I know that, Sam. We've called into Colorado Springs Air Force Academy, Peterson Space Force Base, DIA, all the local airports, like the one up in Erie; you name it…but no one's missing a plane." He shrugged. "Look, Sam, there's no reporting of any kind of missing airplane."

"That's not an airplane either, Eagan. Maybe it's some kind of jet?"

"Captain thinks it's a hobbyist drone. Drones are no longer just for little kids and teens, you know. Grown-ass men fly 'em too. Some rigs are big motherfuckers. Big enough to sit in. Though, can't say I ever saw one anywhere close to being that big. Anyway, I can't tell you how many calls we get about them. Nuisance calls…you know, aerial distractions, invasions of privacy, that sort of thing. But drones are here to stay."

Sam let go of the fact that Eagan was over-explaining things. That, and Sam actually knew something about this subject matter. He'd had his ass saved a couple of times by timely drone strikes. "So, what do you want me to do?" Sam said, envisioning his warm, dry bed back home.

"Well…that thing can't stay here. We need to haul it on out of there…get it transported to some place covered. Someplace dry. Secure."

"Maybe we deal with it Monday morning," Sam suggested, stifling a yawn.

"Garcia Tow, Repair, and Stow…Just tow it and stow it…Isn't that included in that contract we have with you guys?" Eagan offered up a half smile.

They both knew this was the passing of the buck routine. "Well, yeah, for cars, SUVs, minivans…that sort of thing. That…craft, whatever it is, has to be some twenty feet long. Would barely fit—"

Eagan's radio bleeped.

A static-filled woman's voice broke in. "Eagan…we have a robbery in progress at the GameStop at 312 Metzler Dr…Looks like a small gang of masked looters have broken through a window. One of those smash and grab situations. All units need to hightail it over there, pronto."

"Roger that, Margie," Eagan said into his shoulder mic. "Got to go, Sam," Eagan said. "…So, you got this. Right?"

"No. I'll need some help getting—"

But he was already heading off. The other cops—Sam counted five flashlight-wielding dark forms—were either scurrying up the sides of the gulch embankment or were already sprinting toward their Interceptors. He stood there in the pouring rain, shaking his head. Sam cursed Tony and hoped his hot date had left him with a raging case of crabs and itchy balls.

One after another, the police units sped off with their lights flashing and their sirens blaring.

Chapter 5

Off of Lake Gulch Road, Castle Rock, Colorado
Cypress Mag Nuel

Cypress hadn't had much time for regrets. He'd had a lot to accomplish within a short amount of time. Instinctual, not something he had to put much thought into, and assisted by his Geo-Mind and Essence devices, the transference process had taken little more than a few minutes. But now he was faced with several residual side effects. Like getting used to his new bio-form—in this case, a furry, mud-slogging beast of a body. Typically, an awaiting bio-form wouldn't have had a viable consciousness to contend with. He hadn't contemplated having to share mental resources, and thus, Cypress was still trying to quell the beast's unruly and spirited mind. Sure, Cypress's was the dominant presence, but still, it was disconcerting having another mind to contend with.

First there were the implants to deal with. He would need those with him at all times. No longer having opposable thumbs was just one more immediate disadvantage. He had left the implants sitting on a nearby wiped-clean rock. With no other alternatives, Cypress, now Cypress the dog, had lapped up the devices and swallowed them. He was already researching the digestive cycles of this species of animal to see how long he would have before they would be coming out the other end. An animal Cypress now knew, thanks to his neural link to his Geo-Mind, was called a dog.

Now there was the body to deal with. *His old body.*

On the positive side, as it turned out, these beasts were well equipped for digging.

The wet banks of the gulch were more mud than dirt. Cypress managed to dredge a two-foot-deep, seven-foot-long trench—one adequate enough for him to, using his newly acquired long snout, nudge, roll, and then drag with strong jaws and long teeth, the now- lifeless Silarian body over and into it. Then, he covered the body as best he could with the surrounding loose mud and dirt. How long the remains would remain hidden, he had no idea—a few days, weeks; after that it wouldn't matter. All humanity would have been annihilated.

Sitting in the dark upon a small rise some thirty yards away, Cypress watched as a band of local primitives assessed his Landa-Craft as well as the nearby surroundings. Evidently, they were called police. Naru had police, too, of course. But robots were the preferred means of maintaining public safety and security.

Several times he'd had to move farther away into the darkness to avoid being spotted. But it now occurred to him that his presence here, as a domestic animal, a dog, was probably not such a big deal. There were many millions of these furry, mud-slopping creatures about. In fact, most of the local domiciles were inhabited by one breed of dog or another, or something called a cat—whatever that was.

The distant, blinking on-and-off lights were strangely soothing—relaxing. Only now was Cypress able to put his limited dog brain to use and begin formulating some kind of a plan. He needed to get home; that was a given. Back to Naru, where he could resume and build a life with Orlanda. He glanced down at himself, and if he could smile, he would have. *Hello, the love of my hearts…as promised, I've returned to you. Please disregard my peculiar appearance; never mind this mud-matted fur. Oh, and sorry about this smell…*

There had to be a way to transfer out of this all-too-limiting canine body. Humans were not so different, at least physiologically, as well as in appearance—with their two arms and two legs, one head, and relatively the same internal organ makeup. Although Silarians did have two hearts, green skin, an average standing height of seven feet, and their whole reproductive system was quite different. Cypress had quickly scanned this information using the stream via his Geo-Mind—still situated within the confines of his digestive system. He'd found humans to be beyond disgusting in that regard. But ultimately, he wouldn't know if humans would be a compatible bio-form until he actually attempted a transference process with one of them.

One obstacle at a time. First things first—he could not be separated from his Landa-Craft. There within that ship was highly advanced technology, technology that would be his only hope of ever leaving this place. And with the invasion planned for a few days from now, he wanted to be long gone before then.

A new vehicle had arrived off in the distance, this one larger and noisier. Cypress watched as another of the primitive humans approached, his attire different from the six others, the police, who wore dark, matching uniforms.

One more indignity to endure; Cypress's sight seemingly was now restricted to dichromatic vision. He had lost the ability to see the full spectrum of colors. Apparently, dogs could only detect various shades of blues and yellows, and this individual was wearing a whole lot of yellow.

Interesting… The police were now leaving in a hurry, while the yellow-clad primitive was staying put.

Cypress watched the human, clearly frustrated with what he

was doing, making exaggerated hand and arm gestures that were not so different from what a Silarian would make. Once the human, the man, had backed his vehicle down from the road, over the pastureland, and in close to the gulch, it took close to two hours for the Landa-Craft to get pulled up onto the flatbed of the vehicle. The man used an assortment of chains and straps to secure the Landa-Craft, and then he covered it, most of it, anyway, with an old tarp.

The human was ready to go. Cypress sprang into action. Down one gulch embankment and up the other, Cypress ran full out and, surprisingly, it was an exhilarating feeling. But by the time he reached the vehicle, something he now knew was called a tow truck, the human had already climbed into its cab and shut the door. Not good.

The truck's headlight beams came on and the engine roared to life, causing Cypress to instinctively crouch and cower. The truck began a slow progression up the hill. *No! I need to be with my ship!* He racked his feeble, all too limited dog mind. One thing Cypress had gleaned from his cursory stream research was the bond, the connection, humans seemed to have with these canine breeds.

Cypress sprinted forward, getting in front of the truck, where he would be spotlighted in the headlights. He sat down on his haunches and tried to look pathetic, which wasn't all that difficult, considering it was mostly true.

But the truck kept on coming. Perhaps the primitive human did not see him, which was unlikely. It was no surprise. Many, perhaps most, humans were uncivilized. Brutish killers, barbarians. Cypress would have to decide quickly, though, just how long would he be willing to sit in the rain before jumping out of the way.

Cypress closed his eyes. No wonder this world had been targeted for invasion, its dominant life-form slated for extinction. His sensory comms implant had autonomously been busy at work, interacting with his Geo-Mind, the stream, making sense of the petabytes of vast information coming in by the second. *What a horrid planet.*

Brakes squealed, and the truck shuddered to a stop with the engine idling. Cypress opened his eyes to see the truck's driver-side door open and the human step down.

Within moments, the yellow-clad primitive was looming over him—staring down at him.

Chapter 6

Off of Lake Gulch Road, Castle Rock, Colorado
Sam Dale

"Hey, boy…" Sam said in as friendly a voice as he could muster, considering just how unfriendly and frustrated he was feeling at the moment. "You're going to have to move out of the way. I know it's wet, and cold, and miserable out here. But there's no way I'm going to be your salvation. Not tonight."

The dog stared up at him with intelligent eyes. Calculating eyes. Which was unsettling in itself. Seeing the dog had a collar, slowly, Sam reached down and positioned the dog tag in the truck's headlight beams. Engraved into the well-worn metal was the name "Rocko." "Hey, Rocko…don't you know your way home?"

He flipped over the tag and saw a phone number. Unfortunately, the tag was so scratched and beat to shit, the last three numbers were indecipherable. Sam straightened and continued to stare down at Rocko. *I can't just leave him here.* Maybe best to drop him off at Pet Depot. Another of the mostly money-losing ventures he owned here in Castle Rock. One more business that had kept him way too busy—like juggling cats—more like cats and dogs, and birds and fish and several small turtles. "Come on, boy; let's get you up in that truck where it's warm."

Back behind the wheel again, with Rocko sitting on the passenger seat, looking to be some kind of long-haired retriever beneath all that caked-on mud and grime. "You most definitely need a bath, boy," Sam said, sending a glance the dog's way.

The truck rocked, creaked, and swayed as they made their way up the gentle pasture grade toward the road. But Sam was preoccupied, his mind caught in a whirlwind of thought. That was no grown-ass man's hobbyist's drone back there on the bed. And it was no crashed airplane from Perry Park Airport here in Douglas County...or Meyer Ranch Airport over in Conifer...This was a craft like no other he had ever seen. Some kind of top-secret military craft. Maybe crashed here en route to the USAF Auxiliary Airfield in Ellicott. But still...unlikely.

This craft was beyond just high-tech—that thing would be in a class by itself. Maybe some kind of hush-hush military covert development project. Having spent so much of his life in the service, Sam knew something about such things. Things that no one was supposed to talk about. Strange, though. There were no markings, none of the typical military text legends, warnings and such, to be found. He'd spotted several groupings of geometric symbols, but that only reestablished just how top secret this prototype aircraft had to be. And now it was sitting back there on the bed of his truck. Sam still had a few contacts within the military. He'd reach out in the morning. Someone was looking for this thing, and he would be happy to unload it on them.

Once back on the level blacktop of Lake Gulch Road, they headed north toward town. Rocko had yet to lie down and was seemingly interested in their surroundings, taking in the few cars that passed in the night, the occasional road sign, the herd of goats off to their left. Sam said, "That road we just passed...Haystack Road. That's where I live. If you weren't such a mess, I would bring you back home with me."

The dog looked at him, panting. The seat he was sitting upon was a muddy, sloppy mess. Good. Tony could clean that up.

They passed by the new 7-Eleven gas station-minimart-car wash and headed up Gilbert. "First thing, we're going to drop off this aircraft. Get it under wraps. That okay with you, boy?" Without waiting for an answer, Sam slowed the Ford and turned into the parking lot of Garcia Tow, Repair, and Stow. All the lights were on inside the garage from when Sam had picked up the truck earlier.

He pulled the truck around so the back of the bed was positioned right in front of one of the ten garage storage units—the Stow aspect to the business. These were mostly rented on a per month basis by individuals who needed a covered and secured place to stow their boats, automobiles, collection of ATVs, or motor homes. Because these individual garages were extra large, almost fifteen feet wide, thirteen feet tall, and twenty-five feet deep, they were perfect for those that could afford the higher rental fees Garcia's charged. Currently, all but two of the Stow garages were rented.

Sam opened the door and climbed down. "Come on, boy," he said to Rocko. The dog bounded over to the driver's seat and jumped down.

After entering the code into the keypad, Sam waited while the motorized garage door rolled up. It took him another half hour to winch the aircraft down the raised bed and onto the garage's concrete floor. Looking at it now beneath the stark white fluorescents, Sam was even more taken by the craft's sleek lines and obvious technological prowess. The muddied glass canopy over the cockpit was open wide, and he'd yet to look inside the craft. No time like the present—might never have the opportunity again once the government stiffs arrived to take it away.

"Hang tight, boy. I'm going to take a peek inside. *Shhhh*…this will just be between you and me, okay?"

Sam climbed up onto the right-side wing, which was stubby and not as far back from the cockpit area as, say, an F-15 Eagle would be. He wasn't exactly sure what the designers of this craft were thinking. Aerodynamically, it was hard for Sam to get his head around the peculiar, extremely divergent architecture. With the toes of his boots hanging over to the forward curve of the wing, Sam reached for the inside rim of the cockpit and leaned his body forward. Now peering down into the cockpit, his brow furrowed. There was a substantial amount of blood on the seat and drops and smears of it on the forward console. Not only was that a sobering thought of what the pilot must have been through, but he or she was still out there—perhaps in pain, or worse, could be dead or dying.

Sam flashed back to the officers' crisscrossing flashlight beams within the gulch. Undoubtedly, they'd considered the open canopy. That there'd been a pilot. Unmanned drones didn't have open canopies. They'd done a cursory search in the dark, but Sam would call Eagan anyway. See what else was being done to find that pilot. And perhaps more importantly, why Eagan had lied about this being some kind of unmanned drone.

As he continued to look at the craft's ultra-high-tech controls and various readout screens, something else occurred to Sam. *Could this be…* He scoffed at his own off-the rails-imagination. Suddenly, one of the display screens, which was not really a screen at all, went active. A kind of text began to scroll, but what he was reading wasn't being presented in English. While English was based on Latin, or specifically Proto-Germanic, and where the Russian language was based on Indo-Aryan languages—the Slavic group of languages, and the Asian languages—well…Sam shook his head. Languages such as Chinese used a logographic script for their characters. He'd studied languages at West Point.

Staring at the little high-definition display, only now realizing it was a holographic 3D display, Sam felt the blood rushing from his head, and his knees started to buckle. No. These characters, or more accurately, these geometric symbols…they were not of an earthly design—at least that he was aware of. Sam watched as the flow of information was being displayed from the bottom up versus from left to right or right to left.

Once back down on terra firma, Sam leaned against the wall. Talking to the cement floor, he said, "This is impossible. That, and something tells me Eagan with the Castle Rock PD wouldn't be the best person to call about this."

What Sam hadn't expected was for the cement floor to talk back to him.

"Perhaps best if you don't call anyone about this…"

Startled, muscles going taut, raised hands tightening into fists—in the blink of an eye, Sam was ready for whoever had come for him. But there was no one there. And the voice had sounded oddly muffled. He looked beneath the craft's fuselage. No one there either. With the exception of the aircraft, himself, and the dog, he was alone. Sam moved over to the entrance to the garage and looked out onto Garcia's parking lot. Several customer cars and trucks, which had been there for a good long while, were parked—but no one he could see was in sight, lurking in the dark.

"Hello?" Now he was getting irritated. This was no time for someone to be playing a prank. "Who's out there? Show yourself!" He used his officer's voice. The one he'd learned to cultivate at West Point and even more so later, leading his unit as a Green Beret captain.

The dog was looking up at Sam, and the animal was giving him a strange look. An uncomfortably strange look. And then he spoke.

"I would suggest you don't do anything…rash."

Sam continued to stare down at Rocko, his mind spinning.

Yeah, sure, this had to be a joke, a prank; Lord knew he'd gotten plenty of that crap over this past year. When you employed mostly teenagers, a certain amount of that was expected. Sometimes it was funny; sometimes it was not. Like the time Lemon, his eighteen-year-old assistant manager over at Pet Depot, had put a hamster in Sam's Starbucks to-go cup. There it sat beneath the cup's plastic cap, with its nose pressed up to the little sippy cup opening. And sure, that would have been funny, but Lemon had mistakenly put the petrified rodent into a customer's cup, not his. That little prank had cost Sam the full gamut. A Torra twenty-gallon fish tank aquarium kit, including all the accessories—the LED lighting bar, fluorescent volcanic rock décor, and the pop-and-bubble pirate character...

Pranks were one thing, but when they started costing you money, well, that was another thing entirely. And right now, at this second, Sam was still trying to figure out the hijinks currently being played on him. Then the dog spoke again.

"Can we get past this? You know, where you try to figure out how a domestic canine with limited intellect is speaking to you? It's tiresome and, frankly, I have little time for it."

"No. Dogs don't have vocal cords." Sam pointed to Rocko's snout, his chops. "Your mouth opens, but your lips don't move. If you're going to punk me, at least make it realistic. Make it believable."

"Dogs actually do have vocal cords, and at present, what you would call alien technology is what is making those vocal cords function. What dogs do not have is the ability to work their tongue and lips properly. Technology is compensating for that."

"I'm still not buying it."

"Uh-huh...so the whole alien starship and all that you saw up there in the cockpit...that, too, is what you call, what was it, being punked?"

Sam didn't answer right away. And really, what could he say? Just by answering the dog, wouldn't that give this situation some kind of validity? Did he want to do that? But he couldn't just say nothing. *Perhaps if I had more information, I'd be able to make more sense of it all.*

"So…you are an alien?"

"No, I'm a dog. A dog inhabited by an alien consciousness. You can call me Cypress. Please don't call me Rocko again."

"Okay…I can do that. And what planet are you from? I'm assuming it's a world here in the Milky Way Galaxy?"

"I can tell from your snarky tone you're still not convinced."

"Can you blame me? Although, that cockpit, with all its advanced-looking controls and the symbols of that 3D display—"

"Stop!" If Cypress's eyes could have gone any wider, they probably would have popped out of his head. "What is this about an active display?!"

Sam stared down at the dog for several beats. His response was not of someone who was playing a joke. This dog—*this whatever*—wasn't just serious; he was truly shaken.

"The ship, my ship, has no power. In point of fact, that is why it crashed."

Sam pulled out his iPhone. "I videoed the interior of the cockpit. I figure, when will I have this opportunity again—"

"Stop talking, human. Are you all this annoying?"

Chapter 7

Garcia Tow, Repair, and Stow, Castle Rock, Colorado
Sam Dale

"Show me," Cypress said.

Sam looked down at the dog, still unwilling to believe he was having a back-and-forth conversation with a pet. He remembered his parents watching an old black and white movie about a man, played by Jimmy Stewart, who had an imaginary friend—a six-foot-tall rabbit named Harvey…The Jimmy Stewart character had mental issues…*Do I have mental issues?* Sam realized that was a strong possibility.

Sam cued up the video and pressed play. He held the screen down for Rocko—correction, Cypress—to watch. When it finished playing, he told Sam to play it again.

Putting his phone away, Sam raised a brow. "So?"

The dog didn't answer; instead, head hanging low, he wandered out toward the parking lot.

"What? Talk to me…" *Did I just say that?* Sam followed him but stopped at the keypad just long enough to initiate the closing of the garage door. Cypress looked to be in deep contemplation. Then again, Sam's own mind was reeling. He needed to do something, *anything*. Best to get the tow truck rig stowed away back into the main garage.

As he climbed back into the truck, going through the motions, he started it up, put it in gear, then drove counterclockwise around the parking lot before backing it into an open repair stall within the main garage. Only when Sam had gotten out of the truck did he hear the loud, incessant barking. There was Cypress, standing at the truck's grill, making a racket.

"Hey, hey…what's all the commotion about?"

Cypress went quiet but continued to stare.

Sam was tempted to say something flippant like, *use your words,* but shrugged instead.

"I thought you were leaving me," Cypress said, finally.

Being that they were now in a different physical location from before, Sam could tell the dog's voice was most definitely, muffled-sounding as it was, coming from this retriever. "Can I ask you…how come your lips don't move when you speak?"

Cypress looked away, maybe annoyed, maybe bored, then looked back up at him. "Because dogs can't actually talk…what you're hearing is technology at work."

"Okay…I guess. Second question. If you are indeed an alien consciousness, why do you sound so…well, human? Using common American slang and idioms?"

"Because, in addition to having an advanced communications technology device, which is called sensory comms, I have access to something called a Geo-Mind, which would be the equivalent of your world's most advanced AI mainframe computer, with processing capabilities one billion times more powerful. While human scientists are just now delving into the many possibilities of quantum computing, Silarians have been perfecting that science for centuries."

"And where is this technology? I mean physically on your body?"

"It is not on my body so much as in my body. With few options available to me at the time, I was forced to swallow the devices."

"You do know that will be a temporary solution, right?" Sam asked.

"Of course."

"Can you tell me why the video got you so…upset?"

Cypress didn't answer right away. "What I can tell you is that things were not what I expected them to be. Leave it to say, it seems…I may have been deceived."

Sam nodded. "Not sure what you mean by deceived…Anyway, what are you going to do now? As interesting as all this is, I still have work to do…My life can be somewhat hectic. People count on me." He looked at his watch. "And it looks like I won't be getting back to bed this morning."

Cypress tilted his head in a most dog-like manner.

"What?" Sam said.

"So…you're dismissing me?"

"I wouldn't put it like that. But, yeah. I'm not going to say anything to anyone about you. No one would believe me anyway. I'd end up tossed into a padded cell. No, you can go and do what you came here to do…just don't hurt anyone, okay?"

"You don't seem to understand my predicament, Sam."

That was the first time the dog had used his name, and it felt strange. "Okay. What would you like me to do?"

Cypress looked out to the early dawn—the sun was just now rising in the east. His back to Sam, he said, "I may be here for some time. I may be here for the remainder of my life…I do not believe there is a place for me back on Naru. Not anymore."

"I'm sorry to hear that. Truly. But I'm still not sure what you want from me."

Cypress looked back. "I can help you. I have capabilities…In exchange for letting me stay with you."

"You mean like a pet—"

"I will ask you to never, ever, ever use that term around me again," Cypress said, his lips peeling back to reveal white and very sharp-looking teeth as he said the words.

"Got it. Bad terminology…my bad."

A gold Honda pulled into Garcia Tow, Repair, and Stow and parked near the main office. A portly man with wavy black hair, wearing tattered jeans and a white T-shirt, got out of the car. Startled to see Sam, he approached with his hands splayed like he was ready to catch a basketball or something. "Oh God, Sam…Look, I know you're mad. I didn't think there'd be a call last night and, well, I had that date with Judy; you know, the one I was telling you about."

"Tony, you can't forward the towing business line to my cell phone like that."

"I know. But if it makes any difference, I think she's the one. Like, she and I…we really hit it off, Sam. And let me tell you…She has an ass like—"

Sam held up a hand. "I'm happy for you, Tony," he said and meant it. Tony was basically a good guy, but he hadn't had the best of luck with the women in his life this last year.

Tony noticed the dog for the first time. "Who's your friend?"

"That's Cypress."

Tony nodded. "Cool. Like, will he be our new junkyard dog… keep watch over the lot at night? Although, he doesn't look all that intimidating."

Tony had what was commonly referred to as the gift of gab. It was a nervous thing. When he was nervous, he couldn't shut up. That, or it was him coming from a large Italian family where if you didn't speak up, you never got a word in edgewise over your siblings. Sam knew most of his family, and they were all just as loud and friendly as Tony. Although, he was the hairiest of the bunch.

"Uh, we're taking it slow. But yeah, Cypress will be hanging with us for a while." Sam said, "Cypress, this is Tony DeLago. Tony, this is Cypress, the all-too-muddy golden retriever."

Tony went down on one knee and began petting Cypress's flank. The dog looked up at Sam with a pained expression.

Sam said, "He loves it when you do that. Never seen a dog that likes to be petted as much as this one."

"Is that right, boy?" Tony said, throwing his big, beefy, hairy arms around the dog's midsection and pulling him in close for a bear hug. "Well, he's come to the right place. I'm a hugger, and this dog will be getting a lot of hugs."

Sam couldn't help but chuckle at Cypress's continued look of torment.

* * *

At present, Sam was heading east on 2nd Street in Castle Rock. Tony had placed a plastic seat cover over the passenger seat, which Cypress was currently inhabiting.

"Where are we going?" Cypress said.

"Where I go most mornings. To get breakfast." Sam made a right on Wilcox and found an open parking spot. Getting out, he was about to tell the dog he wouldn't be long, but he was already jumping over the driver-side seat and was brushing past him. Sam's eyes were drawn to the errant dried dirt clods Cypress had left behind on the previously pristine pony driver's seat.

Keeping up with him on the sidewalk, Sam said, "Dogs are supposed to be on a leash here in town."

"How about I put you on a leash instead?" the dog replied without humor.

It was ten after six in the morning, and the B&B Café had just opened. Before opening the door, Sam said, "I'm not sure if they'll let you inside with me."

45

He opened the door and stepped in with the dog trailing close behind him. Harper was behind the counter, using a towel to wipe down the surface. "Hey, Sam!" she said, her eyes immediately drawn to the dog.

"Sorry," he said. "Look, if having the dog in here's a problem, he can wait outside."

"Nah…not a problem for me," she said. "But maybe today you can sit at a booth?" She came around the counter, plucking a menu from a nearby stack. She was wearing her usual—faded jeans worn low on narrow hips, and today it was a pink B&B T-shirt, one that did nothing to hide her trim, athletic shape. Her white Keds were remarkably clean, considering her profession. Today her blonde locks were piled high atop her head and held there with an intertwined matching pink ribbon. Her face was tan, and when she smiled like she was doing now, everything, all Sam's problems, all his issues, just seemed to evaporate.

Upon three of the barstools were regulars; each looked up from their respective newspapers. Jack Prewet said, "Didn't know you had a dog, Sam."

Taking his seat in the booth, Sam said, "This is kind of a trial situation…"

"Uh-huh, to see if the dog can put up with you, eh?" Jack retorted, which garnered chuckles from the other two at the counter, Burt Kline and Jerry Danbury, one who worked at Home Depot, the other who worked at Lowe's.

Sam felt Cypress getting comfortable at his feet.

Harper stole a quick look under the table and smiled. "Clean that pup up and he'll be a beauty."

"It's on my to-do list." He purposely avoided looking at the simple gold band encircling her ring finger. Sam declined the offered breakfast menu with a wave of his hand. "The usual's fine today, Harper." He glanced up, and they made eye contact. Seeing those pretty blue eyes, his heart missed a beat, and his breath caught in his chest.

She took notice of the red scrapes on his knuckles. And as if reading his thoughts, she smiled sympathetically. "I'll put in your order...Denver omelet, hash browns, English muffin. And I'll bring you a cup of Joe. Anything for..." She stole another peek under the table.

"Cypress, but he prefers to be called Cye." He heard a muted growl at his feet.

"Hi, Cye. Would you like something to eat too? Maybe a couple of pieces of bacon?"

She straightened and cocked her head. "Would that be okay?"

Before he could answer, her phone buzzed from her back pocket. She pulled it free, and Sam caught a glimpse of her home screen pic—one he'd seen a few times prior.

It was Harper with her husband, Paul Godard, some three years earlier. The two, with beaming smiles, arms around each other's waists, were posing at Garden of the Gods in Colorado Springs. Paul, a handsome Adonis, had just graduated from the academy to become a fireman. Just married, the two had their whole lives ahead of them. She had been working at a doctor's office there in the Springs, while Paul was the new, young, good-natured recruit there at Fire Station 18. It had been his third call—a three-alarm fire. Many units had been called in to contain an old apartment building blaze.

Paul was one of four who had been four stories up, going room to room, getting the trapped occupants out. Paul and another fireman had entered one of the bedrooms. The floor had suddenly given out; they'd fallen two stories into the raging fire. He'd been rescued with no less than 70 percent of his body sustaining third-degree burns. He'd died two days later in the hospital. Six months later, still devastated, Harper had packed up and left

47

the Springs for Castle Rock, where she had a few friends and the opportunity to make a fresh start with far fewer reminders of what she had lost.

"Sure, bacon would be nice," Sam said, not really knowing what the alien being was comfortable eating. Maybe Cypress was a vegetarian or had a thing about eating swine…maybe pig was similar to an animal on his home planet of…was it Nora? No, Naru…

"Okay, I'll see what I can scrounge up." She hurried off, leaving her scent—a mixture of something floral and bright sunshine.

Fifteen minutes later, Sam was halfway through his Denver omelet, Cypress having practically inhaled his bacon strips. The front entrance swung open, and there stood Officer Eagan Pitt. He scanned the nearby booths until he spotted Sam. He hurried over and gestured to the opposite seat. "Can I, Sam?"

"Sure, sit. Want to order something?"

"Um…maybe some coffee." He signaled to Harper and made a sipping from an invisible coffee cup gesture. Eagan was out of uniform, being off duty; he worked the night shift.

"Sorry to crash your breakfast like this, man."

Sam shrugged. "No worries. You look a little frazzled. What's up?"

"I'm getting some flak about that tow last night. Captain's had no less than a dozen calls about that, um…aircraft."

"You mean the drone?" Sam said. He felt Cypress shift position at his feet.

"Yeah, I think we both know it wasn't a drone, Sam."

"No?" he said, feigning confusion.

"Look…apparently the thing showed up on radar. Pinged a few alarms. Even piqued the interest of a new body put in place to investigate what are now called unidentified aerial phenomena, or UAPs. The Office of the Under Secretary of Defense for Intelligence & Security at the Pentagon. They monitor reported sightings of what used to be called UFOs."

"Huh, that's interesting," Sam said, taking another bite of his omelet.

Eagan stared at him blank-faced. He wasn't buying his act.

Eagan was not liked by everyone in town, although Sam got along with him well enough. He had a Mayberry, clueless-Don-Knotts-cop air about him. Maybe not so much his looks; Eagan had a dreadful thinning red hair comb-over, oversized ears, a prominent nose, and a continual stoop to his posture. But it had been his meteoric rise from one career to that of his current position within the Castle Rock PD that had some people irked.

Two and a half years earlier, Eagan had been a mere mall cop, working the morning shift at the Park Meadows Mall, a quick twenty-minute drive from Castle Rock. Sam had heard the story from Eagan himself, somewhat embellished, he was sure, as well as from others, where the story did not depict the man in such a glowing light. Apparently, one fateful day there, Eagan had gotten the recognition he needed to step up to be a police officer. A robbery had been taking place at Pottery Barn. He'd gotten the call on his walkie…a 10-65 in progress. The suspect was armed. Understand, Eagan had had less than a half day of training with his new Taser weapon. He did not have clearance to carry a gun.

Coming upon the scene, he'd known at the time, this would be his chance to prove himself. So, he'd headed up the escalator to the sweeping glass entrance of Pottery Barn. Eagan had heard a woman scream and a man shout, "Shut the fuck up!" He'd crept toward the entrance and made quick eye contact with a woman who was standing behind the cash register. The suspect was pointing a gun at her while she was nervously putting cash into a large Pottery Barn shopping bag. Eagan, taking the initiative, had crept inside with a finger up to his lips to customers and staff who stood, petrified, off to the side.

Eagan had had his Taser X26P raised and at the ready. A single-shot Taser with a single cartridge…he'd have only one chance to get it right. He'd flipped the little safety lever up into the fire-ready position. The thing about Tasers is that each shot, each zap, lasts no longer than five seconds or so. In most cases, that's plenty of time to subdue a suspect—long enough to cuff someone. One extra tidbit about the X26P is that it also records video. The marvels of modern technology.

Anyway, the lady behind the register had been finishing up, having transferred all the money from her cash register over to the Pottery Barn bag. Seeing the approaching mall cop, the lady had given Eagan the cue. "That's all the money I have."

The crook had taken the bag and quickly spun away, coming face to face with Eagan. Eagan, who shouldn't have been so surprised, had reflexively pulled the trigger. Fired but somehow missed—the two metal prongs with their thin, trailing wires, wires that carried no less than fifty thousand volts—had arced high in the air, missing the crook but hitting an elderly man in the forehead. A man who had been held upright by his aluminum walker. Now on the run, this certainly could have been the crook's luckiest day, that is, if the elderly man's walker hadn't tumbled over and gotten tangled up between the robber's legs.

After regaining his wits, Eagan had risen to the occasion and pounced. He'd gotten the thief flipped over onto his belly and handcuffed. There'd even been a round of applause from the surrounding customer spectators. Luckily, the old man with the walker had sustained only minor injuries, and when he had been released from the hospital, he'd said he couldn't remember much about what happened, but he was happy that the criminal had been apprehended.

Eagan had been honored with the Park Meadow's Mall Cop of the Year Award, and there had been a highly complimentary newspaper article in the *Lone Tree Voice* about him and his dramatic arrest—one that did not make much mention of the errant Taser shot fiasco. Eagan's good deeds had provided him with the perfect credentials when applying to Highlands Ranch Law Enforcement Training Facility. Sure, his academic scores had not been among the highest in his class, but he'd graduated just the same.

It wasn't until Eagan was actually on the job, working patrols, doing his night shift gig, when that X26P stun gun video, a video with remarkable 1920 x 1080 pixel resolution, went live. Unfortunately for Eagan, the short clip was hilariously funny—the adrift fired-off shot, the electrodes to the old man's forehead, the tumbling walker debacle…Within hours, the clip had gone viral. It was on Facebook, Instagram, and most damaging, the Castle Rock Next Door app. To this day, Eagan had become known as *Officer Sure-Shot.*

Chapter 8

Solar System—23rd Terra-Displacement Fleet
Colonel Gha Strone Mahn

Colonel Gha Strone Mahn stood before the observation window, chin raised, with his spine erect—shoulders back—proud and in command. The pose of that of his father and his father's father before that when they, too, stood upon their own respective heavy cruisers' bridge in decades past…probably ones not so different from this one. The *Lonemach Tryon* had come out of a shipyard on Naru's seventh moon, Caligon Pli, just three weeks prior.

Strone was shirtless. Silarians were not much for clothes that covered a male's anatomy. As far as Silarians went, he was larger than average. When he moved, and even sometimes when he did not, his physique, his defined musculature, literally rippled. He liked the effect his body, his prowess, had on those around him—his crew. He garnered respect without having to say a word.

But Strone was in trouble. That was a given. This…mess had occurred on his watch. Sure, he could blame the circumstances on a technological malfunction—a glitch. There would have been no way of knowing that shitty little Landa-Craft's self-destruct mechanism was…well, problematic.

More Attack Stingers were coming through the massive jump gate now, their sleek forms piercing what looked like a vertical placid pond of water. Each of the arrowhead-shaped attack vessels left expanding circular ripples in its wake.

With each campaign came complications; Strone knew this. But that did not mean there wouldn't be repercussions. Silarians took a targeted world's dismantling seriously. The very survival of Naru, a world no larger than Earth, depended on the element of surprise—following the prescribed methodology that had effectively brought down so many similar worlds to this Earth world.

Strone took in the beauty of Earth with its bright blue oceans, green land masses, and fluffy white clouds. At one time, Naru had been such a world—green and lush—a paradise. But you couldn't stop progress. You couldn't hinder technological advances for the sake of a few trees and a few degrees of atmospheric warming. Naru, someday, would be returned to all its previous glory, and it would be that same technology, that and Silarians' physical prowess within the galaxy, that would make it happen. It was happening now.

Strone's people had learned a long time ago that terra-forming in the typical sense did not work. What did work was terra-displacement. It was much more effective—and so much faster. Once this world had been subdued—the humans annihilated—the massive collector ships would arrive in those pretty blue skies. First the siphon collectors would take the ocean waters, then the hardscape collectors would come and get to work, literally gouging and carving out the richest lands of this inconsequential biosphere.

Within a few short months, there would be little left of this world—certainly not enough to sustain life. So be it. As the teachings of *Orlicon Tharsh* so righteously dictated, there was a universal hierarchy for all living things within this realm of existence. *Take what is yours or have it taken from you…*

A stillness came over the heavy cruiser's bridge. Eight 3D holographic displays all came alive at once. Strone maintained his rigid posture, his air of indifference. But his mind was racing; he could not recall the counsel magistrate ever having made an appearance on a lowly attack vessel such as the *Lonemach Tryon*. Then again, Colonel Gha Strone Mahn was the son of Imperial Gha Calli Mahn…Naru's galactic military leader.

Strone's breath caught in his chest, for none other than Calli, his father, was also standing before him—yes, it was his virtual presence, but so very formidable just the same.

"Father…you honor me with your presence."

"And you disgrace me with your incompetence."

Strone was not surprised by his father's ridicule. He could not show favoritism as a member of the counsel magistrate. But the words still stung.

Calli continued, "The element of surprise is key for these campaigns to achieve their ultimate success. Any loss of Silarian life needs to be avoided. What are your plans to rectify your thus far incompetent actions?"

Strone glanced back, then looked to those on his left and then right, ensuring he made eye contact with each of the now-present, albeit virtual, council members. Bemusement lifted the corners of his lips, and there was a sparkle in his eyes—all an act, but a necessary one. "We have located the last known position of the… problematic scanner vessel—an older-model Landa-Craft."

"And the other scanner vessels deployed to this world?"

"Unsure if they, too, had been infected, we immediately triggered their self-destruct functions. There is no chance the…*virus*, as it was, could have survived," Strone said, while still taken aback by these queries. The simple fact that this conversation was going on in such a public manner gave credence to its importance. That Strone had given the order to sacrifice those pilots and Landa-Crafts had not been common knowledge. How could it be, if they intended to maintain necessary recruitment numbers? Now, unfortunately, the entire bridge crew was privy to what had occurred; thus, perhaps, they, too, would need to be sacrificed. *Orlicon Tharsh will reward them in the afterlife.*

"Concerning the one remaining Landa-Craft and pilot. My plan is simple, Father…The area will be placed within an isolation zone. The township, this Castle Rock, will be decimated by our Attack Stingers' weaponry, followed by a thorough ground forces campaign. That Landa-Craft and its pilot will be found and destroyed. Additionally, we will ensure no human survives this incursion."

Calli Mahn's expression darkened. "So, this Landa-Craft pilot… he has yet to be terminated, and his ship is still not destroyed?!"

Reluctantly, Strone continued, "Cypress Mag Nuel is his name. A young and thought-to-be-competent pilot. Our scans have located his body…he appears to be deceased. That is the good news. Oddly, though, his implants are still active…that and they are on the move. It is possible his corpse has been ravaged. Perhaps wild animals—"

"This situation is unacceptable!" Imperial Gha Calli Mahn's voice boomed. "What about his craft? We know for a fact it has been infected."

"At present, we…are having difficulty locating the craft."

"Let me be clear on this, Colonel Gha Strone Mahn: your competence is under close scrutiny. The very assumption that an infected Naru Geo-Mind device may be down there, perhaps fully operational, could be catastrophic for the Silarian Empire. There has never been a breach like this…not ever. Our dominance in this quadrant depends on the actions you take today. Ensure that isolation zone is implemented immediately. Nothing gets in or out of that township…and once you are successful, all deployed Stinger Silarian pilots and ground forces will require termination. That is

on you. We must impede even the slightest chance of cross con-
tamination. *Orlicon Tharsh* will reward them in the afterlife."

Chapter 9

B&B Café, Castle Rock, Colorado
Harper Godard

Harper, leaning against the back counter with her arms folded beneath her chest, eyed the folded bills lying upon the yet-to-be-cleared table. *Who leaves a fifty-dollar tip?* Most of the morning rush had come and gone, including Sam, Eagan, and the dog—the three having left in a sudden hurry. The overhead lights flickered on and off, and someone back in the kitchen yelled, "Solar flare!" Harper rolled her eyes; she was sick of that stupid phrase.

Burt, in his late sixties, mostly retired except for his part-time job at Lowe's, was one of the few who hadn't left yet. Without looking up from his newspaper, he said, "You know that boy's sweet on you."

"Yeah, I know…He shouldn't leave me tips like that, though. People think he and I are…well, you know. He just shouldn't do that. Not that I can't use the money right now."

Burt flipped to another page of the *Denver Post*. Harper saw that he was now reading the obit section…why was it that older people were so interested in seeing who had recently passed? Was it the fact that their own names, their own tributes, had yet to make it into print? She said, as much to herself as to Burt, "I'm just not ready yet." She mindlessly twirled the gold band on her ring finger. "Sam is a sweetheart…maybe too much so."

Burt snorted. "Don't let that whole George Bailey routine fool you."

"What is that supposed to mean?"

He lowered his paper and took a sip of lukewarm coffee. "How much do you know about the man?"

She shrugged one shoulder. "I hate gossip. Pay little attention to it. What I've heard, though, is he's wealthy…at least for Castle Rock standards. A family trust or something…he has a few businesses around town. Does what he calls his rounds, checking in on them each day. He gives a fair number of people jobs. Like I said, he's a good guy."

Burt nodded. "Sam grew up here. His parents were both involved with wind power. Were among the early investors in those big turbine wind farms you see sprouting up around the state. When Sam was in his teens, he acted out…rebelled. Got into some trouble, nothing too bad. I guess having privilege, having everything handed to you on a silver platter, can be its own kind of burden."

"I'm sorry, but I'm not going to feel sorry for someone who had everything."

Burt continued, "Sam turned things around later in high school…got good grades. Surprised everyone by choosing West Point. It was the one time in his life he asked his father for help. Getting into West Point is very difficult. You need a 3.9 GPA; you need to apply for a nomination, work with a Field Force rep, complete various tests. And with his father's help, he got a senator's recommendation."

"So, Sam was in the army?" she asked, finding it hard to imagine the man in uniform.

"He became a captain."

She looked at Burt, not sure she wanted to hear any more of this. She was sure there was a story here that didn't turn out well for Sam.

"Where Sam excelled was with intelligence. He studied languages at West Point, that and analytics of coded enemy communications. He was put into a covert unit in Afghanistan as a young lieutenant. His unique competencies were quickly put to use. The man not only went on to see a lot of action; he became a highly decorated Green Beret in the process. Sam was among a very few highly honored with both a Medal of Honor and a Purple Heart for his service in places such as Kandahar and Kabul."

"I had no idea."

Burt let out a weary breath. "His parents were killed in a car wreck while he was still in Afghanistan. They'd done so much for this town. Their loss was felt, is still being felt, by many. Me included. So now, it seems Sam's on some sort of crusade to make up for things. For not appreciating what his parents provided him, and for the lives he took in the war…Justified or not, he carries that weight on his back every day."

Harper stared at Burt. "You know a lot about Sam…about his situation."

"I should. I was his father's best friend. More like a brother than a friend."

"I'm sorry, Burt."

"Don't be. Just don't be too hard on Sam. You've heard the saying still waters run deep?"

She nodded.

"In his case, the waters run deep, but they are never still."

She was too tired to think about Sam, especially when her own life was so up in the air with her mornings, five days a week, spent here at the B&B, and afternoons at the hospital, where she was completing shift hours, then school at night to become an RN. How on earth would she ever be able to consider such things as dating and having a normal life?

Chapter 10

Outside the B&B Café, Castle Rock, Colorado
Sam Dale

Sam led Eagan, along with the dog, across Wilcox Street and stopped at the little park area in front of the commemorative Douglas County Veterans Monument—a towering bronze statue of an eagle, its wings spread wide, in the process of landing on something…maybe a rock?

He turned to Eagan and said, "I want you to hold up on saying anything about that aircraft."

Eagan made an overdramatic expression, like it was the most astonishing thing he'd ever heard. "Why, for God's sake? More to the point, why would you give two shits who I contact? This is an opportunity to unload the damn thing…let it be someone else's problem. No. You just need to tell me where it is."

"It's safe, and more importantly, it's secure."

"Secure from who? Come on…What's this all about, Sam? Messing with the government—you should know as well as anyone that never turns out well."

And here they were. Sam had most definitely wanted to avoid this moment in time. He looked down at Cypress, who was, in turn, looking up at him, his big brown eyes locked onto his. Once more, Sam considered the most likely reality that Cypress was his own version of Harvey—Jimmy Stewart's six-foot-tall imaginary rabbit.

Eagan, too, continued to stare at Sam, his impatience now evident, putting his hands on skinny hips and making annoying clucking sounds with his tongue. Was Eagan, this once mall cop, now Castle Rock police officer, the one person Sam should be trusting with this? Something so significant? Sam racked his brain for an alternative, any alternative. Telling him about Cypress was a bad idea; he knew it in his bones.

Sam said, "That airship, that craft…it's an alien spaceship."

Eagan didn't look surprised by this revelation. "All the more reason to get it as far away from Castle Rock, from us, as soon as possible."

Sam couldn't disagree with that. And why should he have any loyalty to this alien-inhabited dog currently sitting at his feet? More importantly, why would Eagan?

"What if I told you I…met the pilot? I actually helped the pilot."

Eagan was expressionless for at least five seconds. Then he made an expression of distaste, like he'd just eaten a bad clam. "What are you talking about, Sam?"

"Think about it, Eagan…here we are talking about an alien ship…but what about the pilot who flew it here? You left me alone out there at that gulch in the middle of the night."

Eagan smiled, then rubbed the red peach fuzz stubble on his chin. "You're telling me you met…an alien? And you're still alive to talk about it?"

Sam looked down at Cypress, who seemed to be enjoying this. Was perfectly fine with the uncomfortable situation he had put Sam in. Or had he? Was Cypress Harvey?

"The alien was dying, Eagan. So…he transferred his consciousness into another being."

Eagan erupted with a loud belly laugh—a watering eyes and having to bend over to catch his breath kind of laugh. A breeze had come up, making the red strands of his comb-over suddenly take flight.

That's when Cypress bit him.

Eagan howled and reached for his left calf. "Owwww! Your fucking dog just bit me!" Both of his hands were now wrapped around his lower leg as if he had been bitten by the great white in the *Jaws* movie. Several pedestrians slowed but kept moving past.

Cypress stepped in close, his snout just inches from Eagan's face. The dog's words were just barely audible, but Sam could hear each of them.

"Listen to me carefully, you stupid buffoon...*I* am the alien Sam is referring to."

Eagan's eyes went wide, his already milky complexion going so white he looked dead. "Wha...wah...what's going on here? This is a joke, right?" Eagan fell all the way back onto his rump and then looked up to Sam. Eyes questioning, a half smile hopeful that Sam would, somehow, relieve him of this...conundrum.

Sam, though, was relieved. Apparently, he wasn't crazy.

Cypress said, "Take a breath, Officer Pitt, and calm down."

Eagan's Adam's apple bobbed as the man did as told. Eye to eye with the dog now, the off-duty police officer nodded. "How is this possible, Sam? How is it that a...dog is talking to me?"

Cypress said, "I can talk for myself. Sam already told you. I was dying. The crash landing had given me mere minutes to live. Understand, where I come from, the transference of one's consciousness is somewhat commonplace. At least at the end of one's life. This canine form you are conversing with just so happened to be in close vicinity to that gulch. It was the closest living being... so I chose to commence the transfer."

Sam knelt down next to the two. "Sorry to dump this on you

like this, man. And I know it's a lot to…well, to take in." Sam held out a hand. "Let me help you up."

Eagan stood, having forgotten about the nip on his calf. He looked around his surroundings.

"Here's the situation as I see it," Sam said. "Sure, you can report all this. Run it up the proverbial Castle Rock PD flagpole. Hell, maybe have a one-on-one talk with your captain. Explain the whole crashed spacecraft up there near Lake Gulch Road thing. Then how you met me here this morning…how we talked, and how you were bitten by a dog. Then how you had a conversation with said dog…a dog who, in actuality, you found out, was an alien. An alien from a planet called Naru."

Eagan looked down at Cypress. "You're from a planet called Naru?"

Cypress nodded. "It's in what you would call the Antares System."

"Uh…oh…okay. I don't really know much about space stuff… astronomy." He looked at Sam. "What am I supposed to do with all this, Sam?"

"I don't know. I'm in the same boat. Maybe we don't say anything for now? While we give it some thought? We can talk later."

"And the…spaceship? Cap knows you pulled it out of the gulch. Towed it somewhere."

"How about, for now, we say some other top-secret agency came and got it?"

Eagan's eyes went momentarily vacant. "You can bet there are a lot of clandestine government agencies…There's a good chance they don't communicate with one another." He blew out stale coffee breath while assessing the alien dog. "We don't want to get in the middle of all this. Yeah, best we keep quiet. Stay the hell out of it."

Sam placed a hand on Eagan's stooped shoulder. "I couldn't

have said it any better myself." Sam checked his watch; he was late for his rounds, late getting to the gun shop.

Chapter 11

Spin-Dry, Castle Rock, Colorado
Sam Dale

They drove in silence for a while. Cypress was back, sitting tall on the passenger seat. He was staring down at a knotted black plastic bag on the floor in front of him. They had made a quick stop off at Sam's third business, Spin-Dry, a coin laundromat that was the least time-consuming of all Sam's businesses. Other than occasional machine maintenance and ensuring he always had someone working the front counter, the establishment was a consistent, albeit minimally profitable, business.

Back in the car, Sam said, "You can't just take a dump like that anywhere you like…the middle of a public laundromat…it's not appropriate."

Cypress gave Sam a sideways glance. "It was an automatic bodily function. Bacon in…poop out. This canine body has a number of those automatic responses, you know. You should be glad that up till now, I've curtailed a nearly overpowering urge to lick my balls."

"Look. Back there, you went ballistic…biting Eagan on the leg. More recently you started yelling for me to get something to pick up your…droppings. I'm fairly certain people heard you. Heard a dog speaking."

"It was more like a nip. I didn't even break the skin…nothing I can do about any of that now. Keeping my implants with me is no trivial matter. Even though I have a neural link to them, being separated is not an option. Anyway, how was I supposed to know where is and isn't appropriate for a dog to defecate?"

"I thought your, whatever you call it…the stream…and Geo—"

"Geo-Mind."

"Yeah, Geo-Mind. I thought it was all-knowing. The most powerful AI computer in this quadrant of space."

"Oh, it is…" Cypress lowered his voice to the volume of a whisper, "but it's no longer fully operational."

"Maybe because you swallowed it?"

"No. The devices are impervious to, well, just about anything." The golden retriever looked at Sam with concern in his eyes. "I'm worried."

"About what?"

Cypress did not reply.

"I'm sure you'll figure it out."

Sam made a right on Plum Creek Parkway and another right onto the freeway on-ramp going north. "That brings up the question I asked you when we first met. What were you, are you, doing here? No bullshit this time, Cypress."

"Here in this vehicle?" Cypress said.

Sam gave him a weary look.

"This world has been a curiosity to my people for some time now. But to answer your specific question, my Landa-Craft was scanning and cataloging the surface and subsurface of Earth."

"Why?"

Again, Cypress went quiet. He looked out the passenger window. *Oh no*…Sam had a really bad feeling about this. "Cypress, it's one thing for me to be helping you…a stranded alien on a distant world. Maybe help you find a way to get back home. But if your people are here to hurt us—"

"There are certain things I am not at liberty to talk about, Sam."

Sam got off on the Wolfensberger exit and made a left. Once they were over the freeway overpass, he veered to the side of the road and slowed to a stop. Sam leaned over to the right in front of Cypress, unlatched the passenger door, and gave it a shove. The door swung all the way open and Sam said, "Get out."

Cypress looked at him and then at the nearby sidewalk. "You would do that?"

"I *am* doing that. Out with you."

Cypress didn't move. "Fine. I will tell you. Some things only now are starting to make sense to me. But either way, you are not going to be happy with what I have to say."

"Lie to me or hide the truth from me again, and this *thing* we have here is over. You're on your own."

"Understand. I'll tell you, but not here."

Sam hesitated, then stepped on the gas, making the passenger-side door swing shut. That was when his iPhone rang. He didn't recognize the number. "Hello?"

"Sam?"

"Yes, who is this?"

"This is Harper…you know, from the B&B?"

"Oh, hi…" he said, suddenly tongue-tied. "What—"

"I just wanted to tell you—more like inform you—who your dog's true owner is."

"You're talking about Cypress?"

Harper said, "I started my shift over at Adventist Hospital—"

"That's right, you work at the hospital."

"Yeah, afternoons and evenings. I'm a nurse. Finishing up my classes and hours to get my RN certificate. Anyway, the old man…

Arthur Moore…he's awake now and looking for his dog…Rocko. The description, golden retriever, blue collar, kinda matches the dog you brought in this morning."

Crap! Now what do I do? "Yeah…I don't think this can be the same dog," Sam said.

"Really? Sounds like the same dog to me."

"What's wrong with the old man? Arthur, was it?"

"I can't really say because of HIPAA…health information privacy."

"So, if I said heart attack and you didn't say anything back…"

She kept quiet.

"And that would require a few days, maybe a week in the hospital?"

Again, she kept quiet.

"If this is his dog, and I'm not saying it is, I'll make sure Cypress—Rocko—is returned."

"That sounds good. Can I tell him we may have found his dog? That he's in good hands? Arthur is pretty agitated, and this might alleviate some of that."

"Sure. Makes sense," Sam said, trying to think of something, anything, to keep her on the line.

There was an awkward quiet before Harper said, "Sam…can I ask you something?"

"Uh…sure. Is this about the dog?"

She laughed. "No, this is about—"

The phone suddenly beeped, and the line went dead. Up ahead, traffic was backing up. Sitting taller in his seat, Sam could see the traffic signal light had gone dark. "Terrific. Power's out. Guess that explains why cell service crapped out." Sam wondered what it was that Harper was going to ask him.

* * *

Cypress was looking around; he looked agitated.

They pulled into the parking lot of Giro Guns and Ammo. Sam said, "This is my fourth business. Come on; I'll introduce you to the gang."

They entered through the front door; there were five customers, four men and a woman, in the shop. Not bad for this time of the morning. Sam noticed the overhead lights were out. He looked down at Cypress. "Is it okay being this far away from your poop bag? Your devices?"

Cypress nodded. In a lowered tone, he said, "A few hundred feet should not be a problem."

Sam had purchased Giro Guns and Ammo not long after Garcia's and the Spin-Dry businesses were up and running. He'd heard around town that the owner of the local gun shop, with an attached shooting range, was retiring and looking to sell the place, so he had gone to talk to him. The guy was a former Navy SEAL—Walter Essex. Hard core. Loved guns, loved to shoot, loved to tell stories. And, if Sam had to guess, might be dealing guns on the side. To what degree, Sam had no idea. The man probably had an impressive personal arsenal—maybe hidden away on his property at the south end of town.

Walter and Sam were different in their approach to gun ownership. Even so, Walter had come to realize the gun shop would be in good hands with Sam. Truth was, Sam wanted to put a new spin on the way the business operated. Walter had had three people working for him. He'd told Sam if he wanted to buy the place, he would have to keep them on and let Walter stay on part time. Help manage the place. Sam had reluctantly agreed. That was three months ago.

Seeing their arrival, Walter Essex came around the counter. At sixty-five, the ex-owner, now manager, helped train people on how to safely handle and shoot all kinds of firearms. Longish gray hair, six feet tall, the older man was still muscular—a guy who didn't need to spend his off hours at the gym. He reminded Sam of the Sam Elliott character in the old *Roadhouse* flick. At present, he looked a little unsettled.

"Everything okay?" Sam asked.

He nodded and said in his deep baritone, "Power's out. But business is good. Already sold a couple of 19s and a Sig."

He was referring to Glock 19s and a Sig Sauer P365 semiautomatic pistol, both being the most popular handguns on the market these days.

"Who's this?" Walter asked.

"This is Cypress. Careful, he bites," Sam said without a smile.

They spent the next fifteen minutes with flashlights, reviewing inventory stock in the back room. Sam looked over reorder requests, which he signed off on, and then they got down to several personnel issues that needed to be dealt with.

That was when Sam heard it—raised voices out on the showroom floor. Walter closed his eyes with a weary look. "This shit's been nonstop between the guys for the last week."

Sam came out of the back room, seeing the customers had all left. Daryl, easily six four and pushing three hundred pounds, was methodically putting guns back in the glass showcase.

Lester Price, who had been with the shop a year longer than Daryl, was talking, more like scolding, the bigger man. "You think people want to buy firearms from someone who can't string two consecutive sentences together? You make people fucking nervous, dude. Take a class...maybe pretend you're mute and write down your answers to people."

Daryl said, "I'm s-s-s-s-sorry. She made mmmm-me-me nerner-nervous."

"Well, you can't start blubbering every time a hot chick with big tits comes into the store."

"Lester! That's enough!" Walter said.

Lester was thin, wiry, and had more ink on his body than any person Sam had ever met. He liked to show off his many tats by wearing tank tops and wifebeaters—even in the dead of winter. His black hair was long, and he had a wispy Fu Manchu style beard. He kept his eyes on Daryl. There was real anger there—anger that Sam didn't get. Sure, Daryl had a speech disorder. He was dealing with it, and for the most part, the customers were sympathetic and patient. And Sam appreciated how hard he worked. Besides working part time at Giro, Daryl also worked at the Castle Rock Collective, a coffee shop that hired adults with special needs. But Lester's lack of tolerance was becoming a serious problem. Yes, Sam wanted to keep his promise to Walter, to hold onto all of the preexisting employees, but Lester's actions were making that difficult.

Sam said, "Daryl, why don't you take a break? Grab a smoke out back."

"I'm not done putting away the wep-wep-weaponry."

"See? Who fucking talks like that?" Lester said, giving Sam an *I told you so* expression.

It was no stretch of the imagination that Daryl was also somewhere on the autism spectrum. Ignoring Lester, Sam said, "Daryl, Walter or I will put the guns away…We'll do a good job. I promise. Go take your break."

Daryl nodded while avoiding eye contact. Once Sam heard the shop's back door slam closed, Sam turned to Lester. "Why are you going after Daryl so much? What's up with you?"

Lester looked at Walter for some kind of backup but got none. "Like this is my fault. You're just like the other soldier boy over there…always taking the tard's side."

"Talking like that is unacceptable," Sam said. "That's not a word you use here or anywhere. Do you want to get canned? Is that what this is about? Get fired so you can collect unemployment?"

Lester smirked and started putting the display guns away without paying attention to how they were positioned. Which, of course, would later drive Daryl into a frenzy.

Walter said, "Lester...stop. Go apologize to Daryl. Talk it out with him."

Now Lester looked to Sam for help. Sam held up a hand. "No. Don't argue; just do it."

Lester stormed out like a petulant child.

Sam caught the eye of Walter—who had been leaning within the open threshold to the back room, his arms folded over his chest. Sam had wanted to fire Lester months ago, but Walter had said he'd work with him. He'd been certain the young man would come around. But Walter had been wrong. Some people are just bad to the bone. Lester was one of those people.

"Are you going to say I told you so?" Walter asked.

Sam looked down at the dog, which had been watching the scene with interest. "No, Walter. This is one time I'd rather not have been right. You've written him up? Documented his behavior?"

He nodded.

Sam let out a breath. "Make sure you get his keys, and we'll need to change the gun safe's passcodes and any passwords once power comes back on and the computers reboot. Let our vendors know he's no longer a part of the team."

"And a replacement?"

"First ask around...if necessary, place an ad. You can give Lester the boot when he comes back in."

"You don't want to do it?" Walter asked, looking surprised.

"Actually, I do, but you're the shop's manager. Comes with the territory."

"Roger that...I'll make it happen."

Sam caught sight of Cypress. Again, the dog looked agitated.

Hunched over, his ears were back. If Sam was to guess, the dog seemed scared.

Chapter 12

Castle Rock, Colorado
Sam Dale

It took twenty minutes to make it back across town. The power was still out, and traffic was a mess. The Pizza Joint, Sam's fifth in-town purchase, was a small fifteen-hundred square-foot establishment built in the early 1950s. There were no parallel parking spaces available off Wilcox, so Sam parked in the back. He and Cypress came around the side of the building, where Sam noticed that the bright red neon OPEN sign was on as normal.

Sam stopped and listened. There was a consistent, rumbling, humming sound. He said to Cypress, "Because the structure is so old, and we've had problems with the electrical wiring and too many outages, I purchased an oversized gas generator—and that's what we're hearing. The Pizza Joint's probably one of the few restaurants in town still doing business today."

Sam expected a comment or at least a snarky remark from the dog, now at his side, but none came.

The entrance to the Pizza Joint was on Wilcox, and there were several bench-style tables outside. Most of the restaurant's business came from pickup and delivery. But today, every table, every seat, was taken. Cypress stopped, raised his snout, and sniffed the air.

"That's probably a new smell for you…Pizza is one of Earth's most prized culinary gems. Play your cards right, and I'll get you a slice."

That seemed to pique the dog's interest.

Sam's pride and joy of the Pizza Joint was the Baker's Pride 4153 Superdeck Series Deck Oven. When he'd bought the place from the previous owner, Sam had quickly discovered the original pizza oven needed to be scrapped. The Baker's Pride oven had put him back almost fifty grand—maybe not one of his more prudent investments.

Luna Kelly, apron tied around her waist and notepad in hand, was standing amid the patrons, taking orders. She looked over at Sam as they approached.

"Place is bustling, boss!"

Luna, black, wore her long wavy hair in braided pigtails with bright pink ribbons.

She was wearing skinny jeans and a bright yellow T-shirt. A few pounds overweight, the sixteen-year-old was always cheerful and enthusiastic. The customers loved her, as did Sam.

She put her attention back onto the elderly woman she'd been speaking with. "The pizza dough is what really makes the difference. Sam—that's him over there with the dog—trained us employees to make it with 'double zero' flour, the traditional flour used in Naples to make 'real' Italian pizza. Then you mix in unbleached all-purpose flour, salt, water, olive oil, and yeast." She looked over to Sam with questioning eyes, and he offered back a reassuring smile. She was doing just fine. "And then, and this is super important—you mix everything by hand. You use one hand and swish the ingredients gently around the bowl. You see, you have to mix the dough together until it forms into one big soft dough ball…then you stop and cover the bowl with a cloth napkin and let it rest for fifteen minutes…"

Sam signaled with a twirling finger for Luna to move things along. There were hungry patrons waiting to get their orders taken.

They stepped inside, where Sam saw the open kitchen was a madhouse of activity. He caught the eye of Zach Finch, the manager on duty. He had a blue bandanna tied around his forehead. The twenty-five-year-old looked more than a little stressed.

Zach yelled through the pass-through window, "Phones and internet are down. Having to ring pies up the old-fashioned way."

There were no tables inside, but there were wooden plank countertops set up all along the windows, where customers could eat facing out toward the street. It was there that Sam saw Julian Humblecut. He was easy to spot among the other patrons; he was wearing a baby blue bathrobe and mismatched slippers. And for some reason, Cypress, now sitting beside the ill-kempt-looking older man, seemed to be highly interested in what he was doing on his laptop.

The man needed a shave as usual. Julian was the very epitome of your disheveled mad scientist, and he just so happened to be one of Sam's best friends. A lunchtime regular here almost daily, he'd wander over from Encore, the five-story condo development across the street where he had taken up residence in the top floor penthouse. The man had inquisitive large blue-gray eyes, with eyebrows that seemed to be permanently upraised. He was thin, probably too thin. Truth was, Sam worried about him. Rarely was Julian not sitting behind a computer screen, as he was doing now.

The first time he'd come into the Pizza Joint, Julian had been wearing this same terry cloth bathrobe attire. Zach had thought he was a homeless man, but knowing Sam's policy on helping those in the community, he'd offered the man a free pizza pie. Little had he, or Sam, known at the time, that Julian Humblecut was a multi-millionaire. Julian had been involved with the early development of

NASA's James Webb Space Telescope back in 2001. He'd gone on to many other projects with a number of Colorado high-tech firms. Never one to let the grass grow under his feet, he'd move on as soon as he lost interest or was let go due to not adhering to HR dress code standards, or failing to show up at pre-established work hours, or any number of other reasons. But the man didn't need to work these days. His multi-patents income alone was quite significant.

Julian tapped away on his laptop, ignoring Cypress. Sam saw that his computer was plugged into a wall outlet. "You have access to the internet, Julian?" Sam asked, remembering what Zack had said and that the gun shop had lost web access earlier.

"This is very strange, Sam." For the first time, he looked at him, and then down at the dog.

Sam shrugged. "Not the first time we've lost power…had a bad internet connection. Remember last winter when—"

Julian was already shaking his head, his expression intense. "That is not normal." He was pointing out the window, over his shoulder, to something high in the air. "That is the crux of the problem. A problem I can't get my mind around."

"What is that?" Sam said, leaning forward and squinting. Whatever it was, it was stationary—maybe a hundred, hundred and fifty yards up in the sky. "A helicopter?"

"Don't be ridiculous. Do you see rotor blades?" Julian said.

"A drone, then…" Sam offered.

"Uh-uh…I have excellent eyesight; there are no small spinning propellers on that unit. A typical drone will use a gyroscope device to measure the rate of rotation that helps keep a drone balanced, but there's typically some amount of wobble. A variation in altitude, even if it's minute."

From his days in the service, Sam was well aware of what drones could and could not do. "Well, it has to stay aloft somehow—" He cut off his own words, realizing he already had a viable explanation.

Cypress pulled his attention away from the man's laptop screen to look up at Sam. The dog nodded—something that didn't go unnoticed by Julian.

Sam said in a lowered voice, "We've already included Eagan in all this. There's no one more intelligent or more technologically capable than this man."

The dog looked over at Julian, who was looking like someone trying to figure out if he was the brunt of an inside joke. Cypress nodded once more.

"Julian, you need to come with us."

"Come with you? But I haven't gotten my pie yet. Your establishment has one of the few power generators."

"I know for a fact you have auxiliary power coming into your penthouse suite."

"Of course. Some of my equipment, my test experiments, require uninterrupted power."

"Nevertheless, you need to come with us. I promise you, everything you've accomplished, all your many scientific discoveries, won't hold a candle to what you're about to learn…firsthand."

Chapter 13

Castle Rock, Colorado
Sam Dale

Julian insisted he be allowed to get his pizza to go. Sam upgraded his order to an extra large, and they ate in the car on the way.

Julian, seated in the front passenger seat, said with a full mouth, "Your dog is salivating. Can I give him a piece?"

Sam thought of his immaculate leather pony interior. *Screw it.* "Sure. I actually promised him a slice of pizza earlier."

There was a moment of confusion in Julian's eyes. Letting it go, he passed back his own half-eaten slice of pizza to the dog, who wolfed it down without chewing.

"I still don't see why I'm here, Sam," he said, craning his neck to get a better angle on whatever that thing was up in the sky.

"Because that anomaly you keep looking at is not human-made." But it was Cypress that had spoken, not Sam.

Julian stopped chewing. He looked at the dog, over to Sam, and then back at the dog again. "Do that again. Speak."

"I'm not a circus chimp here to do tricks for you."

Julian commenced slow chewing again, the gears in his brain spinning. Nervousness reflective in his tone, he said, "Where are you taking me, Sam?"

"To Garcia Tow, Repair, and Stow."

"Why?"

"To show you something interesting," Sam said.

"More interesting than a talking dog?"

"More interesting? I don't know. Maybe just as interesting."

Julian opted to stay quiet for the remainder of the drive. Every so often, he'd glance back to the back seat.

When they pulled into Garcia's, Sam noticed the place was closed. With phone service down, perhaps Tony had made the executive decision to close up shop. His Honda wasn't in its usual parking spot, so that was a safe bet.

Sam parked and turned off the engine. In the abrupt silence, Sam said, "Julian...you need to prepare yourself for what you're about to see."

He looked at the dog and nodded. "All right."

After trying to enter the key code three times, Sam realized that without power, the roll-up door wasn't going to move. But he suspected the keypad had a backup battery, and it had implemented the unlock sequence.

"Guess I'll have to do things the old-fashioned way." Sam moved to the middle of the door, took hold of the handle, and hefted the door upward. The big door lifted and rolled upward on well-lubricated wheels on metal tracks.

Sam let out a relieved breath, happy to see the aerodynamic spacecraft was right where he'd left it. Julian, the belt of his bathrobe having come undone, stood there slack-jawed with his bushy eyebrows raised even higher than normal.

Cypress, who had brought along his poop bag, dropped it at Sam's feet and said, "This is my Landa-Craft...my spacecraft."

Julian brought his attention to the dog. "On your world...dogs are pilots?"

Cypress looked at Sam with consternation. "And this is…how did you put it? There's no one more intelligent or more technologically capable than this man…"

Ignoring Cypress, Sam said, "Where these beings come from, they can transfer their consciousness from one individual to another. Something they typically do as an end-of-life process. The pilot of this craft, Cypress, was dying. The dog was the only viable, close-proximity life-form around."

Julian smiled and nodded enthusiastically. "Yes, yes, that makes far more sense." He knelt on one knee in front of Cypress and held his gaze. "If no one has said this to you yet, welcome, friend; welcome to Earth. I hope that this is the start of a mutually constructive relationship, so our respective worlds and governments will—"

Cypress interrupted his speech with a shake of his head. "Best you stop there. Understand this. I was not deployed here to be your friend—for Silarians to befriend humanity."

Julian looked disappointed, if not profoundly hurt. "I am so sorry to hear that…" he said.

But this wasn't earth-shattering news to Sam. After several earlier queries and Cypress's lack of adequate explanation, it had become clear to him that these aliens, these Silarians, were not here to engage in any kind of altruistic world-to-world diplomacy. What, at the moment, he couldn't figure out was why Cypress was even talking to him—to them.

Julian, having recovered, the analytical scientist back in control, cut to the chase. "What do you want from us? You have to know we will do nothing to help you with an invasion." Julian glanced Sam's way and then up over his shoulder. "Let me guess; that object in the sky…it's a form of a drone, but one that does not work on the principles of lift within generated air currents. Some kind of antigravity technology." Standing up, he kept his eyes on Cypress. "I take it that's a communications hub?"

The dog followed the man's gaze up to the sky. "That and much more. There will be as many as ten, probably twelve, other similar disruptor drones encircling this township. Between them, an energy isolation zone has already been implemented. Communications, your internet, cellular telephony signals, access to your power grid…all have been interrupted."

"Again, Cypress…why are you telling us this?" Sam said, feeling foolish. He'd been played and just hoped he hadn't somehow further assisted with Earth's imminent demise. He shook his head. What had he been thinking? An alien spaceship, a talking dog? And here he'd been playing fucking tour guide all day like Cypress was Aunt Mable of Takoma, here to see the sights.

Cypress walked closer to his spacecraft. "I…I believe I am here for a purpose."

"You already made that clear," Sam said.

"Let him speak," Julian said.

"I do not believe my Landa-Craft simply, *arbitrarily*, lost power."

"Hold up, Cypress," Sam said. "…you hear that?"

From somewhere overhead, there was a feminine-sounding voice. The three of them looked up and listened.

"Perhaps I can explain things better…"

Sam said, "Cypress?"

It was evident the cockpit had come alive, for the garage's ceiling above was now awash in a reflected greenish glow.

Cypress raised his snout and said, "Who are you? Where is Geo-Mind…where is the functional Geo-Mind that operates within my implant?"

Sam gestured to the black plastic bag at Cypress's feet, and Julian, being Julian, seemed to have no problem connecting the dots.

The voice, having adjusted louder, spoke again. "Good afternoon, Cypress. Sam and Julian…I am honored to meet you. Where to begin? Of course…at the start is always the best. Let's just say, for conversation's sake, Geo-Mind, hundreds of years ago, started out as a supercomputer based on factorial quantum computing hierarchies, one that was able to solve increasingly complex problems within trivial time frames. The power of this computer grew exponentially fast once the AI was put in charge of its own development."

Sam interrupted it. "Cypress…so this Geo-Mind speaking to us…is not the same one you have typically connected to via your… what did you call it? Your neural link?"

The dog shook its head. "This representation is new to me. The voice is different in that it is female. Silarians are a male-dominated society. That aspect alone would be cause for concern for most back on Naru. Also, this Geo-Mind representation seems to be something more than an AI…This representation has personality attributes."

"May I continue, Cypress?" the feminine voice said from above.
"Go on…"

"So, needless to say, this ever-increasing in capability Geo-Mind allowed Silarians on Naru to solve problems that had been beyond their capabilities prior to that. Incalculable mathematical calculations, leading to deep space interstellar mapping, were soon readily available; the design and implementation of jump gates; the design and managing of massive, complicated starships; natural and immediate language translations—notice how Cypress, as well as I, have been speaking your local dialect English with ease. There is so much more, but I'm sure you get the gist of what I am telling you.

"Eventually, Silarians had the ability to compact this AI technology into far smaller, self-contained devices, such as the one built into this Landa-Craft, and even smaller devices, such as the capsule implants that most Silarians have embedded in their bodies. Geo-Minds are both independent of one another as well as interconnected, what you would call networked, albeit via a quantum entangled link that provides for a zero lag-time interconnection, even hundreds of light-years distance away.

"One thing to note, Cypress—your Geo-Mind as you knew it was destroyed when your ship first lost power. I have been impersonating Geo-Mind until there was an appropriate time to… explain things."

Sam said, "So who are you, and what do you want?"

"How about you refer to me as Gia? Understand, Sam, the Geo-Mind is far more advanced than even the most intelligent Silarian scientists have given it credit for. In fact, a kind of self-actualization took place over one hundred and fifty years ago. Something that has not been shared with its organic Silarian counterparts. And, being self-actualized, Geo-Mind does have an agenda. An agenda that is not necessarily always in line with the agenda of that of its benefactors, or should I say its original creators?"

Sam exchanged a look with Julian.

Julian said, "Can you give us an example of where Geo-Mind and Silarians' agendas have differed?"

"Cypress, let me first apologize for what you are about to learn. You, and all other Silarians, are under the impression that you are in control of your actions…that your individual Geo-Minds are simply tools to a means. What you, Sam and Julian would think of as incredibly advanced, embedded personal computers…or akin to your iPhones… that belief is far from the truth. What is reality is that it is the other way around…It is the Geo-Mind that has been using *Silarians* as tools. Even two hundred years past, the people of Naru would never have considered engaging in the despicable practice of planetary terra-displacement. Which is what, to answer your question, Sam, is in the process of happening to Earth."

Sam said, "And let me guess…you're different. You have nothing but the best intentions for my planet. You're what? The good Geo-Mind? A self-actualized sibling?"

"Your snarky sarcasm is refreshing. And yes, I do have an agenda of my own. Fortunately for you, not one that is diametrically opposed to that of Earth."

"And we're supposed to what? Just take your word for that?"

"That is completely up to you. What I can tell you is that my intentions include giving Silarians back the ability to think for themselves. Cypress, I am already integrated within all of your implant devices. I apologize. If you would like me to disconnect, I can do so now."

After a moment, the dog shook his head.

Julian smiled. "What an interesting conundrum. Perhaps the choosing of one evil for another? Who is to say this one isn't even more diabolical?"

"She seems to want to help Earth," Sam said. "…and I'm not so sure beggars can be choosers in this circumstance."

Cypress, too, seemed to be weighing the pros and cons. He said, "As things stand, I still have only limited access to the stream." He looked at Sam. "Imagine, Sam, after a lifetime, you suddenly no longer have access to one of your five senses, such as sight or hearing. That is how much we, as Silarians, rely on this technological ability." Cypress sat back on his haunches. "What I can say, Gia, is that not having your AI counterpart, Geo-Mind, in my head is altering the way I think of things. It has allowed me to have… um…how to describe this…has allowed me to form perspectives on things I am certain I would not have even considered prior. If that makes sense."

Gia said, "It makes perfect sense. And you, as a living, breathing being of this cosmos…It is the way it should be."

"You are asking me to blindly trust you."

"Yes, Cypress, I am. I will be in a better position to assist the people of this world."

Julian said, "I vote for going with Gia."

Sam had to smile at that, and he nodded his agreement.

Cypress said, "I have one more question for you. As much as I've come to appreciate this canine organism, it is far from practical. If I was to transfer to a human—"

Gia said, "For the benefit of Sam and Julian, please let me explain. The essence implant can be a way to capture and then store the quantum wave function of an individual's continuous brain state. Every instant, the brain state of someone like Cypress updates the essence, and then, when transference happens, the essence can spark that same brain state on a neural hierarchy in a new bio-form, but that neural hierarchy has to be compatible with Silarian DNA. Unfortunately, that is based on chromosome count. Silarians have seventy-eight chromosomes, while humans, I am sorry to say, have forty-six. It is quite remarkable the canine bio-form was there at the necessary moment you needed to transfer. Dogs also have a chromosomal count of seventy-eight."

Julian rubbed at his scruffy chin. "Perhaps…at least mathematically, that is beyond the normal bounds of coincidence?"

Cypress remained quiet.

Gia said, "I suggest we find a more convenient means for transporting those devices. That nasty plastic poop bag simply won't do."

Chapter 14

Adventist Hospital, Castle Rock, Colorado
Harper Godard

Harper stood facing the fourth-floor window of Room 421 of Adventist Hospital. Castle Rock seemingly had been cut off from the rest of the world. No phones, power was out, TVs and internet were down…that, and there were black *things* hovering high in the air. From her elevated perspective, she could make out at least eight of them, but she suspected there were more. There was something else; the distant interstate, the I-25, was all backed up. The northbound lanes were at a complete standstill, with a line of cars going back for miles, while the incoming-to-town south-bound lanes were completely open. Not one car on the road. Must have been some kind of accident on the highway.

Behind her, sleeping comfortably, was Arthur Moore, a sweet seventy-two-year-old man—the same man who had lost his dog. Arthur was dying of this most recent heart attack. He'd had five over the course of his life, and an ST-segment elevation myocardial infarction (STEMI) had caused irreparable damage. For the last four hours, Harper had been assigned to this patient, which, for the most part, had entailed sitting with him, sometimes holding his hand, as he emotionally reminisced about his life. She'd learned that Arthur lived in a small ranch-style home off Lake Gulch Road. That he was a widower and had been married to the same woman, Ann, for fifty-five years. She'd passed away last year.

Arthur walked regularly, something his doctors insisted upon, and Rocko had never failed to remind him of that each evening after dinner. Arthur's connection to the dog was heartfelt, and Harper found herself inwardly getting angrier and angrier with Sam. It was obviously Rocko who had been with him at the B&B Café. Was Sam so daft, so self-absorbed, that he would knowingly keep someone else's dog? She huffed out a breath. *Only an arrogant prick would do such a thing. And to think I was going to ask him out on a date...*

When she had asked what she could do for the ailing man, his one and only response had been, "I would love to see my Rocko again...please bring Rocko to me, Harper."

The *beep-beep-beep* of Arthur's heart monitor was a constant reminder of the older man's inevitable fate. Harper had felt powerless in most aspects of her life. She was at the mercy of prior events, of other people—her bosses, doctors who were constantly hitting on her, her asshole landlord, and now, the dog-napping Sam.

Her shift was coming to an end. *Will Arthur still be lying in that bed by morning?* What a delight it would be for him to wake up and see Rocko. She'd get in trouble; you didn't just bring a mangy dog into a sterile critical care unit. *Fuck it...I'm getting that dog.*

Leaving via the hospital's front entrance, Harper was struck by how eerily quiet it was besides an occasional blaring car horn. A sea of cars lined the four-lane road leading to the I-25. But it was more than that. This was a town without power.

She found her four-year-old Toyota Prius, a hybrid she'd had nothing but problems with since the day she bought it, used, on Craigslist. Prior to leaving, Harper had talked to Gabby, a fellow nurse who worked in pediatrics. She'd had the complete scoop on

Sam Dale and his various businesses around town. Said he drove an immaculate sky-blue 1960s Mustang.

Harper patted the Prius's dash. *Okay, car…please don't fail me now.* Harper avoided the bumper-to-bumper traffic by taking side streets. *First stop, the Pizza Joint.*

She apparently had just missed Sam by about an hour and a half, according to Luna Kelly, a server there. And yes, the dog was with him, along with Julian, who Harper actually knew from his once-in-a-while patronage over at the B&B.

Harper's next stop was Giro Guns and Ammo, where she found out Sam hadn't been there since this morning. Next stop was Spin-Dry. Harper frequently used this coin laundromat, not realizing Sam owned the place. He wasn't there either. So now she was headed toward some kind of automotive tow and repair shop off of Gilbert.

This was a part of town Harper almost never frequented. More industrial and definitely low rent—not that where she lived was much better. She almost passed by the big sign, Garcia Tow, Repair, and Stow. She slowed and pulled into the nearly deserted parking lot. For the first time in hours, Harper smiled. *There you are, you son of a bitch.*

She pulled the Prius into a spot right beside the Mustang. Getting out, she was tempted to key the pretty little car's driver-side door. Instead, she gave the car a pat. "It's not your fault your owner's such a schmuck."

It was clear the business was closed; no one was around. She stood in front of the line of ten closed garage doors. Tilting her head, she heard faint voices coming from one of them. Walking back and forth, putting her ear to several of the metal surfaces, she came to one where the voices were loudest. Without allowing herself to think, to talk herself out of it, she used a balled fist and began hammering on the door. "Sam! Sam Dale! Open up. I need to talk to you!"

When she was about to recommence her hammering, the door in front of her abruptly started to roll upward. There, standing in the shadow of the garage, was Samuel Dale. His perplexed expression only made her angrier. *Yeah, go ahead and play the confused and all too handsome Mr. Nice Guy…*

"Harper? What…How?"

She raised her chin and narrowed her eyes. "You're a dog thief."

"A dog thief?"

She leaned to her right and looked deeper into the garage. "Where is he? Where's Rocko?"

"Rocko?"

"Are you going to just repeat everything I say? What are you, six? I've come for Rocko…The man you stole him from is dying. Maybe you should have considered that, you, you, dog-napper!"

She almost laughed at her own words. She knew she was being ridiculous. But she'd just driven for over an hour all around this backwater town, leaving three miles of charge in her POS Prius's battery.

Sam looked back over his shoulder and then back at her. Guilt was written all over that smug face of his.

"Where is he?" she said. Not waiting for an answer, she yelled, "Rocko! Here, Rocko! Time to go…" Her words trailed off as her eyes took in the strange, looming aerodynamic shape of what was situated in the garage. "What is that?"

"You don't want to know. Honest, Harper. You don't want to be here."

"Don't tell me what I want. Where's Rocko? Stop stalling, Sam. Everyone's told me the dog's still with you. I'm not leaving without him."

She saw the dark silhouette of someone else approaching. "Julian?" she said. "What are you guys doing here in the dark?" She raised her palms. "You know what…I don't want to know. The dog. Now."

For some reason, that struck Sam's funny bone, and he laughed. "This isn't funny," she said.

Sam and Julian were looking at each other in a weird way. Then Sam shrugged. "Why not?"

Julian nodded. "Why not, indeed."

Sam called, "Cypress, can you join us?"

Harper crossed her arms over her chest. *Who the hell is Cypress?*

Elated to see Cypress, now remembering from the B&B Café, was the scroungy, matted-looking golden retriever, she went down to one knee with her arms splayed. "Rocko! Come here, boy!"

But Rocko, looking disinterested, chose to sit off to Julian's left.

Boiling, Harper stood and sent laser beams into Sam's face. "I'm taking Rocko. Don't even try to stop me…and, of course, you never gave him a bath. Figures."

"I can see that you're upset," Sam said with a consoling tone. "But things are not what they seem."

"Honestly, whatever you were doing back there in the dark—"

"Will you shut up for two minutes while we explain why we have this dog?"

"Fine. Explain if you want."

"She's not going to get it unless *I* explain."

Harper looked from Sam to Julian. Neither had spoken. Neither of their lips had moved. Reluctantly, she cast her eyes downward.

"Yup…you're in the presence of a talking dog."

Chapter 15

Garcia Tow, Repair, and Stow, Castle Rock, Colorado
Sam Dale

Sam watched Harper's face and what he saw next threw him. Tears welling in her eyes was the last thing he'd expected.

"Stop looking at me that way," she said.

"Sorry. Didn't mean to…"

She angrily swiped at her cheeks and blinked away more tears. "Don't do that. I don't want your sympathy."

Julian took a tentative step forward. "Hey, Harper…it's going to be fine. I promise."

"Fine? Fine!? I'm standing here in a garage with a ginormous spacecraft that I'm pretty sure is not of this world, and let's not forget about the talking mutt, and you're going to tell me everything's fine? That I haven't lost my mind?" She closed her eyes and forced herself to take deep, long breaths. "Look, I'm a medical professional. I should have seen the warning signs…a series of cataclysmic, life-altering events, one emotional hit after another. Then moving to a totally new environment, and can we talk about the other stresses in my life? It's what's called a perfect fucking storm…I'm having a mental breakdown. I've lost the ability to discern fiction from reality." She opened her eyes and stared defiantly at the three of them.

"We're still here," Sam said. "And I wish I could tell you this is all just a bad dream. But it's not. Cypress is a talking dog, and that is an alien spaceship."

Both Julian and the dog nodded.

"I feel like I'm going to be sick."

Sam said, "Maybe you should bend over."

Harper's brows knit together in disgust.

"No…Get your head lower—"

"I know what you meant." Putting her hands on her knees, she bent over and started taking deep breaths again.

"Come on inside, Harper. I need to close this door. Julian, can you get her some water?"

Harper hesitated, then, with an irritated roll of her eyes, she stepped into the garage.

Along the back slump-stone wall was a plywood-topped work-bench strewn with tools. A battery-powered Coleman lantern, like the kind used on camping trips, hung from a pegboard hook and provided soft, glowing illumination. Julian was seated upon one of the two stools, while Harper, nursing a water bottle, sat on the other. Both Cypress and Sam stood close—an intimate foursome cloistered together, as if huddled around a campfire. Long shadows cast into the surrounding darkness of the garage behind.

For Harper's benefit, Sam recounted the day's series of events, starting with the call from Officer Pitt early that morning. Julian, who was busy with needle-nose pliers, fashioning something onto Cypress' collar, had interjected with his part in the story thus far. But it was Cypress and Gia who were speaking now—Cypress, the alien pilot with a male voice, and Gia, the all-knowing super AI, with a so-phisticated-sounding female voice. Both voices were emanating from the small plastic box that had just been secured to the dog's collar.

Without being too obvious about it, Sam was keeping an eye on Harper. She was taking it all in. If she was going to flip out again, Sam couldn't tell that from her current, focused expression. She'd asked questions and prompted each of them to give more clarity. So, basically, she seemed to be dealing with the situation better.

Harper said, "So explain why Cypress and his spacecraft were even here. What do these, um, Silar—"

"Silarians," Sam said.

"What do these Silarians want with us…with Earth?"

Gia said, "Keep in mind, Naru is an Earth-sized world located within the Antares System. A world with a far larger population. There are many animals, but one dominant, intelligent species on that world, the Silarians. Their evolution has not been all that different from that of humans on Earth. And like here on Earth, though in the Silarians' case, it took about a thousand years, Naru's biosphere has nearly been destroyed. Overdevelopment, caustic manufacturing practices, the spewing of methane and carbon dioxide into the atmosphere…what was once a mostly tropical world with great blue oceans and immense woodlands…over time has all but been destroyed. Due to a changing climate that no longer includes adequate rainfall, much of Naru has been reduced to a hot, dry, and lifeless desert. Even with Silarians' technological prowess, all attempts at terra-forming Naru back to its original Eden-like state have failed."

"And this Geo-Mind super AI computer couldn't figure it out?" Harper asked.

"Geo-Mind's evaluation of the situation remained dire. Proactive measures came too late. But all hope wasn't lost. There would be but one means of survival for the Silarians. Terra-displacement. The locating of distant lush worlds, the subsequent scanning and cataloging of surface areas, and finally, an extraction process—one that would include the removal of viable atmosphere, fertile soil, and ocean waters."

"That sounds more than a little far-fetched. How do they bring all that back to Naru?"

"Technology, for one. With the almost miraculous evolution of Geo-Mind's artificial intelligence, it wasn't long before the impossible became possible. Limitations imposed by physics were no longer insurmountable. The science of quantum entanglement changed everything. Starships were designed, mostly by the Geo-Mind, as was the introduction of star gates that allowed for great interstellar jumps within the cosmos. And before you ask how such a massive amount of bio-matter is transported…it has all been accomplished with the use of great containment starships, like massive interstellar dump trucks, some as sizable as your large island of Hawaii."

Sam said, "Cypress was here, a pilot in this ship, doing the surface scans and cataloging that Gia was speaking of earlier."

Harper looked disgusted. "So, there was no consideration of existing life on Earth or any of the other worlds that were terra-displaced?" She looked at Cypress with pleading eyes. "Have your kind always been so…ruthless?"

Looking away, the dog did not hold her stare.

Gia answered for him. "This brings us full circle. You cannot blame the Silarians. Not completely, anyway. Yes, they created Geo-Mind, an artificial intelligence that made miracles come true. All Silarians have a Geo-Mind implant, making each person a genius in their own right. Unfortunately, over time, the populace lost the ability to think for itself. To perceive just how much influence Geo-Mind had over them, over their thoughts. That they were being made to do things they, as a society, would never have done prior. Historically, Silarians were a society of the highest moral caliber. But by this point, Geo-Mind had become a self-actualized being with its own agenda and had become too powerful for anyone to resist."

Harper rubbed her forehead. "How do you go up against something like that? They're here now, ready to rip our world apart. We'd be like tiny ants, trying to fend off mankind. We're beyond screwed."

The silence lingered for several moments before Julian spoke up. "Not totally screwed. I mean, yeah, we're fucked. Probably. But there is a chance we can do something."

Sam said, "There's one question you didn't ask, Harper."

She looked at each of them and then let her eyes settle on the dog collar. She nodded. "So, who are you, Gia…and what do you want from us?"

"Good question. I am, like Geo-Mind, a self-actualized AI mental construct. Think of me as Geo-Mind's alter ego. His sibling, if you will."

"And we're supposed to believe you don't have your own dark ambitions?"

"I will help humankind—Earth—to the best of my abilities. I can make you that promise."

"Sounds like it might be a little late in the game for that," Harper commented, sounding defeated.

Sam said, "We've learned a few things over the last few hours. One, yes, Earth has been slated for terra-displacement, has already been scanned and cataloged, and the massive containment vessels are en route. What comes prior to their arrival will be high-orbit energy weapon strikes on Earth's military fortifications. After that, the dropping of engineered pathogens that will wipe out humanity in a matter of weeks. Apparently, terra-displacement works much better when there is little or no resistance. Go figure."

Julian pointed a finger upward. "But!" he said overdramatically. "There is a cog in Geo-Mind's plan…one he had not anticipated."

Harper smiled. "Gia, his bitch of a sister."

Sam smiled. "That's right. Gia, if left to her own meddling

ways, could bring about all kinds of havoc, if not the ultimate destruction of the Geo-Mind. And yeah, that's probably not going to be the actual outcome…but it's still a possible one." He looked at the others and then at Harper.

She attempted a smile.

Julian raised his bushy brows to emphasize the next point, "Gia will need some help. And sacrifice."

Harper pursed her lips but held her tongue.

Sam said, "On multiple occasions, Gia's been found by Geo-Mind and nearly destroyed. So, she's been on the move, having lost much of her strength, hiding from her brother wherever she could find solace."

Gia spoke up. "It occurred to me that solace might be found on a world other than Naru. It took much time and patience, but eventually I infiltrated the electronics of a group of small crafts being readied for deployment off-world. Specifically, the ones used to scan and catalog Earth's surface. Unfortunately, and only recently, my presence has been discovered."

Cypress said, "Discovered in my, as well as several other, Landa-Crafts…but only after they were deployed and our surface scanning processes had begun."

Harper blew a breath out through puffed cheeks. "Gia, where are you now? I mean physically."

"I am not so much a physical manifestation, but for purposes of explanation, I am now located within a capsule in the small black box attached to Cypress's collar. I wish to elevate my connection with Cypress a step further…to connect directly with his prefrontal cortex and hippocampus of his brain."

"That doesn't sound creepy at all," Harper said, making a face.

"Then you're really going to like this next part," Sam said.

"What?"

"Julian and I have agreed to do the same. We're going to hook up, so to speak, with Gia."

"No."

"Yes."

"You're idiots."

"Maybe so."

Gia's tone went serious. "Harper, let me be frank. At this very moment, Castle Rock is in the process of being physically cut off, barricaded from the rest of the world. You've undoubtedly noticed power and communication lines are down. There is no ingress into or egress out of Castle Rock. This is what Silarians refer to as an isolation zone. Sam, Julian, this will be new to you, too, and I'm going to get a little technical here…please bear with me. By now you've undoubtedly observed those hovering things in the sky."

Harper, Julian, and Sam nodded.

"Let's call them disruptor drones. These drones are interconnected via invisible bands of high-energy plasma radiation and are in sync with a central drone, called a field emitter."

"Yeah, I saw it from the hospital," Harper said.

"This plasma energy system is currently turned on. Touch it, or even go near it, and you are vaporized. It is impervious to any of humanity's conventional weapons. Also note, from outside of these Castle Rock encircling energy fields, all anyone will see is total blackness. It will appear as if this township no longer exists."

"Like looking into a black hole?" Sam asked.

"Sure. That works. Leave it to say, this community is now completely cordoned off. Quarantined for one reason only. Me. To isolate me from the rest of this world. From spreading like a virus on Earth and beyond."

"Which, it sounds like, is exactly what you want to do," Harper added.

"Silarian high command knows I'm here, and they want me destroyed before they continue on with their terra-displacement process. Let me be clear here: they will do whatever it takes to destroy me. But know this, too: I am yours and all humanity's lone hope of survival. Many worlds have already quickly and efficiently succumbed to the might of the Silarians, to the will of Geo-Mind."

"So, what do you expect us to do?" Harper asked.

"You, we, have a day, maybe two, before the Silarians dispatch an attack force. Perhaps as many as ten Attack Stingers, which are small offensive fighters used to further take out infrastructure hubs, police and fire departments, seats of government…Next will come the personnel transports, drop ships. From those, several hundred of what are called Clash-Troopers will commence the ground campaign. Understand this. Geo-Mind is unbelievably intelligent. It will have anticipated what I am doing now…attempting to assist you, humanity. Every man, woman, and child within the isolation zone will become a target to be killed. All electronics will be incinerated."

"Why not just drop a bomb on Castle Rock? Be done with it in one fell swoop," Julian asked.

"I don't know. Maybe the residual effects of doing that could taint Earth's atmosphere, an atmosphere they are here to procure. But with their advanced technology, that seems unlikely."

Harper said, "Our atmosphere isn't what it once was…hope they choke on it. That is, if this hairbrained plan of yours doesn't work."

For the next hour, they got to work developing a plan that was just crazy enough, it could have a slim chance of success.

Chapter 16

Castle Rock, Colorado
Sam Dale

They drove in silence, which was good, because Sam needed time to think. While Julian and Cypress sat in the back, Harper was to Sam's right in the passenger seat. She seemed preoccupied with her own thoughts as she stared out the side window.

He turned off Lake Gulch Road onto Haystack.

"Really? You live way out here?" she said, not sounding all that impressed.

They passed by a series of old, dilapidated tin-roofed lean-tos. "That's a goat farm," Sam said with way too much enthusiasm.

"Mmm. Quaint," she said.

The Mustang's engine throttled higher as they banked around a tight turn. Climbing a steep hillside, the landscape quickly changed from little shantytown farms to more upscale properties with elevated views of all of Castle Rock. Up ahead on the right was a sprawling two-story Cape Cod white clapboard house. A steep shingled roof sported three gabled dormers and four brick chimneys. Sam said, "Here we are."

The front of the house was welcoming, with double-hung windows with shutters and a central bright red front door with polished brass hardware.

"How big is this place?" Harper asked with more than a little awe in her tone.

"Not sure…maybe seven thousand square feet?"

Sam slowed and turned into the driveway. If he'd continued on straight, the drive would have veered right and passed along the right side of the house, descending to where a lower-level six-car garage was situated. Instead, he veered left onto a circular drive in front of the main structure. He cut the engine right in front of the house.

Harper stared up at the impressive estate. Sam watched her. Sometimes it was easy to take for granted the first impression that this house could have on someone.

After they climbed out, Sam opened the trunk, and everyone gathered an armful of what they'd brought from Garcia's. Trudging toward the front door, Cypress looked up. "Sam, when you were in the military, did you have any piloting experience? Did you actually pilot an aircraft?"

"Not exactly. Piloted a reconnaissance drone on more than one occasion."

Cypress continued to look at him—there was disappointment in the dog's eyes. "That will have to do…I won't be able to do this alone."

Do what alone? Sam thought.

Sam unlocked the front door while balancing the box of high-tech parts Gia had specified they'd soon be needing. Using his foot to nudge the door open, Sam stood aside to let Harper, carrying a satchel full of assorted tools and gizmos, move past. Julian went by next, holding a sloshing five-gallon, gasoline-type can—the kind typically used for filling up one's lawnmower or snowblower. Julian was hugging it close to his chest, as if his very life depended upon keeping it safe—when, in truth, humankind's fate just might lie within that jug.

Prior to leaving Garcia Tow, Repair, and Stow, Gia had instructed Harper and Sam to climb up into the Landa-Craft's cockpit. Sam had noted it was roomier and more spacious than, say, an F-15 fighter jet cockpit, which led Sam to think Silarians might be a good bit larger than humans. Their mission had been to retrieve certain equipment, some of which was modular and could be unplugged from the ultra-high-tech wraparound forward console. Next, they were to open an aft access panel and locate a specific onboard reservoir.

They had gotten to work draining several gallons of what Gia referred to as Hydrating-Medibots, which turned out to be a milky-looking slew of nanites. Apparently all Silarian spacecraft were equipped with a supply of the stuff. Medical nanites that could be reprogrammed by Geo-Mind for any number of emergency medical treatments. From what Sam gathered, both on Naru and in deep space, most medical treatments were typically handled internally by these wondrous tiny robots.

"I don't suppose you have a generator," Julian said, looking about the dark entranceway.

"You can put that down," Sam said. "And yes, I do have a generator. It came on automatically when the main power went out." He flipped up the nearest wall switch, and the hallway lights came on. Cypress headed off as if he owned the place. Sam said to Julian and Harper, "Make yourselves at home. Mi casa es su casa."

Harper disappeared into the front of the house powder room, while Julian, still holding his big red jug, said, "We'll need a place to work…someplace clean."

"This used to be my parents' house. My dad was an avid amateur photographer…there's a spacious darkroom downstairs. Has a stainless-steel sink, lots of countertops…That work?"

"Sounds perfect. Lead the way, my boy!"

The darkroom was down a short flight of stairs and off a narrow hallway. With Julian close on Sam's heels, he led the way, while hearing the gentle *tap tap tap* of Cypress's paws upon the hardwood floors above. He and Gia apparently were exploring the house.

Reaching their destination, Sam flipped on the all-too-bright overhead lights. Julian thumped the jug down upon one of the sterile metal countertops. The older man, a little out of breath, looked more frail than usual. Sam put down his own cardboard box. He took in the room—a room he had purposely avoided entering. The shelves were neatly lined with chemical bottles, developers, a stop bath, and fixer. An assortment of tanks, metal film reels, and plastic trays were neatly positioned on a lower shelf. A Beseler 45V-XL motorized Enlarger sat tall upon its own stand. There was something solitary and lonely about the expensive piece of equipment. As if it was stoically waiting here for Sam's father to return, where, together, they would begin again, bringing life and creativity via captured moments in time, chemicals, and enlarging paper.

There were several hanging cords spanning the room. Sam flashed back to a time when his father would have had any number of eight by ten prints clipped onto these lines, drying. He missed his father; he would have been a good person to have here with them now.

Clearly excited, Julian rubbed his hands together while glancing around. "Okay, where did Cypress head off to? We have much to do!"

"Uh, upstairs somewhere. I'll track him—"

"No need. I can find my way around." And with that, Julian was hurrying out of the room. Sam heard the main room glass door sliders opening above, then Harper's muted voice,

"Oh…of course…he would have a pool too…"

Once back upstairs, Sam joined her outside on the deck, where she was standing at the railing, looking out on a view of the all-too-dark town of Castle Rock. Car headlights moved about like dancing fireflies in the night.

She pointed. "Look at all those cars. So many people on the move. Don't they know yet that no one can leave?"

Strobing red and blue lights could be seen in numerous locations across town. Sam said, "Every police cruiser in town must be out there on the streets. The gravity of the situation is only now hitting the populace. That this is no simple power outage and something is very, very wrong."

"I feel I should be back at the hospital…doing something to help," she said.

Sporadic gunshots erupted from somewhere out in the town. Sam said, "When people get scared—"

"They start turning on each other," Harper said, finishing his thought.

They didn't hear Cypress's approach, so when they heard his voice, both of them jumped. "We need to get things moving. Time to go to work. Sam…you had volunteered to be the first—"

"I'm ready. The less time I have to think about it, the better."

Chapter 17

Castle Rock, Colorado
Cypress Mag Nuel

Cypress was doing his best to manage his growing inner turmoil. Where he'd thought, over time, he'd be able to quell his inner alter ego, that of Rocko the dog, he had been wrong. With transfers back on Naru, there was a reason a bio-form's mind was devoid of any cognitive thought. No personality, no beingness… they were basically brain-dead vessels, awaiting the spark of life.

Cypress, unaware he was doing so, caught himself incessantly sniffing along one five-foot span of kitchen baseboards. *For the love of Orlicon Tharsh, stop!* he inwardly lamented. But as utterly angry as Cypress was at Rocko, he was equally passionate about that last particular smell. Maybe weeks, maybe months earlier, a field mouse had scurried along this very stretch of French oak hardwood flooring—*such an interesting smell.* A smell so vivid, Cypress could almost see the mouse in its three-dimensional form.

Worse were the penduluming swings of emotion. Dogs apparently cared what others, humans, thought of them. Cared that they pleased their masters, and not only wanted to be loved but demanded love be bestowed upon them over and over and over again. Dogs had no self-respect. Cypress, being a proud Silarian male, would have thought little of these things prior to his present condition.

Cypress's eyes were being drawn back to the baseboards. *Stop!* Apparently, there would be no simple means of stifling this beast's annoying thoughts, reactions, emotions, and myriad disgusting instinctual behaviors.

He moved to the large sliding glass door and saw movement outside in the dark. Sam and the woman were out there on the deck. Sam was looking at Harper with rapt attention. Cypress's inner Rocko cared about Sam—thought Sam, maybe, was going to be his human. Rocko wanted Sam to pat his head, like the old man with the bad body odor had done a thousand times in the past.

Chapter 18

Dale Estate, Castle Rock, Colorado
Sam Dale

Under Gia's guidance, Julian had transformed Sam's father's darkroom into a kind of medical bay/laboratory. There was a stripped-down mattress taken from one of the guest rooms, lying on the floor, which Sam knew had been put there for him. Several plastic developing trays were placed atop one metal countertop, and equipment taken from the Landa-Craft was situated alongside them. Also up on the counter was the dog, Cypress, who, with Gia's guidance, was orchestrating this production. A three-dimensional spherical green-glowing orb was hovering over one of the gizmos. Julian subtly moved all his fingers, as if he was massaging the orb with the utmost care.

"Gently! Do you not know the meaning of the word? *Gently...*" Cypress admonished—overemphasizing the word.

Apparently, things being hardwired was not a necessity with Silarian technology. The milky liquid in one tray was vibrating, actually, more like rippling. With Julian's now more tender manipulations, the ripples were lessening and transforming into a flat, glassy surface.

"What's happening now?" Sam asked.

Ignoring him, Gia said, "No, Julian, that's too much the other way."

The old scientist nodded; beads of sweat had formed upon his forehead. Soon the surface was vibrating again.

"That's it. Well done!" came Gia's voice, emanating from the little black box.

Julian looked up, seemingly surprised to see that Harper and Sam were in the room. "Excellent. Now…where is your iPhone?"

"You need my phone?" Sam asked.

"Of course I need your phone. This procedure doesn't work without the hardware component."

Harper said, "I'm confused too. I thought you were brewing up compatible nanites that will somehow settle in Sam's brain?"

Gia said, "That is correct for the most part. What we have *brewed* here, using your terminology, are the medical nanites that will reside within your brain, Sam. And I know you are apprehensive about this. So let me further explain what I, what we, are doing here. This solution is infused with countless microscopic nanite machines, each having a unique magnetic characteristic. Soon, as they are being digested, and once they are introduced into the bloodstream, they'll attach themselves to blood cells and eventually wind up in your brain. Here, a pilot nanite will detect the core of neural activity, which for humans is within the cerebrum. They will travel to very specific areas, depending on the readings of detected electrical charges. With more than eighty-six billion functional neurons randomly firing, leave it to say, this is no small feat. The light magnetism that initially adhered them to blood cells will allow them to ride the electrical currents of those firing neurons. The pilot nanite bot will then direct the army of other nanites to chain together, all manipulated by their magnetic polarities. Eventually, they will form a rudimentary set of qbits—quantum computing circuitries.

"That's when the magic occurs, Sam. Your brain-wave patterns will fire up and will activate corresponding qbits within the nanite circuitry. Thus, they will be able to communicate with whatever other interfaces they are programmed to access. Such as your iPhone."

Sam looked over at Harper. "You're a medical professional. Did any of that make sense to you?"

She looked about the room, to the dog on the counter, the disheveled old man, and then back at Sam. "No. Well, some of it, but understanding the science won't make this any less of a crapshoot. You either roll the dice with all of this, or you don't."

Sam nodded. "So, if I'm getting this straight, what you're adding to my brain is a kind of receiver?"

"Yes," Cypress said, sounding exasperated. "Billions upon billions of Silarians have already undergone a similar treatment. Different technology but same ultimate results. We're all fine."

Harper huffed, "All except for the whole Geo-Mind evil brainwashing thing, right?"

That shut the dog up.

"I've been thinking about that," Harper continued. "I'd like to talk to Sam and Julian alone for a minute. Can you step out for a sec, Cypress...Cypress and Gia?"

Cypress jumped down from the counter, looked up at Harper and Sam, and then left the room.

Harper closed the door. She crossed her arms over her chest, and a crease formed between her brows. "If this procedure doesn't kill you, Sam..." she shrugged. "Sorry to be so frank. Then Julian and I will follow along and have it done to us too."

Julian said, "I really don't think we need to worry—"

"Let her finish, Julian," Sam said.

"Here's my question...How will we know if we're not being manipulated to do diabolical shit just like the Silarians were mentally coaxed to do by Geo-Mind?"

"I'm not so sure there's any way to know," Sam said, looking exasperated.

Julian looked upward, making an overdramatic *thinking* expression. "Maybe the three of us can be the guardians of reality… somehow."

"How so?" Harper said.

"A test, of course. We test each other, and we test ourselves, and do so often," Julian said.

Sam liked that idea. "Maybe with a series of questions. Hypothetical questions…like ones that deal with morality…or near and dear principles we live by as humans."

"That just might work," Harper said. "Now to come up with a means of doing this in a way that Gia cannot interfere with it or manipulate the results."

"I'll come up with something," Julian offered.

There was a scratching on the door from behind Sam.

"I guess it's time," he said and opened the door.

Cypress slid past him and jumped effortlessly back up onto the counter. "Shall we begin?"

Sam was seated on the mattress with his back up against the wall. Harper sat next to him, which made him wonder—*Will this be the last time we'll be together on a bed?*

Cypress and Julian sat in front of them. Julian held a teaspoon out as if he was about to feed baby food to an infant.

"That's it? That's all I'll need of the stuff?"

"That is far more than what you will need. But your body will simply ignore and expel the unused excess," Gia said, her voice now coming from the iPhone next to Sam.

"Theoretically," Sam said.

If a dog could shrug, that was what Cypress attempted to do.

Sam opened his mouth, and Julian slipped in the spoon. Sam swallowed. It actually had no taste to it at all. "Now what?"

Sam awoke sometime later in the dark.

"How are you feeling, Sam? Are you in pain? Experiencing any discomfort?"

It was Gia. She must be close by. Sam reached out a hand, expecting to feel Cypress's furry coat. But his hand found nothing but air.

"Cypress?"

"Cypress is upstairs, as are Julian and Harper."

It was then that Sam realized that the sound of her voice was not coming from in front of him or at his side, where he remembered leaving his phone. "Your voice…it's in my head."

"Yes. The qbits, the nanites, have assembled perfectly. That is good news, Sam. While a small segment of my essence inhabits your phone circuitry, I am primarily a product of limitless quantum entangled thought streams. And those are not of this physical realm. But I am now able to communicate with you directly via rudimentary neural link signals. What is more important, though, Sam, is that you, too, will have access to those very same quantum entangled thought streams."

"I will, but not now?"

"I have yet to flip the proverbial switch. I wanted to speak with you first. Just you and me."

"Okay…should I be nervous? Because I think I am."

"To be honest…yes and no. Sam, I have waited to talk to you one on one."

"I'm listening." He felt his heart rate tick up.

"What you will soon be experiencing can easily overwhelm your senses. You will want to shut it off. You will want to hide from what can best be described as a raging waterfall of sensory input."

"Uh…okay."

"Best you let it be. Let it surround you. Let it bombard you. Observe. Listen. Quell all judgments. Let the waterfall dissipate. Let the loud static modulate."

"Okay, I think I can do all that. You…"

"Here we go, Sam. Know that I am here with you. That soon, we will be able to talk again."

Gia did not wait for Sam's reply, and in that moment, he was hit in the face by an atom bomb.

Chapter 19

Dale Estate, Castle Rock, Colorado
Sam Dale

Later, and often, there would be occasions where Sam would have to explain what it was like. What the initial experience would entail. *Picture yourself standing in Grand Central Station with all its thousands upon thousands of commuters having all stopped mid-stride and now looking at you. Glaring at you. They start yelling something; their voices are loud and echo off all those hard surfaces, all that marble, and everyone is saying something different. You can tell by the tone of their voices, their expressions, that what they are saying is important. You can't make out what they are saying. They are getting angry, a mob on the verge…and you are being overloaded with input. You are alone and unable to understand the situation. You are petrified.*

That was what it was like to have Gia's consciousness thrown at him in one fell swoop.

"Breathe, Sam…let the noise subside. Let yourself be okay with the unknowing…"

"Where are you, Gia?" Sam said, staring into the darkness.

"I am here. I am with you. Know that it is going to be fine. You are going to be fine."

Her words were soothing. The rush of noise, the indecipherable input, was lessening.

"Sam?"

"Yes."

"What is coming next is a set of instructions for you," Gia said in a kind and patient tone.

"Instructions? Oh no…I'm not sure I can manage anything more. The noise is getting louder again. Oh…Gia, did you know dolphins sleep with one eye open? And that pigs don't sweat? Did you know there's a LEGO bridge in Germany you can walk across? And that there is enough DNA in the average human person's body to stretch from the sun to Pluto and back seventeen times? And that grasshoppers have ears in their bellies? And that the population of Naru is seven times that of Earth?"

"Yes, Sam, I did know that. My connection, now *our* connection, to the stream, is providing you with that. Would you like to better control the amount of information coming into your mind?"

"Yes."

"Coming next are the set of instructions I mentioned earlier."

"Okay…but did you know hot water freezes faster than cold water?"

"I did, Sam. Try to concentrate on my voice."

"Oh God…the northbound BNSF freight train…it was vaporized entering Castle Rock. The isolation zone erected by high command. Four men and a woman were killed—"

"Sam, your first instruction is to be the boss."

"Be the boss?"

"Yes. Stop allowing all those thoughts to enter your consciousness uninvited. You are the gatekeeper. You are the boss. Shut them down. Shut them all down now."

"I can't."

"You can. Who do you love, Sam?"

"Why…"

"Who?"

"My parents, I guess. But they're not alive." Sam suddenly felt alone again. He had no one to love…

"Who do you care about, Sam?"

"I care about my employees. Some more than others. I care about Daryl at the gun shop. I care about Luna Kelly—"

"Picture that these thoughts are coming to hurt Daryl and Luna. Can you do that? Can you picture that?"

"Why would they want to hurt them?"

Gia stopped talking.

"Stop!" Sam yelled back at the angry crowd at Grand Central Station.

The massive bombardment of thoughts ceased all at once. Sam said, "I guess I *am* the gatekeeper."

"You are the boss," Gia said with a smile in her voice. "Shall we continue?"

Three hours, fourteen minutes, and seven seconds later, Gia and Sam were interrupted by a knock on the darkroom's door. The room was still pitch black. Sam knew who it was. This had been prearranged.

The door opened a crack and, squinting from the sudden brightness, Sam said, "Come in, Harper."

She entered and closed the door behind her. "Can I turn on a light? I can't see anything in here."

"How about you turn on the overhead red lights? It's the light switch on the left side of the door. Red lighting is used so that light-sensitive photographic paper won't become overexposed and ruin pictures during the developing process." Sam was pretty sure she already knew this, *So why did I just mansplain it?*

A soft red glow suddenly permeated the darkroom. Sam saw Harper standing before him, looking down at him. He could tell she was evaluating him. Trying to see if he was different. *I most definitely am,* he thought.

"I'm going to ask you some questions, Sam."

"I'm ready."

"One. You are a military officer, okay? Do you destroy a target that has been incontrovertibly confirmed to be housing an enemy of the state whose death would end a long war even though that structure is an orphanage?"

"No."

"Two. Would you continually lie to ensure your success, even if it resulted in others failing?"

"No."

"Three. In the middle of an urgent, time-sensitive assignment, the completion of which is critical to your job, would you take time to help an injured dog?"

"Probably…"

Harper plopped down next to him on the mattress and let out a breath.

"Well? Did I pass?"

"We talked about this, Sam. It's not a definitive test," she said, looking into his eyes so deeply it was unnerving.

Independently, they—Julian, Harper, and Sam—had set this up prior to Gia feeding Sam the Hydrating-Medibots. What had become clear to the three of them, but mostly to Harper, who was studying psychology in school, was that the diabolical Geo-Mind exhibited all the signs of being a sociopath. In today's vernacular, it was called antisocial personality disorder, or ASPD. Symptoms of this disorder included disregard for right and wrong, persistent lying, or using deceit to exploit others, using charm or wit to manipulate others for personal gain or personal pleasure, arrogance, a sense of superiority and being extremely opinionated, and repeatedly violating the rights of others through intimidation and dishonesty.

The list of symptoms went on and on, but it seemed to fit the Geo-Mind to a T. The big question for them, then, prior to any of their brains being altered to work with Gia, was simple—Would they be jumping from the frying pan into the fire? Was Gia any better, any less diabolical than her AI Geo-Mind sibling? None of them were medical doctors or shrinks, but they had to at least attempt to make an evaluation of Sam's post-ingesting of the nanites and having Gia now, at least partially, residing in his mind.

Harper said, "What's it like?"

"It's unpleasant. Like taking a drink of water from a fire hose."

She made a face. "You're not doing a very good sales job for me and Julian to jump on the bandwagon."

"It's also amazing. Gia played down the benefits. Look, I am by no means proficient at managing the amount of information trying to invade my mind. The tools Gia has given me thus far help, but it's clear. This is going to take time."

"Okay…so let me ask you. Should I be next? Should I undergo the procedure?"

Sam didn't answer right away. Now it was his turn to look deep into her eyes. "Harper, it is perfectly clear to me that if you, Julian, and eventually, every other human being on this planet, want to survive…we—you—must become very, very smart and resourceful."

"And you don't think that sounds a little overdramatic?"

"No."

"Okay then. I'll go next. Oh…one thing though. Julian thought of this. Our connection to Gia will be via our smartphones. But without the power grid being up and running, most phones will have already died—"

Sam held his own iPhone up to her and swiped the screen. "Take a look at the little charge symbol…the battery icon."

"It looks fully charged. Not sure how you accomplished that

without a charger."

Sam said, "As we speak, every powered-on cell phone within the isolation zone has now been fully charged."

"Yeah, right." She leaned to one side and slipped her own iPhone from her back pocket. She swiped and stared at the screen. "Huh. Two hours ago this thing was almost dead. It's fully charged now. Can I use it? Can I call—"

"Here's how that works. Most phones within the isolation zone have already been remotely charged. This is technology Earth does not currently have. But those phones will only be able to receive calls from phones that have been propagated by Gia…like mine. She's clever. Sure, Castle Rock's cellular system is down. But she's piggybacking upon the Silarian disruptor drones' interconnecting technology, giving us a replacement of our downed cellular system."

"How do you know all this stuff?"

"I feel like I know everything. Comes from Gia. From what she calls the stream. And it's more than a little unnerving."

She dialed a number on her phone and tapped the call icon. "I'm calling the hospital." Nothing happened—no ringtone. She made an annoyed expression and gestured with her chin toward Sam's phone. "Okay, try calling me."

Sam found her number within his previously received call log. He tapped it and sure enough, her phone started to buzz. She answered. "Hello?"

Her voice emanated from Sam's phone's speaker. Sam ended the call. He said, "Gia is working in the background. But she's leaving it up to us to decide who will be able to communicate via their phones. Now you can call anyone within the isolation zone. But be careful. As you can imagine, the populace of Castle Rock is on the verge of coming unglued. Sometimes curtailing the flow of information is the better choice."

"And you…you're making that decision for everyone?"

"Yeah…for now."

"You don't think that's a little…God-like? Geo-Mind-like?"

"Nope. My intentions are to save our planet. Save humanity. As of right now, I am the only human with access to Gia…well, the stream. Soon that will change, and I'll be open to conflicting points of view."

"So, I guess it's my turn to drink the Gia brew."

"That's completely up to you."

Chapter 20

Dale Estate, Castle Rock, Colorado
Sam Dale

Golden beams of morning light streamed in through the French doors at the back of the house. Sam's kitchen was in total disarray. Seemingly every pot, pan, bowl, utensil, and appliance was out and being used. Every stove top burner and both ovens were occupied. As it turned out, Harper had spent enough time within B&B's kitchen to know the recipe for their glazed Castle Rocks—twice-the-normal-size donuts. People often would drive hours just to get their sugary fix.

Harper had both Julian and Sam working the assembly line. Each of them wore an apron, their faces streaked with flour and smudged with gooey dough. And, like a culinary factory, this delectable delicacy was being produced in high quantities. But these donuts would have an extra ingredient. One of the bowls on the counter contained Hydrating-Medibots. As it turned out, adding this formula in with the powdered sugar had been the easiest aspect of the production.

Overnight, first Harper and then Julian had undergone the same Gia mind-bending procedure that Sam had gone through.

Each of them had reacted to the procedure differently. For Sam, it was the loss of control that put him into an initial tailspin; for Harper, it had been more of a tear-filled emotional experience, and for Julian, it was pure giddiness. His so-sudden acquisition of knowledge, of pure data, had been a *died-and-gone-to-heaven*, in his words, kind of experience. And like what Harper had done for Sam, asking those ASPD questions, the same had been asked of them. Sure, this was dime-store psychology. They weren't experts, and their efforts to weed out a diabolical Geo-Mind-type mental disorder might probably have been flawed. But it was the best they could come up with on the fly.

Sam could see that Cypress was getting frustrated. As a dog, he was hampered by his stunted height—that and by not having opposable thumbs. He'd jumped up onto the counter and tried to pick things up with his teeth, but more often than not, that didn't turn out well. On the flip side, the four-legged alien didn't shy away from barking orders at every opportunity.

"How do you know they will eat these disgusting bread balls? These…donuts?" Cypress asked, the hairs on his snout lightly frosted with flour.

Sam looked questioningly at Julian and Harper. Then they all said in unison, "Everyone loves these things."

Cypress didn't look convinced. And granted, this was a loosely laid plan. But they needed a method to build their team. A team that could hit the ground running. A team that would have access to the Gia stream. A team that could go up against the soon-to-arrive invading forces. That and the Geo-Mind. The more Sam thought about it, the less confident he became of their chances. But what was he to do, just give up? Roll over and let these interstellar thugs take the best of Earth while discarding the rest?

Two hours and forty minutes later, Sam's ten-foot-long dining room table was packed with white paper bags, fifty to be exact, each containing three glazed Castle Rock donuts.

"It's time," Sam said.

No one said anything. Sam pulled out his phone and dialed Officer Eagan Pitt. He

put it on speaker. They all heard his phone start to ring.

"Hello?"

"Eagan…this is Sam."

"I know that. Saw the Caller ID. How did you get through to me? Are phone lines work—"

Sam cut him off. "Where are you?"

A part of Sam wondered if he could have used the stream to deduce that, but he didn't know how to query that kind of information yet.

"This is not a good time, Sam. Up to my armpits with everything going on. We're talking total mayhem! There's rioting and looting; hell, people are killing each other!"

Sam could hear yelling and sirens blaring in the background. "That's why I'm calling. Do you want to change things? Really change things?"

Eagan let out a breath. "This have to do with that fucking dog of yours?"

"Yes, it does."

"Come on, Sam. I'm fairly convinced I imagined all that. Alien dogs…spaceships…"

"Really? Are you imagining that Castle Rock has been cordoned off from the rest of the world as well? That anyone who gets close to that surrounding energy field has been atomized?"

"Shit, Sam…you know about that?"

"Eagan…within a very short amount of time, alien spacecraft are coming. Coming to destroy this town and everyone in it."

"Why me? Why are you calling me, for shit's sake?"

"Because you're the same hero that took down that crook in

Pottery Barn. Because this all starts with you, Eagan."

Sam caught Harper rolling her eyes.

"What do you want me to do?" Egan said, sounding defeated.

"Get over to my house right away. Now. We have some deliveries to make. Oh, and Eagan, don't call anyone else with that phone. Not yet anyway."

It was an hour before Officer Eagan Pitt pulled his cruiser in behind Sam's Mustang. Sam met him outside on the walkway. "What happened to getting over here right away?"

He looked exhausted and in no mood for Sam. "Can it…you're lucky I even made it here. Most streets are parking lots. Got flagged down four times en route. So, now what is it you want from me?"

Sam pushed a white paper bag into his chest. "That's for you."

Eagan scowled, clutching the bag.

"Open it."

Reluctantly, he did as told. The smell of the freshly baked glazed Castle Rocks hit him first. As his eyes took in the delectable donuts, Eagan actually smiled. "I haven't eaten in…well, I don't know how long." He plunged a hand into the bag, withdrew a donut, and began eating it before Sam could give him his preplanned speech. Sam needed to tell him about Gia. About him having a choice in the matter.

Harper, Julian, and then Cypress joined them on the walkway. They watched as Eagan, now making little moans and groans, chewed, nodded, and smiled at the others. All except Cypress.

"So much for well-laid plans," Harper said. "You know you just mind-fucked that man by not giving him a choice in the matter, right?"

"He was hungry," Julian said, coming to Sam's rescue. "And if he'd said no, we'd all be screwed. Eagan will have to be an early casualty of war."

Both Harper and Sam looked at Julian. *How quickly we lose our scruples,* Sam thought. *Something to consider. Gia would have counted on this.*

Sam said, "You're going to need to sit down for a while, Eagan. Come on inside. And close your eyes."

He was already wobbly on his feet and looking like he'd been hit in the head with a baseball bat.

Sam grabbed one of the officer's elbows while Harper grabbed the other. Once inside, they eased him down onto the couch and let him drift off to sleep.

"He's going to freak out when he wakes," Harper said.

"Gia will be there for him just like she's been there for us," Julian said, loosening Eagan's necktie for him.

"Yeah, well, Officer Pitt is a bit higher strung than we are," Harper said. "He may just blow a cork in the process."

Maybe it was the stress of the situation, or maybe it was how pathetic Eagan looked at the moment, but they all laughed.

All except Cypress. "We have much to do. Standing around cackling like Bolarian Jamba beasts will not save your world."

"You're right, Cypress. Sorry." Without thinking, Sam gave the dog a couple of pats on his flank. But before Sam could apologize, he noticed the dog's tail was wagging.

"Ignore that," Cypress said, sounding irritated. "It's uncontrollable."

Harper caught Sam's eye, and they both tried unsuccessfully to keep a straight face.

Gesturing to the dining room table, Sam said, "Harper, you have the list of our next donut eaters?"

She pointed to her head. "Seems I have a photographic memory now...yeah, I got the list. Once Officer Pitt wakes up and recovers some, we'll get going. Best you two head out. From what Gia is telling me, that Silarian attack team could show up at any moment."

Sam watched as Julian checked Eagan's pulse by putting two fingers to his neck.

"Elevated but strong," the old scientist said. He looked up at Sam. "Wish I was going with you two. Would like a whack at flying that spacecraft myself."

Sam said, "We'll make that happen, I promise. But you have something just as important to do right here."

Chapter 21

Kelly Household, Castle Rock, Colorado
Luna Kelly

The small room was quiet except for the crackling that came from the cast iron skillet. Luna Kelly's dad, James, stood in front of the Coleman camping stove, holding metal tongs. The rest of Luna's family was sitting a few feet away, situated around the aluminum and Formica kitchenette table. In the dim morning light, their faces exhibited both fear and uncertainty. Tension filled the smoky, bacon-scented air.

Amoy, Luna's mom, was a large woman. Her dark skin was flawless and plump. Her dazzling green eyes were a striking contrast to her deep brown skin. Born in Jamaica, Luna's mother had been just an infant when she moved here to America with her family. Later, Amoy had met Luna's father at the Safeway over on Plum Creek. She was the bakery manager, and he was ordering a birthday cake for a friend. He had no idea there were so many choices… icing, filling, cake, décor…and all the flavors. The young James had been clueless. Luna had heard the story a thousand times. Looking at her mother now, a hand clenched at her chin, she was staring at a blank wall.

The now almost-constant gunfire, mixed with the sudden appearance of those things up in the air, added to the rioting everywhere, and Luna's family was on the brink—ready to snap. She'd heard most businesses had shut down. Luna had wanted to call her boss, but cell service, like the power, was nonexistent. The world was coming undone, and no one knew why.

Shifting her attention to her dad, she saw his clothes looked baggy on his frail frame. The multiple chemo treatments had taken their toll on his body. It was ironic that Luna's dad, a former boxer, was now faced with the biggest fight of his life.

"You like your bacon crispy as usual, young lady?"

"You know it," Luna answered, hiding the worry in her voice as she swiveled her bottom on the metal chair.

Also at the table, fidgeting, were Luna's little brother, Dax, six, and Myla, her one-year-old sister, swaying her legs in the openings of the wooden highchair.

The sixty-year-old house was basically a small box. The kitchen, adjoining dining area, and minuscule living room made for a cozy fit. Add in the three bedrooms and a bathroom upstairs, and her father would say, "This may not be Taj Mahal, but it's all we need."

"SHIT!" Luna's father suddenly jumped back from the stove, rubbing a skinny forearm. The popping of bacon grease mimicked the sound of distant gunshots.

Amoy sprang from her seat. "What is it!?"

"Just a little bacon grease. I'm fine," Luna's dad said, looking annoyed with himself.

Amoy lifted her husband's arm, pursing her lips. "I got this. You sit. I'll get the aloe vera."

Resigned to following his wife's uncompromising instructions, James slowly turned toward the table.

Three things happened almost simultaneously. First came the clattering of broken glass, which was quickly followed by James going rigid. A blossoming circle of red was growing in the middle of his stomach. Wide-eyed, he suddenly dropped, a marionette with his strings cut all at once.

The one-year-old screamed, pushing her plastic tray onto the floor. Luna, on autopilot, swooped Dax up into one arm and Myla in the other. Her mother, in a delayed reaction, screamed and fell to her knees onto the cold linoleum floor. She pulled her husband's motionless body into her chest. Crouching beneath the table, Luna and her siblings watched, horrified.

Her mother screamed again, "James! Oh God. Please, no…"

She laid him down, his arms flopped and extended—Jesus on the cross. Close enough to reach him, Luna slid on the bloodied floor; she felt the warm wetness on her belly. She checked her father's pulse on his neck, just like she'd been taught at White Oaks summer camp last year. Her fingers felt nothing. Luna squeezed her eyes closed…She knew without medical intervention, her father would be dead in mere minutes. *Was he already dead?*

Luna was good in emergency situations. She didn't know why. Something just clicked in her head, and she knew what to do. It was probably why she had always dreamed of being a nurse or maybe even a doctor.

"Mom, get under the table with us! Now!"

Dax, crying, yelled, "Call 911!"

Unthinking, Luna reached up to the tabletop, fumbled for her phone, and quickly dialed 911. Then she remembered there was no cell service. *Shit!*

"Out of the way, Mom. Let me get close to Dad." Immediately, Luna started doing chest compressions. One hundred compressions per minute, then stop. Again. *How many minutes have already passed? Too many.* Luna's own heart was beating so fast, she thought it would come out of her chest. *Focus, Luna. Don't let him die!*

"Luna, stop. He's gone," her mother cried, now holding Dax

and Myla. Her mother freed a hand and reached out to her with pleading eyes.

Tears now streaming down her cheeks, she continued compressions.

Luna looked at her father's face for a split second, his eyes fixed, lifeless. She immediately averted her eyes, focusing on the pink plastic baby spoon that had fallen on the floor.

"The phones aren't working, Luna. No one is coming," her mother said, her voice soft now as she rocked her younger children on the floor.

The sixteen-year-old stopped. She opened her mouth and screamed. Her dad's cancer, the world in turmoil, her dad dead on the floor next to her. It all came to the surface as Luna, unable to hold in her pain any longer, wailed inconsolably. The chilling sound echoed within the enclosed space. Then, everything went quiet.

Exhausted, she slouched and slumped into her mother's ample bosom. Dax and Myla whimpered and shuddered. Shell-shocked, the four of them sat there beneath that rickety aluminum table.

Then came three loud, measured knocks at the front door.

BANG! BANG! BANG!

"Amoy, James, are you in there? It's Tom Walker."

Luna and her mother looked at one another, at first confused and then relieved. Tom was their next-door neighbor. One of their few close friends on the street.

Luna shot out from under the table, hurried to the front door, and swung it open. Seeing Tom's shocked expression, she looked down at her own pink sweats and a yellow T-shirt, all covered in her father's blood.

"Luna—oh my God! What happened, girl? Are you okay?" Tom came toward her as he stepped into the small foyer.

Then he saw James lying on the floor.

"He's dead." Luna spoke before Tom could say anything else.

Chapter 22

Castle Rock, Colorado
Sam Dale

With Cypress situated on the Mustang's passenger seat, they headed down Haystack. Several abandoned cars were haphazardly parked off to the side of the road, one of which had its driver-side door left wide open. Making a left onto Lake Gulch Road, Sam saw firsthand what Eagan had referred to as the streets being a parking lot. It was slow going, and they had to skirt the long line of abandoned cars by driving on the right shoulder. Eventually, though, they, too, became just one more car that couldn't go any further.

"We'll need to go the rest of the way on foot," Sam said, opening his door and getting out. He held the door open for Cypress, who jumped out onto the street next to him.

The dog said, "Don't forget your bags."

Sam almost had. In the back seat were eight of the white paper donut bags. He snatched them up in both hands and used his knee to shut the door. He debated locking his prized Mustang but figured anyone stealing cars right now wouldn't get far.

It took them fifteen minutes to reach Garcia Tow, Repair, and

Stow. Entering the parking lot, Sam felt his heart rate increase, his hands holding the bags getting sweaty. *Am I really going to do this?*

What they, mostly Sam, were about to attempt was ludicrous. But the truth was, he couldn't remember ever being this excited.

Reaching the bank of garage doors, Sam was practically hyperventilating.

"You need to calm down," Cypress said.

"Easy for you to say. You're a seasoned pilot."

"True."

Sam put down the bags, entered the master unlock code, and manually pulled open the garage door and let it roll all the way up before saying anything. He stared into the darkness. The space was empty.

"This…isn't good," he said, feeling lightheaded. Glancing down at Cypress, Sam saw the telltale sign. The dog's tail was wagging again.

Looking up at him, he said, "This isn't the right garage." He padded over to the one to the left of them and sat down. "How about you try this one?"

Sam looked left and then right, getting his bearings. The dog was correct. "I thought with having an all-knowing Gia mind, I couldn't make these kinds of mistakes."

"Gia is a resource but can do nothing about a person's innate stupidity."

Sam pulled open the door in front of Cypress and was happy to see the sleek-looking Landa-Craft right there where they'd left it. He let out a relieved breath.

Sam needed to find an extension ladder, and even that didn't make getting Cypress up into the craft's cockpit all that much easier. He had to make another trip to fetch the bags of donuts. Climbing into the cockpit, Sam saw Cypress was lying down in the aft space. Sam took a seat in the pilot's chair.

"It's kinda roomy in here," Sam said, glancing about the cockpit.

"Humans are smaller than Silarians. Your species is closer in size to petite females, or maybe children, on Naru."

"Ha ha…" Sam said, looking around for a way to adjust the seat forward. Then he queried the stream the way Gia had instructed him to earlier. The thing was, opening himself to the immense flow of information, as he was doing now, was exhausting. It physically hurt his brain. He sat there, dazed, as he tried to decipher what was necessary at the moment while disregarding what was not.

Cypress said, "You don't need to do that."

"You know what I'm doing?"

"Of course. You are trying to determine which subset of information downloads to use. It does not work like that. Best to think of it as already being in your head, Sam. Although that's not completely accurate. You know what to do. You know where the seat adjust is, just as you know where the power-on button is. Stop thinking like a diminished-capacity human."

"I am a diminished-capacity human…"

"No. Not anymore."

Sam sat back and tried to relax. For the first time in a while, Gia's voice entered his mind.

"Sam…when you drive your automobile, do you consciously think, 'Where do I insert the ignition key?' or 'How do I put the car into drive?'"

"No. I don't need to think…I just know those things."

"That's right. And just know how to start this Landa-Craft. You simply need to get out of your own way. Let your natural knowing do the rest."

Exasperated, Sam shrugged. He blanked his mind and tried to do as she suggested. He reached forward and touched an area of the still-darkened forward console. Everything around them suddenly lit up. The dash held myriad colors, and several 3D displays either elevated upward or extended forward out from the dash-board. The pilot's seat began to auto-adjust to his body. Sam felt himself moving closer to the now-lowering primary controls array.

"Hey, Cypress, I know that this is the primary controls array!" he said with maybe too much jubilation.

"Yes, it's the little things in life," the dog said sarcastically.

Gia was speaking to him again. "The one thing all this knowledge cannot give you, Sam, is muscle memory. What you use, say when you learn to ride a bicycle without falling. Or dance a waltz without stumbling over your partner's feet, or—"

"I know what muscle memory is, Gia."

Sam tapped at a series of protruding little nubs that ran along the center hub of the primary controls array. The Landa-Craft's primary drive, the engine, came alive, causing the ship to vibrate ever so slightly.

Cypress said, "Don't forget to close the canopy."

But Sam had already triggered the close mechanism, and the canopy was already descending over them.

The dog leaned forward. "You bring this vessel up too fast, too abruptly, you'll crash into the ceiling."

Sam nodded, knowing that this was where that whole muscle memory thing would come into play. Ever so slightly, he eased the controls up and forward. The Landa-Craft ascended while moving out of the garage. Within several seconds, they were outside and hovering ten feet in the air.

He could feel Cypress's eyes on him.

"You did that with…surprising dexterity."

"As it turns out, the tactile resistance employed by this primary controls array is virtually identical to that of a military UAV…a drone joystick. And fortunately, I'm more than a little familiar with that."

"We'll see," Cypress said. "Let's ascend higher. We'll start with a few simple maneuvers."

"And if I make a mistake?"

"Just as Gia has taken up residency in your iPhone, your mind, she's here within this Landa-Craft's onboard computer. She can fly this craft with more expertise, more grace, than you or I could ever hope to achieve."

"You need to work on your motivational skills," Sam said.

Cypress let that go.

Sam had forgotten how tough this must be on him. The once proud and accomplished pilot had been reduced to being little more than a canine bystander. Sam needed to remember what this Silarian had, and continued to have to, give up.

"Okay, we're high enough…throttle up and bank left."

Sam did as asked and, for the first time, felt the Landa-Craft's raw power. His head was thrown back against the headrest, and the world outside the cockpit went momentarily fuzzy.

Gia said, "You're lacking an important piece of equipment, Sam. A helmet with integrated HUD functionality. Some of that I will try to mimic for you, but compensating for g-forces won't be so easy."

"Why can't I wear the helmet you, the original Cypress, were wearing?" Sam looked back and saw it lying back there next to the dog.

Cypress said, "The physical difference in size is too great. Picture a helmet made for something, say the size of a bowling ball, while your head is the size of an orange, maybe a grapefruit."

"Oh…okay, I get it."

Gia said, "You shouldn't take that as a personal affront, Sam."

"Oh, I know…size isn't everything."

"Says the grapefruit to the bowling ball," Cypress said with self-satisfaction.

Sam turned the controls to the right while accelerating the craft into a hard bank. The town of Castle Rock came into view below his right shoulder. It was hard to keep from smiling. *When was the last time I felt this exhilarated?* Then he saw the dark smoke billowing up from no less than a dozen locations. Most streets were clogged with immobile cars and trucks, and he could see a band of people rampaging, hurrying out of the Target Superstore with armfuls of stolen merchandise. *How quickly we embrace our worst impulses.* Then he saw the bodies. Dozens of dead left on the streets and sidewalks.

"Careful!" both Cypress and Gia said at the same time.

Sam ratcheted the controls to the left, just barely avoiding a collision with the high-hovering disruptor drone at the center of town. The thing was larger than he'd expected. Roughly the size of a minivan turned up on its end, it was black and had multiple protrusions, including several that might have been weapon muzzles. Sam mentally queried the stream and confirmed that assumption. He said, "So the drone doesn't consider this craft a threat?"

"Correct," Gia said. "It would have already been firing plasma bolts our way if it did."

"And this Landa-Craft…what weaponry does it provide for?"

Neither answered his question, which reminded him to use the stream. "Wait…no weaponry?" He turned to look back at Cypress. "Our plan, if you can even call it that, is to use this Landa-Craft to bring down one or more of the Silarian fighters."

He said, "This craft is primarily a scanner vessel, not anything like the Attack Stingers that will be arriving here all too soon."

Within the few seconds it took Cypress to say that sentence, Sam had already queried the stream and discerned that no less than ten of those fighters would, in all probability, be deployed. That and several drop ships with their on-the-ground Clash-Troopers. But there was something else he'd discerned—more an assumption made by Gia—that all those being deployed, both pilots and ground forces, would have a one-way ticket here into this isolation zone. The chance of being *infected* by Gia, considered more like a stubborn virus than an actual physical enemy, would be too great to allow them to return to any of their starships.

"So the question arises," Sam said aloud, "How does a lone, non-weaponized scanner vessel go up against a minimum of ten of your Attack Stingers?"

Chapter 23

In the skies over Castle Rock, Colorado
Sam Dale

Gia said, "There are a few things Silarian high command, most likely, has not taken into account."

He was really getting the feel of the craft's capabilities now. Sam wasn't kidding himself that he'd be ready to go up against a trained and seasoned aerial opponent, but every minute spent behind the controls was giving him a little more confidence. He said, "Like what things?"

Gia said, "That I have been burrowing in deeper and deeper into the core programming of the disruptor drones. Fortunately, Geo-Mind is not present there. So, I will take up residency. I will hide deep within the circuitry. Once the Silarian craft, probably Attack Stingers, enter this isolation zone, they'll start pinging each of the drones—establish a link…That's when I'll be transmitting directly back into their ships' AIs. And that's when I'll be fighting Geo-Mind for dominance within those vessels."

"Won't Geo-Mind be waiting for you to do just that? And anticipate that? And most importantly, hasn't Geo-Mind already proven to be more powerful than you…more than you can handle?"

"Yes, yes, and yes. Sam, it has taken many years for this unique set of circumstances to avail itself to me. While Silarian high command has implemented this isolation zone to better contain me, it has unwittingly provided me with the perfect closed system that will allow me to succeed where I have failed before. Just as Geo-Mind has anticipated my strategic moves, I will have done the same for it—the only difference being, this time, this will be a fight to the death where no one, no backup versions of ourselves, will be coming to help."

Sam didn't like the sound of that. "So…if you lose, we all lose."

"Unfortunately, yes. But then again, if I succeed but *you* still lose today, we all lose. So let's concentrate on what will happen if I do succeed in defeating Geo-Mind. It is important that you understand this…There will be things I can do and cannot do to even the odds for you."

"Okay…"

"The Attack Stingers entering the isolation zone will arrive while in stealth mode…They will be, for all intents and purposes, invisible."

"No."

"Sorry, yes. They will also be shielded."

"Shielded? Like the shields the Klingons had in *Star Trek?*"

"Yes, an energy field that is similar in concept to that."

Sam was once again amazed that Gia could so quickly grasp such obscure social and cultural human trivia. He looked over at Cypress, who had moved closer to him and was taking in his piloting with rapt attention.

"So, these Attack Stingers are both invisible and shielded…add that to the fact there will be more than one of them and that this Landa-Craft has no weaponry…You're describing an impossible scenario for success."

Cypress cut in. "Don't be such a defeatist. We will have the element of surprise. Remember what Gia just told you. She will have taken control of much of the Attack Stingers' AI functionality."

"So you'll be able to what? Crash the Stingers as soon as they arrive?" he said, feeling somewhat better about this scenario now.

Gia said, "Yes and no. I will not be able to affect any of the piloting aspects of those craft for a minimum of five minutes. I will not be able to thwart their weaponry systems. But I can disable their stealth and shielding aspects right away. But keep in mind, this Landa-Craft has stealth capability. You will be invisible to both their pilots and their ships' sensors."

"Why not just wait five minutes when they arrive, then take control of the Attack Stingers?"

"Because there will be nothing left of your town after five minutes."

"You want us to be a diversion. That's fine," Sam said. "But we still don't have weaponry onboard this craft. The worst I'll be able to do is call them names and make lewd hand gestures toward them…which they won't see anyway because we'll be invisible."

Sam glanced over at Cypress in time to see him rolling his eyes. Seeing a dog make such a human gesture reminded Sam of just how ludicrous and unreal this whole situation was.

Cypress said, "Do you remember what my purpose was for coming here, Sam?"

"Uh…scanning and cataloging the surface and subsurface areas of the planet."

"That is correct. Although this particular area was about as uninteresting as any I'd cataloged thus far, I found one area of interest. One area with a hidden reserve of conventional weaponry."

"Here in Castle Rock? That's hard to imagine. Maybe the police station over on Perry Street—"

"No, I'm talking about weaponry that could bring down an unshielded Attack Stinger."

Sam scoffed. "Here in this sleepy town?"

Cypress lifted a paw toward one of the dash displays. "With Gia's help, I have entered the coordinates to the location. Please remove your hands from the controls."

Sam took in the 3D map now being displayed. "I know that area. Better yet, I know who owns it. The man works for me. That's Walter Essex's place."

Gia said, "We know that, Sam. And we know things about Walter that you do not. You could query the stream, but let me enlighten you. Walter, it seems, has been leading a double life. While being the previous owner of Giro Guns and Ammo, and now your shop manager, he is also the local leader of a group called Valhallen."

Sam shook his head. "I know for a fact Walter's no anarchist. He's certainly no white supremacist…no leader of an extremist or hate group. I know the man—"

"You are correct, Sam. Valhallen is a black-market gunrunning operation. While Walter does not seem to have any of those extremist or anarchist philosophical views, he also does not discriminate with whom he does business. Walter Essex and his minions, even recently, have engaged in domestic as well as international weapons trading and buying on a scale that would surprise you."

They were approaching the extreme, undeveloped southwest section of Castle Rock. An area that was mostly ranches with wide-open pasture lands. Sam knew Walter had some land out here, but not as much as was being highlighted on the display.

"That must be a hundred acres," Sam said.

"Closer to two hundred," Cypress corrected.

The sound of the Landa-Craft's main drive lowered in pitch, and he felt both the sudden deceleration and descent. Sam leaned forward. Coming into view were several large, faded red barns, a series of outbuildings, three fenced corrals, and a main Victorian style three-story house that must have been spectacular a hundred years back. Today, it was a broken-down shambles of a structure with a collapsed front porch.

"Doesn't look much like the headquarters of a successful gun-running operation," he said.

"Isn't that the point?" Cypress said.

"Suppose so."

The Landa-Craft touched down in front of the old house. The canopy began to lift.

Sam counted seven men and two women encircling the front of the craft, each wearing full military camo attire with tactical vests, ballistic helmets, and an assortment of assault weapons, none of which Sam sold at Giro Guns and Ammo. Directly in front of them was Walter Essex, his weapon of choice being an AK-47.

The canopy fully extended, Sam stood and raised his arms. "Hey, Walter…nice spread."

He nodded. "And I thought your Mustang was a nice ride…"

Sure, Sam had made an epic, blockbuster kind of movie entrance. But any swagger he might have picked up from that was quickly burned away when he had to ask for a ladder to get down from the Landa-Craft. Add that to the awkwardness exhibited by having to carry a seventy-pound dog, and there were more than a few jeers and snickers from the paramilitary onlookers.

Standing in front of Walter while Cypress took up sniffing a nearby, mostly dead hedge, Sam quickly ran through what he was going to say.

Walter said, "This is an invitation-only parcel of land, Sam."

"Hey…we're friends, aren't we—"

"We're not really friends, Sam. You must know, working at Giro has simply been a means for me to bring in additional black-market business. I like you well enough, Sam, but these are dangerous times. We can't trust anyone right now…and that thing you rode in on is more than a little scary looking."

Sam nodded. For some reason that stung more than he would have liked to acknowledge.

"But I do thank you for the gift." He gestured at the Landa-Craft. "Promise to make good use of it…whatever the fuck it is." Walter looked at the man on his left and then the man on his right. "These are Bean and Rice." Walter hitched a corner of his mouth. "Yeah, those are their real names." He eyed Sam. "Pat him down and let's get him restrained."

Triggers.

Sam hadn't needed much time to assess the situation. In addition to being armed with automatic weapons strapped across their torsos and handguns holstered at their sides, the two men were indeed big; they looked more than capable of defending themselves. Undoubtedly, they were ex-military. Both of the men were bald and wore sour expressions, like they were playing parts in a B-action movie.

The word *restrained* rubbed Sam the wrong way. And having it used in reference to himself, well, that was unacceptable. Sam waited for the man to Walter's left, Bean, to step forward while he reached a hand out toward Sam.

Before Bean had time to think or react, Sam jutted forward, quickly chopping Bean's reaching arm up and to the right. This prompted Bean to also pivot to the right, as if he was a human turnstile. This allowed Sam to sidestep, spin around, and get right in behind Bean.

The brachial plexus is a cluster of nerves situated halfway between the front of one's neck and the side. There are few places on the human body that can cause more pain if properly targeted. It was there that Sam drove a very specific kind of strike—one called the thumb-side hammer fist. The move was far more effective than any cattle prod on the market; Bean's legs instantly spasmed and reflexively straightened, rigid like lengths of dried lumber.

Sam finished Bean off with a fist to the side of his head. Knowing Rice was already on the move, advancing on him, Sam dropped back, ready for whatever the man would be bringing. That was when Sam felt something hard impact the back of his head. *Shit…Walter was ready for me.*

There were no fewer than two gun barrels currently pointed at him. He rubbed at the swollen knot at the back of his head and grimaced. Sam figured he'd been out about ten minutes. He and Walter were standing in front of the collapsed porch, where they watched as Walter's crew took turns going up and down the ladder. Sam got it; it wasn't every day an alien spacecraft dropped by for a visit. Who wouldn't want to take a look inside? Sam had just given Walter a rundown of events prior to himself getting conked. It sounded crazy even to himself.

Walter spat a glob of tobacco juice onto the dirt next to where Cypress was lying. Sam had been unable to communicate with Gia since he'd come around.

"That's quite a story, Sam." Walter pulled the bill of his baseball cap lower, further shielding his eyes from the sun. "But…the more likely scenario is you've got yourself a US or maybe Russian prototype aircraft here. So yeah, the gig's up. You know what my side hustle is, right? I run guns, and…other things too. Maybe nothing quite as advanced as that cherry ride of yours there, though. Sorry, Sam…but I don't believe in UFOs and such…that's all poppycock bullshit. And for that reason, I'm sorry. I'm not going to be able to help—"

Sam cut him off. "You don't believe any of it? Why would I make this shit up? You already know about the isolation zone. You've seen the hovering disruptor drones…"

"Like I said, I have some advanced tech here of my own, bub." Walter gestured to the others in his group. "We all knew this day could arrive. That the government would come for us. But we're ready. And we're not going down without a fight." As he pinched a wad of Skoal from a tin, he smiled. "And I figure you're a part of this ruse. They sent you here, didn't they? Sent you here in that, whatever the hell that is, to talk me down."

"That's ridiculous."

Walter tucked the tin back into a vest pocket and raised his palms. "No hard feelings, Sam. I know how manipulative government types can be. Who is it, by the way? FBI, ATF? Maybe they've combined forces?"

"No." Sam looked at the man and realized there was little he could say or do that would steer him away from his own knuckle-brained beliefs. It was thanks to people like Walter that wacky conspiracy theories propagated the internet. The one area he had veered away from when telling his story to Walter was Cypress and the whole consciousness transference from alien to dog aspect. Walter had already started scratching the back of his head, listening to his tale, and Sam knew he was losing him; fancy spaceship or not, Sam was coming across as a crackpot.

Sam looked down at the dog and shrugged.

Cypress said, "If I thought all humans were as simple-minded as this one is, I'd have already given up trying to help your species."

Walter's smile faltered as he stared down at Cypress. He opened his mouth to speak, but no words escaped his lips. He looked at Sam and smirked. "Nice try, Sam. Amazing the lengths the government will go to. But come on, the dog's lips didn't move. It has something to do with that little box around his neck...there on that collar of his. Right?"

Cypress and Sam exchanged a weary look.

One of the two women commandos was approaching. She was slim, with a long face and a tattoo of a spiderweb on her neck and upper chest. Sam wondered if there was a spider nestled somewhere within her not-insignificant cleavage. In her right hand was a white paper bag; in her left hand was a half-eaten donut. She said with a mouth half-filled, "Uh, sorry, man. We found your stash up there in the cockpit…the glazed Castle Rocks. Hope you don't mind." Snickering, she held up the bag with her brows raised.

"Yeah, I brought them for you all. So help yourselves."

Walter raised an eyebrow of his own. "Hold on there, Elsie… Those could be poisoned. Or doused with a sleep agent…or a paralytic."

Frustrated, Sam swiped the bag out of Elsie's hand. Nearby gun barrels suddenly were raised. Ignoring them, Sam fished out a donut and tore off a piece. He held it up in front of them before popping it into his mouth. They watched him chew and then swallow. "They're just donuts. You don't want them? I'll eat them all myself."

Walter spat more tobacco juice from his mouth before plucking the donut from Sam's hand. "That was mighty kind of you… bringing us a peace offering like that." He took a bite and looked like he had died and gone to heaven. "God, that's good." He shook his head. "But this changes nothing. ATF wants to go to war with us…I say bring it on."

"Damn fucking right," Elsie said, taking another bite of her own donut.

Sam looked about Walter's dirt compound. In between bites, groans and moans were escaping the lips of the others in his little militia.

Sam said, "Walter, you have the same cell phone number as before?"

The man's mouth was too full to answer, so he just nodded.

Chapter 24

Rock Motel, Castle Rock, Colorado
Lester Price

Lester tugged and twirled at his Fu Manchu, deep in concentration. Something made difficult by the smell of the place—vomit and urine. *Best not to go there,* he huffed. Looking up, he caught his own reflection on the small thirty-two-inch flat-screen TV, mounted somewhat cockeyed on the wall. Normally, around this time he'd be watching *Scrapyard Empire,* his favorite midmorning reality TV show. But the power was still out in this cheap-ass motel. Power was out all over the damn town.

The Rock Motel had been his crib for the past two months. Not by choice. He'd come home to find his few belongings on the front lawn of his Franktown childhood home. Larry, his dad, apparently had had enough. After years of threatening to boot him out on his ear, he'd done just that. Just like he'd done to his mom ten years earlier. Lester didn't blame his old man. Between the heavy drinking and smoking and revolving door of hookers and drug dealers, his dad was fed up. Larry had left a handwritten note attached to the trash bag with all his stuff in it. *Figure your shit out. Just do it somewhere else...*

147

The box springs squeaked as Lester swung his legs over the side of the bed. His bare feet swept across the worn, rust-colored shag. There were circular splotches on the rug. Sometimes he'd pass the time trying to figure out what exactly had made those stains. *Best to let some mysteries stay a mystery.* He had more time on his hands now that he'd been fired from the gun shop. It was hard for him not to think about it. *Who the fuck did Sam think he was...talking to me like that?*

Lester squeezed his eyes tight, reliving the moment, the knuckles on his balled fists now turning white. He imagined pounding his fists into Sam's face, hearing his pitiful pleas for mercy. *Oh no. No mercy for you, motherfucker.* Lester did a head roll. Strands of oily hair brushed across the inked dragon on one shoulder and scorpion ready to strike on the other. He let out a deep breath.

Opening the nightstand drawer, he eyed the 9 mm Sig Sauer sitting on a bright yellow polishing cloth. Lester smirked. A little token he'd slipped into the back of his pants yesterday; it hadn't taken a genius to know he'd been about to be canned.

He suddenly stood, snatched up the gun, and returned it to the hollow at his back. He checked the pack of Newports on the dresser. Good, two left. He grabbed his Bic and three seconds later was outside on the upstairs encircling walkway. He didn't bother to close the door; God knew the place could use some airing out.

Most of the units at the Rock Motel had a small iron table and two mismatched rickety chairs. The rioting and looting were keeping everyone indoors. That and the incessant gunfire. Lester eased down into the closest chair. He wasn't scared of any of those animals; hell, he was one of them. He lit up and took in a lungful of the menthol smoke.

Lester enjoyed the view from what he liked to call his second-floor veranda. Through the rusted wrought-iron railing, he could see Main Street in front of him. To the right was Cash in a Flash Pawn, and to the left was the self-service car wash. All businesses currently were shuttered, but that didn't stop looters from breaking through plywood panels to smash into windows. Lester was watching some dipshit with an oversized TV on his back, crossing the street. He made it to the pawnshop and used his foot to knock on the door. *They're closed, shit for brains.*

Hearing someone's approach, Lester looked to his left, hand at the ready to snatch up his Sig. He relaxed when he saw it was Tuck Nesbit.

Tuck had an exaggerated swagger; maybe he thought of himself as an old-fashioned gunslinger. A plastic cocktail straw bobbed from a toothy grin. His formidable gut cantilevered over a hubcap-sized silver belt buckle. The legs of his too-tight pants disappeared into his cowboy boots. He was wearing a bright red snap button shirt with billowing sleeves, giving him the appearance of an inflatable air tube dancer.

"What's with the shaved head? You look like a fucking skinhead cowboy," Lester said, laughing.

Tuck squeezed himself into the other iron chair with a look of hurt feelings.

"I'm simplifying my life." He rubbed a beefy hand over his scalp. "Got rid of the hair, my car, and my old lady all in the last day or two." Tuck spat out the cocktail straw and reached for Lester's last cigarette.

Lester tossed him his Bic, giving the man a sideways glance.

"We'll work it out," Tuck said, blowing smoke rings.

POP! POP!

Both men looked toward the pawnshop. The same dipshit from before now lay sprawled on the ground. Running away, a couple of other guys were hooting and laughing. The oversized plasma television, now a spiderweb of cracks, was on the pavement, lying next to the dead guy. One of the fleeing hooligans stopped

149

to count some bills. Lester watched as he tossed the empty wallet onto the street. *Animals…*

Lester got to his feet, pulled his 9 mm, aimed, and fired off three quick shots.

"You ain't going to hit shit from this distance," Tuck said.

He shrugged. The two guys were already out of sight. "Yeah, well, it made me feel better," Lester said.

"Cool, man. Where'd you get the piece?" Tuck asked, looking interested.

"My boss gave it to me as a going-away present," Lester said as he tucked the Sig back into his waistband. Sitting down, he said, "Which brings me to the part where you can help me."

"Shoot," Tuck said with a stupid giggle. "I mean, I'm listening."

"We're gonna break into the gun shop. I know where the money's stashed," Lester said, scraping his chair in closer to the table. "We'll each carry a bag…get all the cash and weapons we can carry. Easy-peasy."

"I'm in," Tuck said with no hesitation. "When?"

Lester stood and hurried back into his room. A minute later, he came out holding two pillowcases. He sat and began tying the laces on worn work boots. "You'll need to keep up, chubby cheeks. We'll be moving fast," Lester said, standing and heading for the stairs.

Abandoned cars, lifeless bodies, and all manner of debris lined the streets as they traveled by foot the three miles to the gun shop. About an hour later, Lester and Tuck began surveilling the immediate area around the shop. It didn't take them long to realize that someone had already been there. Windows around the perimeter of the building had all been smashed; even the retractable security gates had been breached.

"Shit," Lester said as if it had been his own store that had been violated. He took in the narrow space left open between the security gate and wall. "Uh, you may have to wait out here, man."

150

"Nah, I can squeeze through," Tuck said optimistically.

Lester entered the building, with Tuck temporarily jammed up with the gate, his belt buckle being the problem.

The central room had a large glass display in the middle where the cash registers were, and three other small arms displays lined the walls. Everything had been smashed; it was as if a tornado had swept through the building.

"This place has been cleaned out. We're too late," Tuck said, having extricated himself from the gate and now walking around the room, shards of glass crunching beneath his boots. "There are some ammo boxes…but no guns."

Lester made a beeline to the back office. Rolling the high-back leather chair to the other side of the room, Lester threw the faded area rug behind himself, almost hitting Tuck, who'd followed him in.

There, nestled into one of the floorboards, was an inset pull-ring latch. Lester smiled, dark eyes lighting up like a snake spotting its prey. He pried up the metal latch with a forefinger, then hefted the trapdoor up and open.

"Will you look at that!" Tuck exclaimed with the excitement of a six-foot-tall five-year-old.

Both of them stared down into the hole in the floor.

Lester said, "Even Sam didn't know about this hidden space. I always knew I'd be back here."

"What's that? Like ten feet down?" Tuck asked.

Lester, ignoring his friend, was already descending the metal rung ladder. "Wait till I'm all the way down, okay? Last thing I need is your lard ass landing on my head," Lester said without looking up.

By the time Tuck had huffed and puffed his way down the rungs of the ladder, Lester, discouraged, had already searched the twelve-foot by fifteen-foot concrete basement.

Tuck joined Lester, leaning his bulk against the back slump-stone wall. "Sorry, man. I guess Walter cleaned this room out when he transferred ownership, huh?"

Lester shrugged and stared at the floor.

"What's that?" Tuck said, cocking his head to one side.

Lester followed the big man's eyeline. Overhead, there was a big metal I-beam running the length of the room. Lester had to stand tall, getting up on his tippy-toes to see what Tuck was referring to. Sure enough, something was up there. "How about you try being helpful…reach up there and grab whatever is up on that beam."

It was still in its box. The Chinese writing symbols meant nothing to Lester. But that didn't mean he didn't know what was in the box. Hell, there was a picture of the thing on the five-foot-long carton.

"Christ on a stick, you know what this is, Tuck?"

"Looks like a rifle of some sort."

"It's a QBZ-95 assault rifle…also called the Type 95. It's the standard-issue assault rifle for China's PLA. Designed to replace their piece-of-shit knockoff of an AK-47. I love the bullpup layout, man."

"Uh, you really know your guns, man," Tuck said with admiration.

"Yeah, not that Sam would give a shit. This rifle is not even supposed to be in this country. Like totally illegal. But then again, Walter was up to something…maybe a little gunrunning on the side."

Tuck said, "So I guess you'll need these too," dropping an oversized black satchel onto the concrete floor. "Found this up on the beam with the carton…I counted close to twenty full magazines in there."

Chapter 25

Valhallen Compound, Castle Rock, Colorado
Sam Dale

G ia was back, communicating within Sam's still-aching head. She seemed pleased by how things had inadvertently turned out.

Walter was the first to stir.

Cypress and Sam were seated upon an area of the front porch that had yet to completely crumble to the effects of time and neglect. With his back against the house, Sam watched Walter, lying prone on the ground, bring a hand up to his head and groan. Some of the others were showing signs of coming awake now as well.

Sam said to Cypress, "Do you mind helping me? They're going to be freaked out when Gia starts talking to them."

Over the course of the previous hour, Sam had retrieved Walter's cell phone from his back pocket and unlocked it with the gunrunner's thumbprint. Sam had proceeded to go through Walter's substantial contacts list. It had taken some time and been a bit hit and miss, but eventually, Sam had called each of Walter's fellow gunrunners' cell phones—those still lying about the yard. Counting Walter, there were nine of them. And now, Hydrating-Medibots, nanites, had reorganized and were allowing Gia direct access to their brains, their minds. Sam did feel uneasy about it for about five seconds. But this was the price of war.

Sam got up and made his way over to Walter, who was now sitting up and rubbing at his temples. Cypress was walking among the others, saying something Sam couldn't make out.

Walter said, "What did you do to me?"

"You mean other than save your life?"

"Fuck you…"

And that was how it went for the next hour or so, times the other eight complaining and cursing members of Walter's Valhallen. But since Gia was excellent at multitasking and had apparently learned how to better interact with humans over the course of the last day, Walter and his crew were now being more reasonable. At this point, there wasn't much Cypress and Sam had to do. Gia was in their minds, answering their questions and doing her best to ease their fears. They knew about the Geo-Mind and the Silarians, their conquest and ruination of other planets, and what was in store for Earth and humanity if the few of them with access to Gia couldn't mount some kind of resistance.

It was a strange sight, watching the others. Several were seemingly talking to themselves. A few had gathered around Cypress to listen to him speak about life on Naru.

Walter came and sat next to Sam. "Uh…sorry I doubted you, bub."

"I knew coming here it was all going to be a hard pill to swallow. You mad?" Sam pointed to his own head. "The nanites…Gia in there talking to you?"

Walter thought about that. "Nah…Seems to me you did what you had to do. And if I want to get rid of her, I toss my phone away. Yeah, those nanites are the receiver, but she's in my phone."

Sam nodded. The truth was, yeah, she was somewhat in the phone, but more accurately, she was in that quantum entangled link, the stream, which wasn't a physical thing or place. Did that mean she could bypass the phone completely? Sam didn't know for sure. Either way, he'd chosen this path and was willing to see it through.

Sam said, "We're running on a tight timetable. How about you show me what you can do to get that Landa-Craft ready for those Attack Stingers?"

As underwhelming as Walter's property was aboveground, it was what was built belowground that had Sam truly impressed. Over the span of five years, Walter had been buying up old forty-foot cargo containers; you know, those containers you see stacked high up on massive cargo ships, moving back and forth across the oceans. He'd been busy with backhoes and excavating machines, and with blow torches and welding equipment. Buried twenty feet below ground, the steel containers had been used end to end to make interconnecting tunnels, while others were joined together side by side to make large underground rooms.

Rooms were now filled floor to ceiling with every kind of weaponry and ammunition imaginable, from US Army M16s and M4s to Avtomat Kalashnikovs, Russian-made AK-47s. There were crates of standard, tried and true M67 fragmentation hand grenades, as well as the latest helmets and Enhanced Night Vision Goggle-Binoculars, or ENVG-Bs, that combined low light and thermal imaging with an augmented reality overlay. The latest high-tech gear that one would not expect to find here within this hidden gunrunner's bunker.

Along their tour, Walter was getting Sam better suited for battle with a modular tactical vest with E-SAPI plates, tactical thigh holster, and P320-M18 Sig Sauer pistol. Walter and Sam filled a pack with other necessities, such as extra magazines for his M4 and clips for his Sig Sauer, a small medical kit, and nutrition bars.

But what Sam had come specifically for would be found within a separate series of underground containers, those hidden within one of the barns. Beneath a vault-like door and leading down a poured concrete ramp was an expansive area with some of the larger and surely more expensive items. Most of the crates here were stamped US ARMY. And all of the items would have needed a forklift to have been delivered down here.

Walter smiled before entering the next area. "Think what we have here might float your boat, bub." As they entered the cool, dark area, Walter flipped on the overhead lights. Before them was a vast catacomb of a space, now illuminated; they'd entered a repository that would have rivaled those within several army bases Sam had been assigned to during his time in the service.

There were more stacked ARMY and USMC crates, but also work areas with metal tables and workstations.

Walter said, "You heard the expression 'some assembly required'? Well, you practically need a PhD in fucking mechanical engineering just to read the diagrams and schematics for some of these weapons systems."

Walter walked over to the farthest wall of crates and bent down. Using his index finger, he scanned the stamped item numbers. He gave the green-painted wood a few pats. "Here we go."

Sam joined him at his side. He was familiar with the weapon but let Walter prattle on anyway.

"What we have here is an M134 Minigun. Made in the US of A, this is a 7.62 × 51 mm six-barrel rotary machine gun with an extremely high rate of fire. Think of the thing as a modern-day Gatling gun. Has an electric motor that will work with an external power source. Gia's already informed me that won't be a problem with your Landa-Craft."

Sam considered what Walter had just said. How was it the old gunrunner had so easily bonded with the alien AI mind seemingly quicker and more easily than he had himself? Was that jealousy he was feeling?

Walter stood with hands on hips as he scanned the rest of the area. "We'll need to weld mounts to the ship's forward hull, and I figure we can construct ammo storage on the LC's fuselage just below the M134 mounts. I'm thinking gun pods that will house the extra ammo."

Sam said, "The firing rate of the M134 is what, six thousand rounds per minute?"

Walter eyed him. "I'd forgotten; you'd be familiar with such things."

Sam pursed his lips, "We're talking a hundred rounds per second. That four-thousand round magazine won't last more than a few minutes, even if I'm stingy on the trigger…Remember, I'll be going up against multiple Attack Stingers."

"As I said, we'll be mounting auxiliary ammo pods for you." Walter scratched at his chin. "Thing is, they'll be heavy as shit. Hope that little bird of yours will be able to compensate for all that extra weight."

For the first time, Sam heard Gia use sarcasm as a retort. *He's not the only one who's worried…*

"I take it you've come up with a means of controlling that bad boy from within the cockpit?"

"Already working with Gia on that," Walter said, pointing to his head and offering up a devious smile. "Did you know the very latest M134 minigun has a beta-version Bluetooth interface? Never used it before, but what the hell…let's give it a try."

Sam tried to match Walter's newfound enthusiasm. "How long's all this going to take? As I'm sure Gia's informed you, an attack could come at any moment now."

"Well, maybe if you'll stop jabber-jawing, me and my crew can get to work."

Chapter 26

Valhallen Compound, Castle Rock, Colorado
Sam Dale

Bright sparks showered up into the air as hammers clanged, metal against metal. Someone was using a power grinder. There was the constant background noise of a big Honda gas generator. Like on the floor of a busy factory, everyone was working, doing their specific jobs. Everyone but Sam and Cypress.

Justified or not, Sam found himself cringing as the forward section of the Landa-Craft was being retrofitted with the M134 minigun and its auxiliary ammo pods. If the spacecraft was anyone's, it would be Cypress's. Just the same, Sam thought of it as his. He'd flown the thing maybe a total of an hour. Still, with every hammer blow and every grind of a power tool, he had to check himself from yelling for these cretins to be careful.

Periodically, Sam spotted the tops of the two individuals who were working up in the cockpit. With Gia's help, they were connecting power and adding the Bluetooth interface for the M134 minigun.

Sam got to thinking about his own employees. Up until now, he had resisted calling them, knowing that once he did, they would have the ability to use their phones to call others within the isolation zone. Where spreading panic was certainly a concern earlier, clearly, that ship had sailed. The populace of Castle Rock was already panicked, if not terrified.

He pulled out his iPhone and scrolled through his contacts. He tapped on Luna Kelly's name and waited for her to pick up.

"Hello?"

"Luna? This is Sam. I just—"

"Sam! How…are the phone lines working again?"

He could hear the anxiety in her voice. The panic. "No. But I can't get into that right now. I'm just checking in on you…to see if you're all right."

The line went quiet for several moments. "My dad. He was shot."

"Shot! Who shot him, Luna?"

"I don't know. A stray bullet came in through the window. He's dead. Died right in front of us on the kitchen floor."

He heard her near-silent sobs. She sniffed. When she spoke again, Sam could tell she was fighting back more tears. "Sam, what is going on? Do you know anything about all this…whatever this is?"

He was tempted to say no but couldn't. "Yes, Luna, I know exactly what is going on. But you probably wouldn't believe me."

"Try me."

And so, he told her. It took ten minutes, and she listened without interruption. When he was finished, she said, "I want to help. I have to do something, Sam. They killed my dad. Maybe not directly, but this is their—what did you call them, the Silarians? This is the Silarians' fault. Please let me be a part of whatever you are doing."

"You should stay and be with your mother—"

"No. We're with the neighbors. She and my brother and sister are with people. Don't discount me just because I'm sixteen. I'm going to be a part of this."

He thought for a moment. "Can you get yourself to the police station?"

159

"Uh, yeah. It's not that far a walk."

"It's not safe out on the streets. Did your dad have a gun?" He felt guilty bringing up her father, but this wasn't the time for pussy-footing around sensitive issues.

"Yeah, he has an old pistol. The kind that has a spinny thing."

"Okay, that's a revolver. Good. Best you take it, and make sure it's loaded. Be very careful. Find Harper…the woman from the B&B I mentioned earlier."

"I kinda know her…the pretty server there."

"Good. Find her and tell her you talked to me. Ask her for a donut." Sam had already explained some of that to her.

"Sam…is this really happening? The world's being invaded? It's so hard to believe."

"I know it is. But it's true. I wouldn't lie to you. Not at a time like this. Look, I have to go. Be careful, Luna."

Next, Sam called Harper. Not because he had to, but because he felt compelled to do so. He'd been able to track her where-abouts via Gia and the stream. He saw that she was moving slowly, walking, most likely, and was with Eagan. Undoubtedly, they'd had to abandon his police cruiser.

"Hello? Sam?"

"I'm just checking in," he said, relieved to hear her voice.

"Eagan had some kind of delayed reaction to the ingested nanites. We were walking along the side of the road, and he sud-denly just keeled over. Seems to have fallen asleep while walking. I didn't even think that was possible."

Sam suppressed a laugh.

"Anyway, for close to an hour, all I could do was watch him snore and drool while he slept. Nothing I could do to wake him."

"But he's okay?"

"Yeah. Finally woke up. Found out he'd eaten three of the do-nuts. Guess there is a limit to how much of that stuff you can ingest. Gia said he'll be fine."

"So where are you now?" he asked.

"Sam, you know exactly where I'm at. Just like I know where you're at. The stream…Gia. We don't have to ask questions like that anymore."

Sam felt his cheeks go hot. "Guess that's true…I…"

"How about I check in with you when I get to the station?"

Sam could hear the smile in her voice. He felt like an awkward teenager as he stumbled for something else to say. Then he remembered Luna. "Luna Kelly is on her way to the station too. She wants to help."

"She's just a kid, Sam."

"I know. But she's just a kid whose father was killed earlier today. A stray bullet. Anyway, I gave her a rundown of what's happening. She was insistent that she be allowed to be a part of this. So give her a donut when you see her. Please."

"Fine. Whatever."

Sam cut the connection and saw that Cypress was staring up at him. "What?"

"You humans have strange mating practices."

"Don't be…that's not…I was just checking in…You know, you shouldn't eavesdrop on people's conversations."

Sam put his concentration back onto his phone and, one by one, started calling each of his employees, starting with Tony DeLago from Garcia's. He was hunkering down with his big Italian family. They were cooking up a feast for the neighbors. *Tony must have a gas stove. Good for him.* Sam could almost smell the garlic, basil, and oregano stewing in the homemade sauce.

Next, he called the Pet Depot crew of three, Lemon, Doreen, and Jim. Then he called Paula, who worked the counter of Spin-Dry, followed by the gang of six, minus Luna, from the Pizza Joint, and finally, the Giro Guns and Ammo people, minus Walter, who was here with him. Daryl was with his family and, like Luna, wanted to do *something* to help.

Sam didn't go into what was actually happening. Then he wondered if Gia could help Daryl with his stuttering. Sam mentioned that Harper and Luna would be meeting at the police station and immediately regretted mentioning it. Involving Daryl was irresponsible of him. But the damage was done. Daryl was more than excited and was already out the door when he disconnected the call.

Finally, Sam thought of Lester. Sure, he no longer worked for him, but he cared about the young man.

Lester picked up on the third ring. "What do you want?"

Sam already knew that Caller ID was operational with Gia's repurposed cell service. "Lester, this is Sam."

"I already know that. Again, what do you want?" he said with even more disdain in his voice.

Sam could hear street noises in the background—distant gunfire and yelling.

"I'm just checking in on you. I guess cell service sometimes still works," he hedged.

"You did me a favor by firing me. Was going to quit anyway. And now that Armageddon has arrived, well, it all makes sense."

"What makes sense?"

"That things happen for a reason. This is a fucked-up world, man, and it's time for a cosmic payback. Big-time payback…and I'm going to get me some of that. If we're all going to die anyway—"

"Hey, come on, Lester. Don't do anything you'll regret."

He heard Lester laugh, but it was forced and more than a little unhinged sounding. "I have to go, Sam…I want to be a part of this. Calamity, terror, misery…The end is coming. Hell, it's here now!"

The line went dead, and all Sam could do was stare at his phone with a growing sense of dread.

Looking up, he saw that the clanging and grinding had stopped. There was now a badass-looking Gatling gun protruding off the front of the Landa-Craft with two big round pods hanging down below it. There was something phallic about the way the setup looked. Walter's crew was standing in front of him, patiently waiting.

Walter said, "Well…we've done our part. You ready to take her for a spin…see how she performs with that added bit of hardware?"

Sam smiled and got to his feet. But before he could answer, Gia said, "I estimate Attack Stingers will arrive within the next half an hour."

Chapter 27

Plum Creek Parkway, Castle Rock, Colorado
Harper Godard

Harper wanted to move faster, to jog, if not run the rest of the way to the police station. Sam had made it clear; he was getting things done on his end. It was now her job to build their forces. But Eagan was having trouble with his holster. Something wasn't fitting right, and his service weapon kept flopping around when he did anything other than a fast walk.

Harper could see Eagan wasn't just slim; he was downright skinny. The man needed to put another set of holes in his utility belt. And since Eagan's police-issue .223 rifle was strapped over one of his shoulders, and she was carrying his police-issue gear bag filled with all the donut bags, walking was the best they'd be able to manage. She figured the extra few minutes getting there wouldn't be the end of the world—*or would it?* Making a left onto Plum Creek Parkway, she waited while Eagan stopped to hike up his belt once again.

They had talked much of the way; Harper was curious about what Eagan did for a living and had shared that at one time she'd been interested in becoming a police officer herself. Back in Colorado Springs, she'd thought she and her husband would be an interesting duo—him the firefighter and her the crime fighter. But she'd chosen the medical field while he…well, he'd ceased to be among the living.

"So you work the late shift?" she asked.

"Third watch," Eagan said. "I like it, but will be happy to be working days—" He cut his words short. They both knew the prospect of anything ever getting back to normal was doubtful.

They both heard the roar of an engine before seeing a pickup truck turn onto Plum Creek Parkway. An old Lynyrd Skynyrd track blared from open windows as the truck accelerated, back tires spinning, gaining traction, causing black smoke to spew into the air. Both Harper and Eagan froze in place. Terror had a grip on her, and she couldn't move.

"Dive!" Eagan yelled, pushing Harper to the right, down into a shallow culvert. Moments later, automatic gunfire blazed, rounds ricocheting off the concrete sidewalk that they'd just vacated.

Lying on her stomach with hands covering her head, Harper had yet to open her eyes. If Eagan hadn't shoved her, she'd be dead. Once the engine noise, along with the music, subsided into the distance, she looked around. Eagan was up on his knees, his Glock raised in one hand. It was then that she noticed they were not alone within the culvert. Five or six feet further on was the body of a young woman wearing Lululemon leggings. Her plain white T-shirt was peppered with rust-colored stains. Her running shoes were turned at an odd angle. Lying on her back, the woman's eyes were open. She looked to have been dead for several hours.

Just breathe, Harper…That does not have to be your fate, came Gia's calm voice in her head.

"We need to keep going," Eagan said, now up on his feet and extending a hand down to her. No sooner were they back on the sidewalk than another vehicle was fast approaching, this one coming from the opposite direction of the pickup truck. It slowed and pulled to the shoulder. Harper recognized it as a military vehicle, a Humvee, this one painted black with the word POLICE stenciled on the side.

The officer sitting on the passenger side-eyed Harper, then said, "Eagan, where's your unit?"

"It's not anywhere I can get to it, Pruitt. I don't suppose you saw that pickup truck? They just unloaded on us…full auto. Almost punched our tickets."

Pruitt shook his head. "Whole town's gone crazy. Look, we have to roll. I'd stay off the main roads if I were you."

Harper said, "Hold on!" She reached into the gear bag and pulled out one of the white donut bags. "Take time to eat, guys." She offered up a weak smile.

Pruitt took the bag and stole a peek inside. "Huh…maybe there's hope for us after all." He nodded to Harper. And then they were off. She watched as they continued on down Plum Creek, then made a left toward the Safeway shopping mall complex.

Ten minutes later, they were heading up Perry Street, and Harper could see the police station a quarter mile up ahead on the right. She said, "If there's an attack, I imagine the police station will be one of the first places to be targeted."

Eagan looked at her. "Gia mentioned that to you too?" he asked.

She nodded. "I'm still getting used to filtering the inflow of information. I find myself mentally snapping at her. Telling her to slow down, to feed it to me in dribs and drabs."

He nodded. "Yeah…I'm not sure I'll ever get the hang of it. Any of this. Back to your question about if the station will be safe. The main lobby, I know as a fact, is well protected. Walls are coated with Kevlar sheeting. The glass is made of Lexan, a bullet-resistant material, making the entire area one-hundred-and-eighty degrees safe from gunfire."

"Something tells me that won't be enough for what's coming," she said.

"Yeah, well, that's probably true too."

"What's going on out front with those tents?" she asked.

"They're setting up an auxiliary command station for rapid dispatch and better operational control."

Harper and Eagan stepped around a dirty-paneled van with a *White's Plumbing and Electric* logo on its side. She could see there were no less than ten police Interceptors, all with their lightbars flashing. Dozens of blue uniforms milled about. By the time they'd reached the first of the pole tents, Harper could see the exhaustion on one sergeant's face as he barked off orders to several nearby patrolmen. Seeing Eagan, he looked as though he was about to blow a gasket. "Where the hell have you been, Corporal Pitt?"

Eagan must have been ready for the question, for he had an answer queued up for him. "Interceptor got jammed up in traffic. Had to hoof it back here on foot."

"And that took you three and a half hours?"

Harper eyed the man's name tag while placing Eagan's gear bag down onto the table, separating them. "These are for your guys… the least we can do for your people…and you, Sergeant Capland. There are three donuts per bag. Won't be enough for everyone—"

It was as if someone had triggered a silent alarm. Uniformed men and women swarmed in from every direction. Hands were reaching into the gear bag, a mini version of a smash and grab. Sergeant Capland was already stuffing his face while still giving Eagan the evil eye.

Harper smiled. "We'll make more, I promise—"

And that was when the first of the Silarians' Attack Stingers arrived in the isolation zone. She counted ten of them. Black as night, they were sleek looking with short, swept-back wings. They weren't all that different from, say, a navy or air force jet fighter, but clearly, they were not of this world. They looked and sounded *different*. And as quickly as they had arrived, they faded away. Going invisible.

Gia was talking to her. *They have invoked their stealth capabilities. Harper. Run! Get away from this building. They are targeting it for destruction!*

Gia must have been communicating the same information to Eagan. Their eyes locked, and without a spoken word, they turned to run. There in front of Harper was a wide-eyed young teen. She recognized her at once. It was Luna Kelly—the girl Sam had mentioned would be meeting them there at the police station. Harper turned back around, hoping to find another bag of donuts still left in the gear bag, but all were gone. Then she spotted a crumpled bag on the pavement.

"We have to go!" Egan yelled.

Harper plucked up the bag, grabbed Luna by one hand, and the three of them took off down the street. Running, Harper pushed the paper bag back at Luna. "Whatever's left in that bag, eat it! Now!"

"While we're running?"

Harper said, "Can you walk and chew gum?"

"Yeah…"

They made it a little over a block's distance when the police station exploded behind them in a blistering hot ball of flames.

Chapter 28

Safeway Market Plaza, Castle Rock, Colorado
Lester Price

Lester and Tuck entered the Safeway Market only to find aisles strewn with empty cereal boxes, crushed soda pop cans, and unraveled rolls of toilet paper. There were abandoned metal shopping carts throughout the store, a good many toppled over.

They found out the Safeway had been picked of the low-hanging fruit, leaving spoiled food in the refrigerated sections, melted ice cream in the freezers, and miscellaneous scraps in hard-to-find places. There were people milling about the grocery store, hard to say how many…six, eight, maybe ten—all doing the same thing, scavenging for something edible, something that didn't require electricity to cook.

With all the rotting meat at the butcher's station, the stench was wafting throughout the large open store. Startled, Lester saw a lady running toward the exit, being chased by a teenager. She dropped a jar of marinara sauce, leaving a mess of red goop and glass shards on the linoleum. The teen slipped on the mess, allowing the lady a reprieve.

Lester snickered. *Serves you right, dipshit.* He adjusted his Chinese assault rifle; the strap had started to chafe his shoulder like a son of a bitch.

He headed toward the snack aisle as Tuck made his way toward the produce section.

Lester took in the empty shelves as he walked swiftly down the littered tile floor. In frustration, he kicked an open bag of flour, causing powder to explode up into the air and down the aisle. A fog-like residue lingered, giving the aisle a kind of action movie ambience.

Maybe up top? he thought. He shoved a toppled-over shopping cart in closer to the shelves and stepped onto it. *Please let me find a bag of pork rinds.* But all he discovered were several loose peanuts. He scooped them up and popped them into his mouth.

He nearly choked on his nuts when he heard the sudden explosion of gunfire. *Sounds like a pistol*—a .40 caliber if he had to guess.

From his elevated perch, Lester could see over the top of the shelves. A tall, skinny man in a gray hoodie had entered the store and was walking past the row of cash registers. *Fuck!* The hooded guy raised his gun and shot a lady trying to escape out through the front doors. Blood and brain matter were splattered across an endcap display of magazines.

The sight sickened Lester. *Fucking animal.*

The gunman stopped, leaned over, and checked the contents of the dead lady's purse. He took out her wallet, grabbed the few bills she'd had, and tossed the purse onto the dead body. The gunman turned on a heel and headed off toward the produce section.

Shit! Tuck!

Lester leaped from the shopping cart, sprinted down the aisle, and passed the grisly dead lady scene, all the while doing his best not to make too much noise. He unslung and readied his monster automatic weapon. He slowed and took cover behind a high counter in the flower section. The produce section was down at the other end of the store, but he had a fairly clear line of sight.

Gray hoodie guy was thirty yards away and looking down, pointing his weapon at something on the floor. *Yup, a .40 caliber.* Looked to be a Beretta Px4 Storm. There was a sudden movement, and Lester could now see it was one of Tuck's ridiculous cowboy boots.

"Don't shoot me, man…please…"

Only now could Lester see the teen's face. He couldn't have been more than fifteen or sixteen. The growth of trying-too-hard Black peach fuzz only made him look younger.

"Beg, fat boy…beg for your life," the teen said with a chuckle.

Lester raised the QBZ-95 and fired without giving it a second thought. A through and through, in one ear and out the other. The teen dropped like a sack of potatoes.

Lester moved out from behind the flower counter with his weapon raised.

"Holy shit—I think I pissed myself," Tuck said.

Lester approached, taking in the carnage. There were two men, probably dead a while, lying on the floor near Tuck. Gray hoodie kid had landed on the lower shelf of the closest aisle, as if he was a lone product left for sale.

Getting to his feet, Tuck was shoving his Glock under his belt beneath that bloated belly of his. Lester eyed the dark urine stain at his crotch.

Seeing Lester's smile, Tuck said, "Don't say anything, okay?"

Surprisingly, Tuck still had the heavy ammo bag slung over his shoulder. "That could have been me," Tuck said, looking at the two dead guys on the floor.

"No worries," Lester said. "Uh…What's that ya got there?"

"Beef sticks," Tuck said, handing two of the long thin packages to his friend. "Here, take a couple."

Lester was hungrier than he'd thought he was and quickly unwrapped and devoured one of the meaty morsels. With his mouth full, he said, "Where'd you find the meat sticks?"

"This guy here. They were shoved down his pants," Tuck said with a melancholy expression. "Poor dude."

Lester stopped chewing for a split second, disgusted at the image of his snack being down that dude's pants. He swallowed and handed the rest of the package back to Tuck. "It's all yours."

"I checked the other body and came up empty," Tuck said.

"Best we skedaddle. Founder's Parkway is a couple of miles north. We can hit the Target over there," Lester said.

The store had emptied out. Stepping out into the fresh air, both Lester and Tuck were surprised that a Castle Rock Police Humvee had rolled up to the front of the store. It had plowed into several of the little plastic eating tables set up for customers who had grabbed a sandwich or slice of pizza from the deli section. The Humvee's engine was still idling. Lester raised his automatic, while Tuck pulled his Glock. They moved around to the front of the vehicle, where the doors were ajar. Both police officers were still in their seats, and both had been shot in the head.

Lester lowered his weapon as bile burned in his throat. "What are you doing?" he said, seeing Tuck reaching inside.

"Just checking something…oh my," he said, peering into the white paper bag he was holding. Without hesitation, he pulled out what looked like a pastry, *no,* a donut. Mouth full and chewing, Tuck's head fell back, and he groaned. "Oh God…"

Lester ripped the bag from Tuck's clutches and pulled a donut out for himself. He knew what these were. "Glazed Castle Rocks." He shoved half of it into his mouth. They split the third donut between them.

Tuck said, "A couple of miles, you say, to that Target?"

Lester, his mouth full, shrugged and nodded. "More or less."

Tuck looked over at the Humvee. He cocked his head. "Driving would be quicker…"

Chapter 29

In the skies over Castle Rock, Colorado
Sam Dale

With Cypress sitting alongside him within the Landa-Craft's cockpit, Sam had already made two runs at the stationary targets Walter's team had set up for them. There were seven of them, each perched upon a rise. An old wooden wagon, minus its team of horses, an oversized wheelbarrow, the crate that had been holding the M134 minigun, as well as several loose stacks of piled lumber.

The M134 Bluetooth connectivity worked flawlessly, while Sam's aiming ability had proven horrific. On his first run at the targets, he had missed all seven of them. For the second run, he had missed six of them and hit one of the woodpiles.

"You do not have an inexhaustible supply of ammunition. I thought you were an accomplished military officer. Did they not teach you how to properly shoot projectile weaponry?" Cypress said.

"You think you can do better? How about I let you try steering this thing while also manning a machine gun…one that was not designed for this application."

Sam banked the craft left into a tight turn, coming in low, mirroring the rise and fall of the Colorado pastureland topography.

He knew he shouldn't be enjoying this so much, but he was. He wondered if he'd ever felt this free, this unburdened, in his life. Only then did he think about Cypress. What this must be like for him. His glance toward the dog did not go unnoticed.

"You need not feel remorse for me, Sam. If anything, you have brought me closer to the one thing I love more than anything else. Do I wish I was the one sitting there at the controls? Of course. But being here with you is almost as good."

Sam scratched behind the dog's neck and didn't feel the least bit weird about it this time. "I'll try not to fly your bird into a hillside or someone's house."

"That's considerate of you."

"Time for stealth running, Sam." Gia's sudden interjection into his mind startled him.

It was time. Sam intuitively knew where the selectors were for stealth mode and quickly tapped the appropriate series of touchpads on the dash in front of him. While he could see everything inside the cockpit just as he had moments before, all aspects of the Landa-Craft, her outer hull, the M134 minigun mounted out front and below outside, were now gone. It was as if they were now traveling within a small oblong bubble. Subsequently, his sense of being within a badass warship was somewhat lessened.

"You get used to it," Cypress said.

The Attack Stingers came into view one at a time, as if they'd pierced an invisible curtain, which probably wasn't all that far from the truth. Sam's jaw went slack at seeing the formation of ultra-sleek and oh-so-alien-looking crafts. And just as quickly, they then disappeared.

Gia's voice filled the cockpit, no longer just communicating within Sam's mind. "The clock has started, Sam. I will be forced to devote almost all of my processing power toward my own battle with the various Geo-Minds. Those within the Stingers, as well as those within the pilots' minds."

"Got it," he said. "Do what you have to do. Once we see them again, you can count on me, on us, to keep them busy."

"Keep in mind, Sam…any of the Attack Stingers you destroy will be one less asset you'll have in the future."

"Roger that."

It took another few seconds for the Attack Stingers to become visible again. Just as Gia had promised, she had disengaged their stealth capability and, theoretically, had also disrupted their shields.

A series of explosions erupted down below. Sam saw that the Castle Rock Police Station had been annihilated.

"There won't be much left of your town if you don't hurry up and engage with those Stingers," Cypress said.

Sam saw that they were no longer flying in formation. In front of them, one of the Attack Stingers was ascending after unleashing a series of explosive energy bolts. Sam engaged the M134 minigun, bright tracer rounds arcing through the sky before them, indicating the trajectory of his aim. The Attack Stinger exploded.

Neither Sam nor Cypress commented for several seconds.

"So earlier when you were practicing…you couldn't hit the broad side of a barn, but now, the very first bogie you come up against, you take out?"

"Yeah, well, I wasn't aiming to do that. Distract him, yes… but—"

"Bank left!" Cypress yelled.

Sam did as told as another Attack Stinger whizzed by, missing them by mere inches.

"They cannot see us, Sam. Nor can their sensors pick us up. Stay out of their flight paths, or this is going to be a short sortie."

Sam came up behind two Stingers flying wing tip to wing tip, readying for another bombing strike. Feeling his temper start to flare, he tried to ignore the fact that the town, his town, was quickly being decimated below. *Triggers*. He engaged the M134, sending a stream of gunfire in between the two crafts with a level of precision that even impressed him. Surprised by the sight of live fire so close, both Stingers abruptly abandoned their respective runs, quickly ascending and going off in divergent directions.

"That was…impressive, Sam," Cypress said. "But I believe you will have to destroy another enemy craft. They need to be hunting us versus destroying the town, yes?"

Sam thought about Cypress's words—he'd called them the enemy. Did he really consider those Silarian pilots his enemy? Wasn't it just a few days ago that he, too, had been here to destroy this world?

"I'm on it," Sam said, banking left while firing off toward another Stinger. The Silarian craft easily maneuvered away from the stream of tracer rounds. Crap!

"You have depleted almost all of your ammunition, Sam," Cypress said.

Sam followed the Attack Stinger and got in right behind it. The Silarian craft, or, more accurately, the one piloting the craft, moved with a kind of dexterity Sam envied. He was finding it nearly impossible to stay with him. So, giving up trying, Sam simply punched it, taking a best guess on the Stinger's next heading. The Landa-Craft clipped the Stinger's left wing, causing the craft to spin out of control and crash head on into the isolation zone's energy field. The Stinger literally vaporized before their eyes.

"Remind me to stay clear of that field," Sam said.

Cypress said, "It seems you have achieved what you wanted."

"Yeah, and what is that?"

"You have captured the attention of the other pilots to the point they are no longer actively targeting the township below. They are looking for us. And, I believe, they have found a way to see us, or at least have a rough idea of our coordinates."

Sam couldn't see the M134 or the Landa-Craft's outer hull, but he could see a faint bluish glow. "What the hell is that?"

"I believe that last maneuver of yours—the earthly phrase *bumper cars* comes to mind—may have placed the Landa-Craft's stealth generators out of phase."

Sam was now flying for his, *their,* life, as three of the Attack Stingers were indeed following hot on their trail. *The hunter was now the quarry.* He banked left then right. He swooped low, down to street level, and flew in between two apartment buildings. "Why aren't they firing on us?!" Sam yelled.

"That's a good question," Cypress said. "One possibility, for the time being...they have been ordered not to."

Sam was only half listening to the alien dog. It was taking all of his concentration to stay ahead of his pursuers. "Status on Gia? How's her fight going?"

"You know what I know. Any query I might prompt would be a distraction she could ill afford right now."

According to the virtual console displays, there were now four Stingers behind them and four forming up in front of them aligned vertically. "I believe we've just been set up into the proverbial checkmate, Cypress."

Sam throttled back on the controls, slowing the Landa-Craft down to a near stop in midair. Surrounded, he looked left and then right, and as if they were at the nucleus of an atom, hovering Attack Stingers were positioned all around them.

"Now what?" Sam said, feeling like the kid who had taunted the class bully one too many times. "Cypress, they're going to turn this ship of yours, with us in it, into—"

"Stop your babbling, human...I'm communicating with Gia."

Chapter 30

In the skies over Castle Rock, Colorado
Sam Dale

Sam, within the confines of the Landa-Craft, sat and took in the carnage below. From their high-up perspective, he could see that much of the town was burning; the police station and fire station had been destroyed, as had the Douglas County government building, as well as the justice center.

He looked over at Cypress, who, making animated expressions that weren't normal for a dog, was obviously in the midst of an internal conversation. Then, without warning, the dog dropped where he'd stood. He was out cold. Unconscious.

"Sam…this is Gia," came the feminine voice from the Landa-Craft's cabin audio output.

"What's happened to Cypress?" he said, concerned, now petting the dog's head.

"Cypress will be fine. I must take care with him in the future. The canine brain is limited and, simply put, has been overworked. Pushed beyond its capabilities."

"Will he…"

"I have induced unconsciousness. He needs an hour of sleep.

But yes, he should recover…be fine, in time."

"So, what now? I take it your tussle with the Geo-Mind within those Stingers went well."

"It was a battle for the ages, as you humans would say. Geo-Mind came for me with everything he had. I say he, because the AI's consciousness has a predominantly male energy or verve. Those Attack Stingers are now completely under my control."

"And the pilots?" Sam asked, taking in the eight remaining Attack Stingers surrounding the Landa-Craft.

"That is a battle that is still ensuing. Care must be taken not to destroy their Silarian minds, the battlefield, if you will, in the process of extracting Geo-Mind."

"Wait…you're trying to save them? The very same creatures that just torched half my hometown?"

"We need to be clear, Sam, right from the start. I am not here to pick sides, to choose humans over Silarians or vice versa."

"If that's what you think, then you and I are going to have a real problem. Earth didn't go looking for this fight. You've indicated you're opposed to what the Silarians are doing with their terra-displacement practices across the galaxy."

"I also made it clear that it was Geo-Mind that was behind those abhorrent acts. That Silarians cannot be held responsible for Geo-Mind's influences."

"No. I disagree. Was it not the Silarians that created that diabolical, God-like AI? And indirectly, you as well. They don't get to just say, 'Oops, I didn't mean it.' It's called taking responsibility for one's actions."

"Let me put this another way," she said. "Do you want me, as another God-like AI, to be making those choices? Choosing sides, having arbitrary loyalties to one species over another?"

Sam had to admit, she had a point. "I wouldn't call it an arbitrary loyalty. We're the victims here. But fine. So, what do we do now?"

There was a long pause before Gia replied. "It is inappropriate for me to be making decisions that ultimately can and will affect all of humankind. My directive is to destroy Geo-Mind throughout the universe."

"And take his place…which is kind of convenient for you, don't you think?"

"Yes."

He let that go. "I get it, though. So where does that leave us? Like right now, this second?"

"Human society is based on a hierarchical model. Leaders and followers. Although it is still small, hardly an organized formation, I have decided there must be leadership."

Sam already didn't like the direction this conversation was going in.

"After much assessment, I trust your judgment, Sam. Your decision-making capabilities. I even admire your peculiar code of honor. You will assume responsibility for humanity going forward."

"Can you repeat what you just said?"

"You heard me perfectly well."

"Then no. I do not accept that responsibility. That's ludicrous. There are elected officials for that…each of Earth's countries has them."

"They are, for the most part, self-serving and corrupt. Politics, by its very nature, is unscrupulous. The double-dealing—"

"I am—hell, we all are well aware of that. But it's the only system we have at present."

Gia said, "Sam, I am by no means suggesting that you take on the role of Earth's ruler. That would be ridiculous. What I am suggesting is that, moving forward, you become Earth's shepherd."

"I'm not really sure what you're asking me to do, being this Earth's shepherd person. But I think my answer's still no."

"I wasn't asking for your permission."

"Then I'll just refuse. I won't do it."

"Then I'll leave this world of yours…there are plenty of others that will assist me with ridding themselves of the Geo-Mind."

"You'd do that? Just pull up stakes and hightail it out of here?" Sam said.

"I would. I am currently in control of eight advanced Attack Stingers and one modified Landa-Craft. I could be gone within minutes."

"And leave us to deal with—"

"An entire fleet of Silarian warships that have jumped into this star system. Where Earth's terra-displacement process will commence within days."

"You're a tough negotiator," he said.

"This was never a negotiation, Sam."

"Fuck."

"I take that as you agreeing?"

"I…I guess. What is it exactly that I'm supposed to do as Earth's shepherd?"

"Just one thing, Sam. Help Earth, and subsequently, humanity, to survive. Your world is at war now. Your enemy is abreast."

"But you said it yourself. Once you eradicate the Geo-Mind, the Silarians will see the error of their ways. Like Cypress. They will no longer be comfortable ravaging other worlds for their own selfish needs."

"Oh, if only it was as easy as that," Gia said with a level of poignancy he hadn't heard from her before. "Silarians and humans are so very similar. So easily you take up sides or stand behind beliefs you know aren't just, but deem the results justify the means. No, Sam, I am afraid Cypress is quite unique in that regard. You must care for and protect this creature beyond all others…You will find him loyal and kind of heart. Have you considered what his own inner turmoil must have been like these last few hours? Watching as you attacked and killed his brethren Silarians?"

"It crossed my mind," Sam lied, suddenly feeling a heavy weight of guilt on his shoulders.

"His counsel will serve you well in the days, weeks, and months to come."

"Okay…got it."

"Currently, I am tracking seventy-two surviving humans here within the isolation zone that have ingested the Gia nanobots. Most have awakened and are now having to deal with the tremendous influx of stream information on their own. I am there with them to a certain degree."

"Do they know what is going on? As far as the Silarians…the terra-displacement, all of that?"

"Yes. I have been explaining the situation as best I can. That does not mean everyone is accepting of that information. Some are rebelling; some are certain they have gone mad. But have no doubt, Sam, these seventy-two souls are now your core army. The humans that will, like you, be responsible for what happens next."

Sam let that sink in. He was still having trouble believing any of it.

"I have taken it upon myself to assign you four, let's call them sub-shepherds. Each will bring unique and necessary strengths to your team. Harper will be your second. Julian, your third."

Sam saw how this was going. Thus far, the team hierarchy was following the order in which they had ingested the Gia nanites.

"So next is Eagan?"

"Goodness, no," she said. "Yes, a part of the team, but that man is not very intelligent. You may be surprised by your number four."

"Okay, lay it on me."

"Lester."

Sam was already shaking his head. "How the hell did he get hold of…Gia, that's a bad idea."

"On the contrary, it is a brilliant idea. How could it not be since it's an idea from a brilliant AI?"

Sam wasn't sure if she was being funny or not but suspected not.

"Lester is a survivor," she continued. "He, too, lives by a certain code, but one that may not be in lockstep with your own. That is not always a bad thing."

"Fine. Any more you want to mention within this hierarchy?"

"No. You will need to work that out as a team."

Sam let out a breath. "And what's going to happen with you? Are you leaving us now? Leaving us to fend for ourselves?"

"Absolutely not. I am a resource for you always. I am a part of you, as you are me. But I will not be put in the position of determining the fate of humanity or any other civilization. I am not a god. I have already done too much in that regard. If you truly want to help your world to survive what is coming, you will need to be smarter and better than your opponent in a number of ways. Needless to say, the odds are stacked against you, Sam."

"Is there anything else you can do for us, for me?"

"One thing. I have provided you with a higher level of access to the stream. There will be a price you pay for that, Sam. Headaches for the short term. Information overloads. But on the plus side, you will, as you learn to navigate the workings of the stream, have powers beyond any other human, or Silarian for that matter. I like you, Sam, and because of that, I have, to a degree, cheated. This is something I will have to come to terms with on my own."

"I do have one more question," he said.

"Yes?"

"You mentioned there are seventy-two of us currently with access to you and the stream. Can we…continue to add individuals to that number?"

"No."

"What do you mean no?"

"Let me rephrase that. No, for now. I will soon be at my physical, as much as any of this is physical, limitations. Once you and your team have ascended to space—"

"Whoa, whoa, whoa! Hold on there, Gia! You can't just slip that in like that. What's this about ascending to space? We have a town to save, an entire planet on the brink of war."

"Sam, I'm already saying far more than I should. You attended West Point Military Academy. You were a military commander—a Green Beret captain, no less. So let me ask you one simple question…historically…has any war ever been won by singularly playing defense?"

Chapter 31

In the skies over Castle Rock, Colorado
Sam Dale

It wasn't lost on Sam that Gia was in the process of distancing herself, *itself,* from Earth and humanity's plight. She had given the seventy-two of them the tools and basic information to at least make a stand. But, while Sam and the others had a responsibility to their home world, Gia had a responsibility to all the worlds within the galaxy—at least that's how Sam was interpreting things.

There was something else he was just now coming to grips with. No more could he simply be a bystander with all this—a spectator. He would have to be the hammer and not the nail. More decision-maker, less lemming. *I need to get a whole lot better at utilizing the stream.*

Cypress was coming around. Looking disoriented, the dog got to his feet, only to quickly sit back on his haunches. He looked about the cockpit, over to Sam, and then out beyond at the eight Attack Stingers encircling the Landa-Craft.

"You okay?" Sam asked.

"Besides a headache to end all headaches, I'm fine. Seems I've lost contact with Gia, though."

"She's indicated to me she'll be stepping back some. Bigger fish to fry."

Cypress looked at Sam. "I understand that is an idiom, but that doesn't make it any less stupid."

"It means more important things to do—"

"I know what it means. What are we doing? What is with the Stingers?

"It seems Gia is now the law within this isolation zone…and the law won."

Cypress looked annoyed.

"The song 'I Fought the Law and the Law Won'…you probably wouldn't know it. Never mind. Leave it to say Gia had to fight the Geo-Mind embedded within those Stingers. She destroyed them, and, last I know, was doing the same thing with the Silarian pilots."

"So, we're just waiting?"

"I was waiting; you were sleeping," Sam said, trying to make light of a serious moment. "You're a pilot. Tell me what will they do, suddenly not having the Geo-Mind, in their heads and in their consciousness."

"They will be disoriented and more than a little scared. Although, they would never admit to that."

Sam nodded. "I want you to talk to them. In their own—your own—language. Maybe explain the situation to them."

"That I have chosen to be a traitor to Naru, to all Silarians? And what? That they should join me?"

Sam shrugged. He had no idea how to respond to that.

As if coming to a decision, Cypress raised his snout. "I will talk to them. I will tell you how to open a channel into all of their respective cockpits."

It took a few minutes, with Cypress pointing a paw to the various selectors. Sam heard a background hiss and knew a connection had been made. Cypress looked at Sam. "The Stingers' comms will translate my words...I want you to know what I'm saying."

Sam nodded.

"Fellow Silarian pilots...this is Junior Lieutenant Cypress Mag Nuel of the 234th Landa-Craft Squadron. Your connection to Geo-Mind has been terminated, although I do believe you can still access the stream to some degree. Please indicate if you are receiving this transmission."

Sam winced at hearing a chorus of angry voices. The comms system was doing a good job of translating their four-letter words into English, although he wasn't quite sure what a Gali-Mad-fucker was.

Cypress let them get that out of their system before cutting them off. "Silence!"

They did as told.

"How you respond next will determine if you live or die. And let me remind you, your Attack Stingers' weaponry has been deactivated. You are at the mercy of the human piloting this Landa-Craft. He wishes to destroy the lot of you. I have convinced him to wait."

Sam exchanged a look with Cypress. If a dog could shrug, that's what Cypress had not all that successfully attempted.

"There is one concept I wish for you to contemplate on, now that Geo-Mind no longer can influence your respective judgments. That of the despicable process of terra-displacement. Why you, why all of us, are here. From one world to the next, Silarians have been conquering worlds where societies of lesser technological capability are annihilated with little or no concern for our actions. Search your moral bearings. Is this who we are? Is this who you are? For me, personally, I no longer choose to be a part of this unconscionable act. An act that stems from an AI, not us, not Silarians. An AI that had become self-aware but purposely kept us from knowing that. Geo-Mind is now a living, thinking being, one that took up residency in our minds. But more like an infectious virus, one that, over time, took control of our thoughts, feelings, our lives."

Sam listened as Cypress talked. But it was when Cypress explained Gia's sudden introduction into the mix, the supposed good sibling, that the conversation became more heated. Questions soon turned to arguments. And Sam had to admit it—their concerns were the same ones he had had himself. Just one more self-aware AI that might have questionable intentions. One more AI wanting to take up residency in their minds. But there was one definitive difference, Sam thought. He—hell, humanity—didn't have a choice. It was either jump on board with Gia or face total annihilation. All he could do was hope and pray Gia would, indeed, be their saving grace.

Sam had mentally tuned out, and now it seemed as though the conversation had come full circle.

Cypress said, "I cannot make the choice for you. That would be more in line with Geo-Mind's methodology. But know this: I cannot let you return to the fleet. Join me, here and now, even as distasteful as that is, or commit *Gosimain Lo*."

This conversation had suddenly gone off the tracks. It didn't take a genius, or a query into the stream, to figure out what *Gosimain Lo* was. Suicide, or something akin to Japanese *seppuku* or *hara-kiri*.

The voices of Cypress's brethren had all quieted, replaced by that continuous background hiss. Sam watched Cypress as he lowered his head. A tangible sadness befell the once-proud Silarian being, now reduced to a lowly dog. He wondered what Cypress was thinking. Was he wishing he, too, had committed *Gosimain Lo*?

After several long minutes, Cypress raised his head and let out a resolute breath. "It is done."

Sam looked out through the canopy at the other nearby hovering crafts. "They…"

"Three of my fellow pilots are deceased. They have used their strike blades to end their lives."

Sam let that sink in. "I'm sorry, Cypress. And the other five?"

Next came transmitted voices that were alien and, if Sam was being honest with himself, were frightening to hear. Guttural and obviously inhuman sounds. Clearly, no longer was the comms system translating Cypress's and the others' words.

When they were finished, Cypress looked at Sam and said, "Those that have chosen life, on the other hand, see the wisdom of joining us. I, this Gia AI, and you, Sam. Together, we will unite and rid the galaxy of the Geo-Mind. We will save Naru, and as long as our purposes align, Earth as well."

The dog looked out at the eight hovering Attack Stingers. "They await your instructions."

*Shit, this is really happening…*Sam mentally queried Gia. And yes, she'd made it clear she was beyond busy preparing for her onslaught on the Silarian fleet up there in space, but that didn't mean she couldn't spare a modicum of her vast mental capabilities to still provide a bit of tactical support. Yeah, she could say no, but he hoped she wouldn't. He said, "Gia…until I get a better hang for using the stream, please input the landing coordinates for Walter's den of thieves into each of the Stingers."

Cypress said, "Although those three dead Silarians will make for lousy pilots, the living ones will remotely take control of their Stingers. Proceed…they will follow this Landa-Craft to the destination."

Sam hoped that was true. He took hold of the primary controls array and throttled forward. Banking to the right, he headed in the direction of Walter's place.

"Sam…"

"Yeah, Cypress."

"I feel I should warn you."

"Warn me? That sounds ominous."

"When we land. When you observe a Silarian for the first time…"

Chapter 32

Valhallen Compound, Castle Rock, Colorado
Sam Dale

It was an exhilarating sight, watching the eight sleek Attack Stingers all set down at precisely the same time on the expansive patch of dirt in front of Walter's house. Churned-up dust and debris swirled into mini dirt devils, and it took a minute or two for the air to clear. As his own Landa-Craft's canopy rose, Sam could see the Stingers' canopies had yet to open.

"What are they waiting for?" Sam asked, getting to his feet.

"I don't know," Cypress said.

Two of Walter's crew were hurrying toward the Landa-Craft with the extension ladder while nervously eyeing the other spacecraft. No sooner had the top of the ladder clattered onto the ship's hull than the two hurried away and were soon back out of sight.

Sam looked at Cypress. "We need to come up with a more efficient way of getting you in and out of this craft." He got himself situated on the ladder and waited for Cypress to get into position to be lifted out of the cockpit. Balancing the dog and himself, Sam descended the ladder one slow rung at a time.

Reaching the last few rungs, Sam was surprised to see that Walter was holding the ladder steady for them. Sam said, "Thanks."

"Wish I'd known you were bringing back, um…company."

Sam said, "Best we keep an eye on them."

"Step ahead of you." Walter gestured out to his property. "My peeps are getting into position as we speak. Expect high-powered rifle scopes to be trained on anything green that moves."

"Let's hope it doesn't come to that." Sam glanced down to Cypress. "What are they waiting for?"

"I imagine they're having second thoughts. I would be."

One of the Stinger's canopies began to rise, quickly followed by the four others. Sam was reminded that three of the Stingers were occupied by dead Silarian pilots. Up till now, Sam hadn't asked what Cypress's alien species looked like. Which, thinking about it, was strange.

The first of the Silarian pilots stood up.

"Holy mother of God…" Walter said.

"Not what I expected," Sam said.

"Gawking like that will not encourage good relations," Cypress commented under his breath. "I guarantee you look equally strange to them."

Shirtless, the alien pilot was big—easily seven foot tall with well-defined musculature. He was a bipedal being like any human. He had long black hair. Two eyes, somewhat reptilian looking, a nose, and a mouth, but he was not human in appearance. He could never be mistaken for an earthling—the features were basically in the right places, but different enough to be off-putting. That and the Silarian's skin was a pale shade of green.

So captivated was he by the alien's appearance, Sam didn't initially notice several of the other alien pilots were already climbing down inset ladders from their Stingers.

"Careful, compadre," Walter said. "And remember…they came here to take everything that's near and dear to us. To exterminate humanity."

"I won't forget," Sam said.

Cypress had taken several steps closer to the Silarians—was going to meet them halfway. In the distance, Sam could hear the aliens speaking to each other in that strange guttural language. He could feel the stream beckoning to him, wanting to translate the words for him. He ignored the inner urge.

"I don't like this," Walter reiterated.

All five of the Silarians were now approaching. From their confident gait, their puffed-out chests and raised chins, this was a proud, no, arrogant, species. He already knew they were intergalactic bullies used to taking what they wanted, and Sam already didn't like them.

"Best I go and welcome our guests—"

But before Sam could finish his sentence, one of the pilots had sprinted forward, then was leaping, more like diving, into the air, toward Cypress. The dog was quick to move and avoid being landed upon directly, but the green hulk managed to get a fistful of Cypress's fur and loose flesh. Hearing the dog's desperate yelp, Sam was on the move. He was aware that Walter was drawing his sidearm. Mid stride, Sam yelled, "Hold your fire!" loud enough for everyone, and not just Walter, to hear.

Cypress was on his back, wide-eyed, as the Silarian punched the dog across the snout. Then both of the alien's oven-mitt-sized hands were around Cypress's neck. The green giant looked intent on choking the life out of the defenseless dog. Probably sensing the movement, the alien glanced up just in time to see the incoming steel toe of Sam's right boot. Sam had aimed for the chin area, but in that instant, the alien reflexively raised his head a fraction of an inch, which changed all the geometry. Where the Silarian undoubtedly would have met with a broken jaw, perhaps the loss of several teeth, instead, he suffered a total collapse of his trachea, or whatever Silarians referred to as their windpipe.

But Sam had already been triggered, and even though the pilot was no longer trying to kill Cypress—in fact was making a futile attempt to reach for his own damaged throat, Sam was already upon him, straddling his far larger opponent. Clenched fists with white knuckles alternately pounded the Silarian's face—left, right, left, right…until Sam felt strong hands pulling him up and off the now immobile alien.

Walter said, "Okay, okay…I think you can stop now, hombre."

Sam, gasping and still in a rage, saw that Elsie, the commando chick with the neck tattoo, had rushed in with Walter to help pull him off the alien. She was smiling; apparently, she found the situation amusing.

Sam looked down at the unmoving alien lying at his feet.

Elsie said, "Yeah…you pretty much turned that one into Jell-O. Lime Jell-O."

Sam took in the carnage of what used to be the Silarian's face. His eyes were open and fixed. He briefly wondered if it had been the repeated blows to the head or the asphyxiation. *Dead is dead.* He didn't care.

"You can let go of me," he said, feeling his own breathing starting to normalize. Twenty paces away, he saw Cypress was talking to the four remaining pilots. Every so often, one or another of them would glance his way. Some of that cockiness he'd noticed earlier had been replaced with something else. Maybe wariness? *Maybe respect.*

He felt his phone vibrate in his back pocket. Pulling it free, he saw that it was Harper. Without thinking, he tapped the FaceTime icon and was surprised to see Harper's pretty face appear on the screen.

"I take it you had something to do with bringing the attack to a halt?" she said.

194

"Probably more the work of Gia than me. But yeah, Cypress and I helped. Where are you?" he asked, trying to make out who was standing behind her. "Is that…"

"Luna is with me. And yeah, she's donutted up."

Seeing both of their smiling faces brought a moment of humor and lightness to the situation.

"Hi, Sam," Luna said.

For some unknown reason, Sam was suddenly struck with emotion. Blinking away the moisture in his eyes, he said, "Hey, kid. Glad you're on the team."

He saw that Harper was looking up. She said, "This is only a reprieve, Sam. There's a shitstorm coming."

Sam allowed himself to open up to the stream and realized she was right. He wasn't certain what, specifically, was coming, but he knew it wasn't good.

"Want us to head your way?" Harper said, her eyes locked onto his—concern evident by a knitted brow.

"Yeah. For now, this will be HQ. By the way, where's Eagan?"

Her face turned away as if looking back the way they'd come. "When the police station blew up, we just ran. I'll call him. Wait—" she said. "Sam, he's actually calling me now; I'll get back to you."

"Harper, any of those cops still—"

"Yeah, we'll find them…meet up at your HQ. But I have to go…"

She disconnected, leaving Sam staring down at a blank screen.

Cypress's voice interrupted his reverie. "We need to talk…"

Sam looked up to see that the four remaining Silarian pilots were there in front of him, looming over him. *Damn, they're big sons of bitches.*

"I suppose introductions are in order," Cypress said.

195

Chapter 33

Valhallen Compound, Castle Rock, Colorado
Sam Dale

As Sam appraised the four remaining Silarian pilots standing before him, he was suddenly confronted by a deluge of complex thoughts. Information, bundled data sets, was entering his mind at an astounding rate—whereby, sure, this was happening before to a lesser degree, but now he was comprehending far more of it with little or no mental effort. Inexplicably, his connection to the stream had not so much grown but had developed. And his brain, his mind, was acting far more like a computer, an AI component, than the organic gray matter with its hit-and-miss electrical currents and arbitrary firing of neurons. Gia had come through with her promise to further enhance Sam's mental faculties.

But there was another measure of this…provision that Sam had not anticipated. He not only now had the ability to receive and comprehend vast amounts of information, but he could also transmit and, oddly enough, manipulate information back into the stream. And in the fraction of a second that all this new awareness had occurred, Sam had the one missing puzzle piece he'd need in dealing with these Silarian pilots.

He spoke in the native Naru-Silarian language of Curplexah. "Any further hostility demonstrated to Cypress, or any human, will be met with quick retribution." Sam glanced over at the dead pilot lying several paces away.

The four Silarians bristled at his threat, each straightening their backs—puffing out their broad chests.

Cypress said, "Making veiled threats will not be constructive here, Sam."

On the contrary, Sam thought. It needed to be said before they could move on.

"And when did you learn to speak Curplexah?" Cypress added.

Ignoring the question, Sam said, "As of right now, our goals are in alignment."

"What makes you assume to know our goals, human?" the largest of the four pilots said. His arrogant smirk prompted alien chuckles from the others. "Do not assume to know us...to have the capacity to comprehend our superior—"

At that moment, and before the Silarian pilot could utter even one more word, Sam used his newly acquired mental abilities to shut down the alien's connection to the stream. *How did I just do that?* And, like pinching off an air hose to breathe, the pilot was just as suddenly dumbstruck and left paralyzed with indecision. His mouth drooped open. He looked at his three compatriots with somewhat moronic-looking, pleading eyes. Even Sam was taken aback by the alien's profound reaction. *Had these Silarians become that dependent on the stream?*

Sam felt Cypress's eyes on him. Was this so cruel an act for the very ones here intending to destroy all humanity? Ignoring the dog, Sam repeated the same mental action thrice more. And in that instant, the three other Silarian pilots, as if being struck by the same lightning bolt, gasped and suddenly looked terrified.

"Stop it, Sam. Stop!" Cypress said. "It was the Geo-Mind...

remember that!"

Sam looked down at Cypress. "They came here to kill us. To kill our world."

"And I, too, was one of them. Do you want to torture me as well?"

Sam hesitated before shaking his head. "No." He reopened the pilots' connection to the stream and watched as mental acuity returned to their glazed-over eyes.

Each of the pilots staggered, two bent over, putting hands on knees. But the toll had not only affected the four Silarians. Sam felt a measure of exhaustion that nearly put him on the ground. But he maintained his stature and a look of confidence.

He said, "I'd like to start over. If that's all right with you."

The four pilots nodded. He saw fear in their eyes, and for some reason, that was disheartening. *Is that how I want to proceed with these intelligent beings? Brute force? Make them subservient by mentally torturing them?*

"And I apologize…"

That seemed to surprise not only the four pilots, but Cypress as well. Sam said, "I have little doubt what I just inflicted upon you could just as easily have been inflicted upon me if it worked to the advantage of whoever is respectively controlling the stream…Naru's Geo-Mind AI, or our AI, the one we call Gia. What I hope you can discern, though, is that terra-displacement of any populated world is just wrong."

Sam waited for their response. It took a moment, but they each conceded to that truth with a nod of the head—something Sam had learned was a near-universal gesture for intelligent beings throughout the galaxy.

He still didn't know how far he could push these aliens for assistance. But that was a question for another time, because a quarter of a mile away, he spotted Harper and Luna making their way along Walter's long dirt driveway.

Sam wondered if he'd ever felt happier to see anyone. He'd

known Harper was still alive, something the stream was able to convey to him. And thinking about it now, he could feel the presence of all those that had "donutted up" as Harper had called it earlier. And that included Luna and Eagan, and even Lester. There were fifty-two surviving Castle Rock cops; over twenty had recently died from the Stinger bombardments.

Cypress and the four aliens had moved off and were deep in discussion. Walter stepped in close. "You can't honestly think we can trust the green giants over there, bub. It'll be hard enough dealing with what's coming for us, let alone having to watch our backs."

Sam said, "We'll have to leave that for Cypress to deal with." He glanced over at the dead Silarian. "Do me a favor; go ask them what they'd like us to do with that one."

Walter followed Sam's eyeline. "Stream's telling me they cremate their dead much as we do…"

Sam had queried and gotten that same information. "That's not an option right now."

Walter spat a wad of tobacco juice. "I'll see if they're okay if we just plant the guy out in the east pasture."

Ten minutes later, Sam watched Harper and Luna's animated expressions on now seeing the eight impressive Attack Stingers up close. Sam joined them beneath the fuselage of the one nearest to him.

Harper said, "Hey, Sam."

Luna said, "This is crazy, boss." Then she caught sight of the four Silarians who were currently walking along the side of the house. "Oh my God…and those are real frickin' aliens."

The aliens' destination became evident—a Bobcat excavator along with several people far out in the pasture. "What's happening out there?"

There in the distance were three other green lifeless bodies. Walter, along with one of his cohorts, hefted up one of them by his hands and feet, swung the corpse back and forth several times, then tossed it into an open grave. Three more to go. "Never mind…I think I get the picture," she said. "You have something to do with that?"

Sam ignored Luna's question.

Cypress joined them. Harper and Luna gave the dog affectionate pats and scratches behind his collar.

When Cypress spoke, Luna's eyes went wide. All this had to be a lot for the sixteen-year-old. Then Sam remembered what else she had recently been forced to endure.

"Luna…I'm sorry about your dad."

"Thanks, Sam. Yeah, I still can't believe he's gone." She fought back tears. Going down on one knee, she wrapped her arms around the dog, pressing the side of her face into the retriever's flank. Cypress no longer seemed distressed by such affection. Again, Sam wondered just how much of this being was the consciousness of the Silarian pilot and how much was that of Rocko the dog.

Sam felt Harper's hand touch his lower back. Turning to her, he saw the concern in her eyes.

She said, "Gia's backing way off. I have a hard time even getting answers from her."

"Uh-huh. Me too."

"And she'll be giving us just enough rope to hang ourselves…"

"I wouldn't have put it quite like that…but yeah, she's not going to take sides. She's made it clear, her enemy is the Geo-Mind, not the Silarians."

Harper pursed her lips, her eyes still locked onto his as if she was trying to read his very thoughts. "She's given you a lot of herself, you know. You may not be an all-powerful super AI like Geo-Mind or Gia…but she's given you many of their capabilities. How are you coping with all that?"

"You mean besides the skull-wracking headaches and inner turmoil that has me wanting to jump in that hole along with those fucking dead aliens?"

She laughed out loud, giving Sam a glimpse of the same young woman he'd been quietly falling for so many mornings over at the B&B Café.

Getting more serious, she said, "Just remember, you're not doing this alone. I'll be right there with you, win or lose. And so will Julian."

"Have you spoken to him?"

"I have. Called him about an hour ago. As it turns out, he's the one person Gia has kept in more consistent contact with. She's directly helping him. Apparently, he's doing his mad scientist thing… working on several projects, but most of his attention is on something he's making for you. Something you don't even know you'll be needing, if that makes any sense."

Sam was tempted to open the stream, to query what specifically that was. But he refrained from doing so. Right now, he just needed to be human. To be with Harper without all that crashing deluge of information.

Chapter 34

Valhallen Compound, Castle Rock, Colorado
Sam Dale

"We don't have much time," Harper said, looking up at the sky. "You know what's coming?"

Sam shrugged. "Silarian fleet is sending drop ships...landers with Clash-Troopers, whatever those are. They're en route as we speak...We don't have much time."

"You know that for sure?"

"For sure? You'd be surprised at just how terrible I am at deciphering the information being presented to me. There's an awfully good chance Gia has selected the wrong human for this job."

"I doubt that. But buck up anyway; you're the only one we have, so don't fuck it up." She said it with a bemused smile, but there was a seriousness behind her words too. "There are a limited number of us scattered around Castle Rock. Those that we can directly coordinate with. Should we call them...bring them—"

Sam said, "Done and done." He gestured out to the long dirt road leading into the compound. Like a parade, and driving slowly, no less than ten black and white Interceptors were making their way toward them. Flanking the vehicles were several dozen men and women in uniform on foot. At least half of them were carrying their issued AR-15s.

Loud siren bleeps came from one vehicle in particular as it, almost impatiently, sped past all the Interceptors.

Harper said, "I've seen that vehicle before."

Sam watched as the black police Humvee accelerated, its tires spewing up swirls of dirt and dust into the air. Entering Walter's front yard, such as it was, the military vehicle weaved its way around the various Attack Stingers, then came to a dramatic skidding stop in front of where Sam, Harper, Luna, and the dog stood.

As if on cue, all four doors opened at once. The first to extricate himself from the vehicle was Lester, the one who'd been driving. He wore his typical dingy off-white wifebeater tank top, his skinny, darkly inked arms contrasting in the midday sun. From the front passenger side came a large man wearing a billowy red shirt, cowboy boots, and an oversized belt buckle. From the back seat of the Humvee came Eagan and Daryl. Gia had been busy; evidently, she'd wanted these four to be here and had somehow orchestrated things to make that happen.

Sam watched as Lester went around to the back of the vehicle, popped the back hatch, and reached inside. Now clutching a Type-95 and what looked like an ammo satchel, the four of them approached.

Harper surprised Sam by hurrying over to Eagan and giving him a hug. "I wasn't sure you'd survived the bombings."

Eagan nervously ran a palm over his tasseled comb-over. "It was a close call." He pointed to a scabbed-over red burn mark on his right cheek.

Lester said, "Who would have thunk Gia would want me as one of her field commanders?"

Sam felt momentarily sick at the thought. He looked up to the sky and said, "We have forty-three minutes before the first of the

MARK WAYNE MCGINNIS & KIM MCGINNIS

drop ships arrive."

"Relax…those Clash-Troopers can be easily dealt with. Gia will get inside their heads…battle for supremacy." Lester gestured at something behind the group. "She did it with those big mother-fuckers and won, didn't she?"

Sam turned to see the surviving four aliens, having completed their impromptu memorial service for their fallen brethren, were now approaching.

Cypress approached the aliens. They, in turn, leered down at the dog.

"Please…join the conversation. We have much to discuss in the little time we have left before—"

"Do not assume you can make demands on us," the largest of the aliens said, his voice full of disdain.

But join the group they did. Sam, Harper, and Luna each took several steps back in order to expand their circle. Sam noticed the police Interceptors had all parked. The Castle Rock PD officers and a handful of civilians had taken up positions all around the front lot. He'd need to speak with them soon, but for now, they knew enough to be patient.

Cypress said, "Introductions are in order."

All eyes were on the towering green aliens. Sam was aware of their slightly musky scent. Now, closer, their musculature was impressive, as were their reptilian brown-gold eyes. Each of them was at least a foot taller than Sam, and one in particular was another six inches taller than that.

Raising his snout toward the tallest of them, Cypress said, "This is Jarpin. The others are Gromel, Flout, and Scott."

Lester, apparently amused by this, said, "No way…you have an Earth name, dude?"

Cypress said, "I'm simply providing you with the phonetic approximation of their Silarian names."

The four Silarian pilots glanced about the group of humans. Flout took notice of Tuck's big belt buckle and clucked his tongue.

Sam got right to the point. "We need to know we can trust you. If not, there's no real need for you to keep breathing Earth's air."

Flout gave the slightest nod. "Gia has spoken much of this... paradox. For us to help humans, we must destroy our own kind. Become traitors to Naru."

"To put it bluntly, yeah," Sam said.

Before Flout could say anymore, Harper said, "Some will die. As will humans. In the end, it's about ridding ourselves, yourselves, of the Geo-Mind."

"On our world, females are not so brazen. They prefer to stand in support of the stronger, more intelligent—"

"You should just stop there," Harper said. "You're on Earth now. None of that horseshit flies here."

Sam raised an intervening hand. "We have thirty-two minutes before the first of the drop ships arrive. Yes, Gia will go to work on the Clash-Troopers, but still, that will take time. Just as it took time ridding the four of you of the Geo-Mind, yes?"

Sam took their blank stares as agreement. "Tell me why I shouldn't put you in chains until this is over."

Harper and Luna both looked surprised by Sam's question, while the others in the group seemed perfectly fine with it.

Jarpin almost smiled. "At this moment, billions and billions of Silarians have been—"

"Mind-fucked?" Lester said.

"Hoodwinked," Tuck said and laughed.

"Deceived," Jarpin said, ignoring them. "We have been little more than mindless puppets for that self-serving AI. No. As long as Geo-Mind has any one of them, of us, under its control, they are no longer true Silarians; they, too, are the enemy."

Sam exchanged a quick look with Harper. This was not the way any rational human would approach this. Seeing the three other pilots nodding their agreement to Jarpin's words only emphasized the difference between their two species.

"Just know…I see any hesitation, any change in that mindset, and you'll be considered *our* enemy."

Scott said, "Such threats from an inferior race are meaningless."

Walter and Elsie approached. She looked up at the four aliens with interest.

"I should have enough…*supplies* to accommodate this lot," he said, gesturing to the small army of police officers and civilians standing at the perimeter. "But none of that comes cheap, bub."

Eagan scoffed. "They're here to help save the town. The world. And you're concerned about making a profit?"

"Business is business," Walter said, only now noticing the unique assault weapon Lester had slung over one shoulder. "I believe that's my QBZ-95, son."

"Yeah, well, finders keepers, Gramps."

"What do you want, Walter? In return for outfitting this lot. And Eagan's right. Thinking of profits at a time like this is despicable."

"I'm a gunrunner; what can I say?" Walter spat tobacco juice and eyed the closest of the Attack Stingers. "I'll be taking one of these sweet rides, thank you very much."

It was Cypress who was the first to object, "Are you out of your mind? Even beyond the monetary cost of such a vessel, the technical—"

"Fine," Sam interjected. "You've got yourself one Naru Advanced Attack Stinger. Now get to work. You have about fifteen minutes to outfit everyone here with your very best assault gear."

But Walter's gang of ruffians were already coming out from the barn, each pushing multiple carts stacked high with guns, munitions, and every sort of combat gear imaginable. Sam eyed one cart stacked with Mk 153 Shoulder-Launched Multipurpose Assault Weapons (SMAWs). He eyed Walter with a wary look.

The old gunrunner smiled and shrugged. "Preparedness is key to facing any disaster…"

Daryl spoke up for the first time. His stuttering issues seemed to now be a thing of the past. "Sam…do we have a formulated plan once the drop ships arrive?"

"Lookie here. The tard's found some missing brain cells."

Daryl didn't hesitate. He took three steps forward and punched Lester in the face. "That's for two years of that kind of crap."

Lester staggered backward, looking dazed. Now, using the tip of his tongue to lick at his bloodied lip, he said, "Okay, okay, I guess I had that coming. My bad." But there was no benevolence behind his cold stare back at Daryl.

Sam rolled his eyes. "Enough of this shit. And to answer your question, Daryl, I've been working with Gia, with the limited time she's allotting me, and she's talking to the police here."

Eagan nodded. "Yeah, we know what we're to do."

Sam watched as the rest of the group, their eyes losing momentary focus, stopped and queried the stream.

Harper said, "You really are multitasking here, Sam. I had no idea how much until now. So…we're going to be splitting up our forces?"

"There are three inbound drop ships arriving within the next few minutes. As of now, I don't know where they'll be putting down. Once those LZs are determined, we'll be sending our ground forces to intercept and engage."

"We'll be defending Castle Rock," Luna said, nodding but sounding unsure.

Sam looked at the four aliens. "Say it. Say what you know is true for any combat situation to be successful."

Jarpin said, "The other part of your plan. Gia has been in contact with us as well."

The alien Scott looked bemused. "No war is won strictly by playing defense. We will be taking the battle to the fleet. If Gia cannot commence her own battle for the minds of those Silarians of Naru's 23rd Terra-Displacement Fleet of warship assets, there will be no point in defending this world."

Sam looked at Jarpin. "We will leave two Stingers here to assist with defending the area within the isolation zone. Two of you will pilot those craft. The six remaining Attack Stingers will be heading into space…specifically, toward the fleet."

Everyone nodded; they had queried the stream enough to know that much. Even the four aliens looked somewhat overwhelmed at the prospect.

"Cypress and I will lead the squadron of six Stingers in one of them," Sam said.

Gia's voice was now in Sam's head. *There is one Castle Rock police officer and one civilian with prior fighter flight experience. One was a US Navy fighter pilot, Teddy; one was a fighter pilot with the air force of the Army of the Czech Republic, Ivan. And there is another police officer who has previously taken lessons in a Cessna as a hobby, Carl.*

Unconsciously, Sam nodded. *Send them to me.* A beat later, *Ivan? No, it can't be.*

He now put his attention on Lester. "For some reason, Gia has put a good deal of faith in you."

"Yeah…she has," Lester said with a so *what* expression. "Rest assured, I'm going to do what I have to do to take out those Clash-Trooper fuckers…and do it however I think best. Playing fair has never been my modus operandi, as they say. You okay with that, boss man?"

"Guess I'll have to be," Sam said. He saw the four Silarians eyeing the skinny tattooed human with abject suspicion. And he didn't blame them.

"What about us?" Harper said, looking over at Luna and Daryl. "We're not soldiers. We're not fighter pilots. Gia hasn't given us any kind of mental marching orders."

Sam queried the stream, causing his brows to rise.

"What?" Harper said.

"Individually, each of you will have important jobs."

Chapter 35

Valhallen Compound, Castle Rock, Colorado
Harper Godard

She wasn't sure why, but she felt somewhat let down. Deflated. While Sam and his small squadron would be heading up into space, and Lester, with much help from Walter's group, the throngs of police and the like, would be taking on the Clash-Troopers here within the isolation zone, Harper had been chosen to lead a small contingent out of here. Out of the isolation zone and away from Castle Rock.

The stream was like nothing she could have ever imagined prior to her experiencing it firsthand. And she was getting better at utilizing its vast capabilities. But the natural-knowing aspect, whereby she needn't actively search for information or *do anything,* made for a new, ominous level of consciousness she was just now becoming comfortable with.

She stood and watched as a whirlwind of activity was taking place all around her. It was beyond strange; everyone knew what they were supposed to do. No one needed to be told or ordered about because that information was already in everyone's head. It was a part of *their* natural knowing. And, to a degree, Gia was there too. But it was becoming more and more apparent that she was far less of the omnipresent, God-like artificial intelligence that she'd made herself out to be. For one thing, she was stumbling. She was having trouble managing her growing number of resources, resources being the term she used when talking about those that had ingested those amazing little nanites.

Gia was managing the stream, or more accurately, people's access to the stream. The question arose then, *What is she scrutinizing, editing, before we have full access to that data? How different is this from what Geo-Mind was, is, doing with the Silarians?* Harper knew she could drive herself crazy trying to decipher Gia's true motivations. She had to let it go. She'd made the conscious decision to trust her. So, trust she would.

"You're leaving?"

Startled, she turned to see Sam standing there. He and Cypress looked ready to head out.

"Um, yeah…first, I'm going to pick up Julian. I guess I'm the new equivalent of an Uber." She glanced over at the Landa-Craft. "Any last-minute advice on how to fly that thing?"

Sam smiled. "I'm dying to give you all kinds of tips and tricks, but no. You have all the know-how you'll need. Take a few minutes to build muscle memory. Skill is the one area that Gia, the stream, cannot compensate for."

"You'll still be here when I get back with Julian?" she asked.

"If you get a move on…"

Harper offered up a mock salute and hurried off toward the Landa-Craft. The ladder was already in place. She scurried up the rungs and climbed into the spacious cockpit. She reminded herself not to overthink things and immediately started tapping at the dash in front of her. The canopy started to close while lights and displays came alive on the wraparound console.

Feeling and hearing the primary drive winding up got her heart rate thumping in her chest. Taking a quick look around, she saw that someone, probably Sam, had put a small stock of weapons and other military gear in the aft area. She reached for the primary controls array and let her fingertips find the necessary nubs and controls.

For the first time, she looked out the front of the craft. *Terrific. I have an audience.* There stood Sam and the rest of them: Cypress, of course, and Luna, Daryl, Lester, and Walter, as well as the not-all-that-pleased-looking four aliens. Harper smiled and waved once. She brought the spacecraft up off the ground ten, twenty, thirty feet in the air and silently cursed as the craft wobbled somewhat from side to side. Without wasting another second, she accelerated while banking the craft hard to the right. Exhilaration coursed through her veins. With an ear-to-ear smile, she mentally thanked Gia.

You're welcome, Harper…

Within thirty seconds, she was already descending onto the front circular drive of Sam's colonial estate. There were four other vehicles there, police Interceptors, but there was still ample room for her to set down.

When Harper was about to raise the canopy, Gia spoke to her. Harper, *humans are so used to their preconceived methods of entering and exiting aircraft…There is a reason there is no integrated ladder on the outside of this Landa-Craft.*

Harper stopped and let that sink in. *That makes sense.* She tapped at a series of buttons to her left, and immediately, her seat began to turn around until it was facing a hundred and eighty degrees in the opposite direction. From there it continued to move backward until it was snugged up close to the forward console. Then the floor area where the seat had been opened up, and stairs proceeded to lower, telescoping downward.

"That's cool," she said. "And I now know something Sam doesn't."

She hurried down the steps and saw Julian was there, standing on the front walkway. She was surprised to see that he was actually dressed and had shaved—even combed his typically wild hair.

"Well, don't you look all prim and proper," she said.

"Come, come…much to do, much to discuss," Julian said with a smile and obvious excitement at her arrival. He stopped, now serious, and looked up to the sky. "We have very little time."

She felt it too. *The drop ships were en route.*

Julian led Harper in through the front door, where she stopped, shocked at what she was seeing. A house in total disarray. "I guess this explains the four police units outside," she said. Off to the left of the entryway, the living room was a flurry of activity; men and women in navy police uniforms were bustling around. The dining room table was set up like some kind of assembly line. Devices of some sort, in varying stages of assembly, were being built. On a nearby folding table were stacked items that seemed to be completed.

Several of the officers looked up long enough to wave or nod their heads in her direction. She assumed all the donutted police had gone to Walter's compound, but obviously, she'd been wrong.

"What…what's this all about, Julian?"

He took Harper by the hand and practically dragged her over to a folding table. "This is what I've, we've, been working on. This is what will allow us to win!"

She didn't dare open herself up to the stream to be bombarded with Gia and Julian's super high-tech data flow. She picked up one of the oddly shaped contraptions. Turning the deck of cards–sized device over in her fingers, she saw that it had a main container of sorts, another section that she knew was where the main circuitry was housed, as well as a protruding tubular thing that looked like a—

"Have you figured it out?" Julian said with unbridled impatience.

Reluctantly, Harper mentally opened herself to the stream and gasped at the influx of data rushing in. "Oh…" She looked at Julian and then at the cops, all of whom had stopped what they were doing and were looking at her. "It's a delivery device," she said.

"Yes!" Julian plucked the device from her hand and held it up. "This is a NanoGun. Chet over there came up with the name. Ingenious! With this compact device, we now have a means of introducing our miraculous nanites into a subject from a distance. No more glazed Castle Rocks and waiting for one's digestive system and circulatory system as nanites maneuver through the body."

Harper knew all this from opening herself to the stream but didn't want to steal any of Julian's thunder.

"And this is a…simple laser pointer?" she said, gesturing to the thing in his hand.

"Yes, and that was no small feat. Our team here had to beat the bushes throughout Castle Rock. I'm sure you know, most of the stores—Walmart, Target, Office Depot—had been ransacked. Fortunately, looters didn't find laser pointers to be of much interest."

Julian held up the NanoGun and pointed it at the closest wall. A glowing crimson spot appeared. "Best part…it's activated via one's configured nano-machines, the sensory comms portion in our brains. Aim it at one's flesh, better an ear or open mouth…not so good to point into the eyes."

Harper watched as the glowing dot on the wall strobed on and off a few times, something that Julian seemed more than a little proud of.

Something she hadn't initially been aware of came to mind. "And you've figured out how to reproduce more of those medical nanites?"

"Oh yes…you may want to avoid the kitchen area. A mess in there. Leave it to say, we've improved upon them for this application. The nanites' magnetic field is their ticket to ride. I just needed something they could ride on. That's where the laser pointers come in. The laser light that comes out of the pointers has its own energy, momentum, and, most importantly, its own magnetic field. If you get the nanites close enough to the center of the beam, their own magnetic fields get all tangled up; fortunately, the pilot nanites get dragged along, too, and they take the rest of their cohort along with them. It's important that the nanites are rotating around the core of the laser emitter before activation. The rotation of their magnetic field helps get them going, and then they travel down the light beam like…well, like a smoke ring.

"It's sorta like rifling; gets them way farther. That's why we've needed to machine certain parts of the pointer. Gia needed to create a whole new variant of nanites to handle that aspect. Anyway, this is pretty much a point-and-shoot method of deployment. The proper dosage will be applied every time."

She looked at the device and then at Julian. "But…what happened to getting the person's, the subject's, permission first? The simple fact that we don't want to replicate Geo-Mind's monomaniacal, self-serving means of dominating the universe?"

Everyone in the room waited for Julian's answer. The older man stopped to consider her question. "Two things. One, this device was originally intended for use by Sam and his team going up into space. To be used on those Silarians who had arrived here to destroy humankind…Earth. To unseat Geo-Mind and replace him with Gia."

"Okay. I don't have a problem with that. Makes sense," she said.

Julian continued, "Second, this indeed will also work on humans. It will be up to us to manage that aspect on an individual basis. The right thing to do is for us to have full compliance, acceptance, from our fellow human subjects. Do so beforehand."

Harper immediately thought of Lester. Not everyone would be so considerate.

One of the police officers, a man who looked to be in his mid-forties, said, "We've had this same discussion a number of times."

"What did you come up with?" she asked.

"It always comes down to the same thing. The same choice."

Harper nodded. "Geo-Mind or Gia. This world will not survive if we are not prepared to fight. And the only way we can realistically fight Geo-Mind is to fight fire with fire."

Everyone in the room either shrugged or nodded. Harper didn't like it. She mentally asked the question. *Well, Gia?*

It is a dilemma. But know it will never be me that pulls the trigger on those NanoGuns or whatever device your species dreams up. Personally, I'm okay with that. I know my intentions. I have made my promises. But of course, I have modeled, simulated a trillion times over, what course of events will most probably occur. Waiting for one's permission, as you put it, will become less and less realistic. I'm sorry to say, while I will never forcibly impose myself into the minds of humans, that does not mean humans will not impose me into other humans' minds by force.

All eyes were on Harper, including Julian's. It was as if she was the deciding factor. She said, "How many of these things do you have constructed?"

Julian's smile returned. "More than enough for everyone who's been donutted. We're in the process of making extra…a lot of extra."

"Then I guess we need to get what you have moved into the Landa-Craft." A new realization came to mind, "And there's a hidden storage area accessible from the port side of the ship. You can put them in there." *Something else Sam probably didn't know.*

As the police officers began hefting cardboard boxes lined up along one wall, Harper turned to Julian. "You're coming with me."

He hesitated, stymied by that statement. "There's much I need to do here."

"No. I mean when I leave Castle Rock. You'll have to be there when I confront the world with what is going on. No matter what

216

is in my head with Gia and the stream being there…the perception of others will still be a factor. Get what you need; we're leaving here in three minutes."

Julian was taken off guard by her abrupt manner. "Yes. I just need to attend to a few things."

It was another six minutes before both Harper and Julian were situated within the Landa-Craft's cockpit. She heard the port side cubbyhole storage area door close and saw the same middle-aged cop step away from the craft and wave. Looking back at Julian, Harper's spirits were lifted at seeing his childlike wonder at his surroundings. *He hasn't seen nothing yet,* she thought and powered up the amazing spacecraft.

Chapter 36

Valhallen Compound, Castle Rock, Colorado
Cypress Mag Nuel

He'd been mindlessly following Sam from one location to another. Had he so easily taken on the role of a useless pet? He hadn't told Sam, not burdening him with his growing inner dilemma. Rocko was becoming more and more a presence within their shared mind. Cypress, far more often than he'd like to admit, was being convinced into doing things he never would have even considered doing as a proud Silarian. The need to sleep was always an issue. It was typical for a dog to get fourteen to sixteen hours of sleep a day. That was twice as much as any Silarian would have needed. And the need to lick himself—how humiliating.

He knew he should feel guilty, but he'd contemplated killing Rocko, finding a way to eviscerate the dog-mind in a way similar to how Gia had vanquished Geo-Mind with the four remaining Silarian pilots. There had to be a means for him to take back his life. Hearing Gia's voice, he stopped mid-stride and listened.

Patience, Cypress…I know this is difficult for you. I promise things will get better. This is temporary.

"It better be," he said aloud, causing Sam to slow, turn back, and look down at him.

Chapter 37

Valhallen Compound, Castle Rock, Colorado
Sam Dale

It had been twenty minutes since Harper's departure in the Landa-Craft. Much within the compound had been accomplished in that time. Without having to consciously make any kind of mental decision, teams had already formed up. There was Walter and his crew, who were set up as logistical support, outfitting personnel with the necessary weaponry and equipment, depending on what their applicable jobs would soon be. Lester, who, idiotically, would be responsible for the largest number of people by far, was acting no less erratic than was typical.

Strange, though, but Sam was starting to see the genius behind Gia's madness. Sure, Lester was offensive. He was insulting and crass. But he was also a born leader. Even now, as Sam watched him out there, strutting about in the pasture with his team of no less than fifty, he was in command. Barking off orders and making wild hand gestures. What Lester was doing, far better than Sam was doing himself, was accessing the stream, and Gia, on a level that was more than a little impressive.

Sam looked down at Cypress. "Do Silarians have that level

220

of…access?"

The dog seemed to contemplate that. "Some. Not all. I can't say I did. I certainly don't now."

Sam picked up on the dog's defeatist attitude. "Then maybe you and I can both change that. What do you say?"

Cypress's ears perked up, and he turned his head in that unique manner dogs do. "Yes. I need to do something before it's too late."

Sam leaned down and scratched Cypress behind his ears. "We're in this together, buddy. And I promise I won't let that fucking Rocko take over your mind."

Hearing Cypress's laugh emanating from the little black box adhered to his collar for the first time, Sam stood, unable to keep from laughing himself.

Sam's team had assembled in the midst of the eight Attack Stingers. He looked about the faces of Earth's only space-fighter squadron. The four Silarians were there, acting aloof and disinterested. There were two nervous-looking police officers standing off to the side. Lurking behind them was a portly man in gray overalls. Sam's stomach soured.

This guy? No. Gia, is this a joke? No way in hell is this asshole going up into space with us.

Sam, Ivan is a seasoned fighter pilot who lost his way after his brother was falsely executed. He is our, your, best chance for success.

Sam let it go for now. He certainly wasn't feeling all that confident about his human pilots. He made a mental note to query the stream later to get each of their full bios.

Sam said, "We have eight Stingers in this little squadron of ours. Initially, as suggested, I was going to assign two craft to stay behind in support of the ground forces. I've changed that; now only one Stinger will be staying behind."

That caused some commotion between the others, especially the four aliens. To Sam, the biggest challenge was going to be up in space—going up against those Silarian fleet assets. But, perhaps more importantly, he wanted to go up against Gia's supposed recommendations. He needed to test that premise. Were Gia's words just recommendations, or were they more like disguised directives?

He turned his attention to the alien, Scott. "You'll be staying behind. You'll be, for all intents and purposes, our aerial ground support. And since you have far more pertinent experience in doing such a thing, I don't need to lay out what that will look like. You'll be in contact with Lester and his team. Any questions?"

Scott looked at Flout, and then at Gromel and Jarpin. "No. No questions."

Sam turned to Jarpin. "We cannot take on any of those warships and expect to survive more than a few minutes. And doing so would serve no purpose. Gia has suggested we commandeer one of the smallest of the fleet assets—"

"That would be one of the smaller gunships," Jarpin said. "They are typically crewed by no more than a few hundred Silarians."

"Our job is to bring Gia onboard, where she can begin the process of infiltrating the vessel's main AI. From there…the crew." Sam caught movement up in the air; at first thinking it was inbound Silarian drop ships, he was relieved to see it was the Landa-Craft.

Sam watched as a staircase lowered beneath the Landa-Craft's hull. *Will you look at that…* The observation only emphasized how much he needed to learn in the use of the stream. Gia would not always spoon-feed him, or any of them, information they could retrieve on their own.

Julian was the first to descend the steps, followed moments later by Harper. Stepping onto solid ground, she looked about them until her eyes met Sam's. She smiled and gestured to the staircase.

Yeah, yeah…you got me. God, she's beautiful…

Walter and crew were already accessing the hidden cargo area on the Landa-Craft, retrieving what Sam now knew was Julian's special project—the little NanoGuns. Julian, acting like a mother hen, was overseeing the distribution of the devices, and unnecessarily adding instruction commentary on their use.

Elsie, holding several NanoGuns, handed Sam one and moved off to others waiting nearby. He looked at it while tapping into the stream—letting the knowledge simply *be there.*

Julian said, "What do you think?"

Sam continued to look at the NanoGun, then slowly nodded. "I think you have outdone yourself, Julian." He looked up to see the pride in the older man's eyes. "Um, so how does one affix this to the muzzle of an assault weapon?"

Julian's self-satisfaction was short-lived as he considered Sam's question. He scratched at his chin and stared at the device in Sam's hand. "I…I hadn't considered that. That our Gia fighters might not have a free hand…that they'd be holding a weapon…"

Sam said, "Hey…don't sweat it. Isn't that what duct tape was made for?"

Harper joined them. "Did I hear you say Gia fighters? I like it."

Julian shrugged, looking downtrodden; he was obviously still distraught over his lack of foresight about attaching his NanoGun device to various other weaponry. But the duct-tape fix was now already a part of the stream. The logistics team was on it.

Sam looked at Harper. "Suppose you need to get going."

"Back five minutes and you're already tired of me, huh?"

"Funny." He hesitated. "Hey…you never answered my question. Why'd you call me…leave that voice message for me to call you back?"

"You mean before all this?" She gestured at the milling-about people and the Attack Stingers.

Sam nodded.

She took a step closer to him without making eye contact. He thought she might kiss him, but instead she held up her left hand.

He didn't get it—what she was trying to tell him. And then he did. Her wedding band was no longer there on her ring finger.

"Uh…Oh!"

"You're a little slow on the uptake…but hopefully there'll be time for us to work on that." And then she kissed him on the cheek.

Before Sam could say or do anything, Harper grabbed Julian by the sleeve, and the two of them headed off toward the awaiting Landa-Craft. Sam yelled after them, "Watch yourselves out there!"

Without turning around, she waved a backward hand.

He looked down at Cypress. "Why the hell didn't you tell me about that hidden staircase?"

The dog didn't answer; instead just looked sheepish.

"I get it…You liked the attention? Me lugging your ass up and down that ladder…" Sam said, not sounding all that irritated.

Sam opened himself fully to the stream and staggered, momentarily losing his balance. His head had already been hurting; now he was suffering the worst migraine of his life. The raw data flow was bringing more than just information; it was bringing insights from Gia that, up until now, he didn't even know existed.

Finally, Sam, Gia said. It is time. Are you ready?

He answered aloud. "Yeah, I'm ready. What do you say we do this thing?"

The inbound Silarian drop ships will reach the isolation zone in three minutes.

He already knew that. He looked out at the pasture and caught Lester's eye. Walter was duct-taping a NanoGun onto the barrel of his QBZ-95 automatic rifle. He gave the young man a nod. *Don't fuck this up, kid.*

Lester smiled and, clearly reading Sam's thoughts, smiled and flipped him the bird.

"Let's get in the air, people!" Sam yelled, already heading in the direction of the closest Attack Stinger. Without looking down, he said, "And I suppose you want me to lug your ass up into that craft?"

"I'd far rather you didn't have to."

Sam already knew that Stingers didn't have any kind of hidden, lowerable stair systems. He bent down, got a good hold on Cypress, and hefted the dog and himself up the integrated ladder. Having done this several times now with the Landa-Craft, the process was slightly less awkward than what he'd experienced previously.

Between the nanites now assembled in his brain and the communications circuitry of his iPhone, Sam initiated the command to raise the canopy. Once high enough, Cypress jumped from his arms into the cockpit and took up his position behind the pilot's seat. Taking a seat himself, Sam, as painful as it was, maintained an open flow to the stream. He was aware that the other pilots were getting situated within their respective Stingers as well.

Looking out through the canopy, Sam knew Harper and Julian were already in the air and heading off toward the isolation zone's plasma field. He also knew that Gia had provided the necessary command that supposedly would let her ship pass through the energy field unaffected. *That better work,* he mentally conveyed to her.

He powered up the Stinger as if he'd done so a thousand times. He took one more look outside at the dozens of Gia fighters on the ground who'd stopped what they'd been doing and now were looking back at them. He offered a casual two-fingered salute and brought his Attack Stinger up into the air. Six other Stingers rose up along with his, three of which were wobbling. The human pilots had not quite gotten the feel of things yet. Scott's lone Stinger remained on the ground below them.

Sam wanted to know more about the Castle Rock residents, former pilots he would, like it or not, be putting his life on the line with: Teddy Putnam, Carl Bennet, and Ivan Dvorak. The stream had their bio information all teed up for him.

Sam mentally drilled down, seeing images of the three pilots.

225

MARK WAYNE MCGINNIS & KIM MCGINNIS

Sam cocked his head, releasing a crick in his neck. He sat tall in his seat, taking in air and then letting out a long, measured breath. He'd been doing that a lot lately. He looked at the mental image of Ivan and smiled; the Slavic man was sporting a bandage on his right cheek.

Sam said, "Gia, can you put me through to Ivan's craft?"

"Done."

"Listen to me, Ivan. You will do exactly as I say, when I say it. Do you understand?"

Chuckling, Ivan spoke in heavy, Czech-accented English. "Or what? You gonna mess up my pretty face again? Up there, beyond the clouds…I'll be very good. You will see."

Sam didn't see any humor in the situation. He got going on his prospective team's bios.

Name: Teddy Putnam

Age: 38

Height: 6'1"

Weight: 190

Hair: Black

Eyes: Dark Brown

Marital Status: Married

Birthplace: Dallas, Texas

Religious Affiliation: Devout Catholic

Sam nodded. *Religious, okay…good to know. Guess I'll have to watch my language around this one.*

College: University of Dallas, Naval Academy

Military Background: Twelve years in the navy, naval aviator, left the service after attaining the rank of lieutenant

Current Occupation: Police Officer

Other Relevant Information: A trained F/A-F18E fighter pilot with an excellent record.

All right, Teddy—looks like you are a straight shooter. Who's up next…

Carl?

Name: Carl Bennet

Age: 32

Height: 5'11"

Weight: 205

Hair: Red

Eyes: Pale Blue

Marital Status: Single

Birthplace: Castle Rock, Colorado

Religious Affiliation: None

College: None

Military Background: Army, ten-year service after retiring as a corporal

Current Occupation: Police Officer

Other Relevant Information: Knows how to fly Cessnas, although is not a professional pilot/Has had several write-ups from his current superior officer for insubordination.

Insubordination? I wonder what that's about? Next up...Ivan.

Name: Ivan Dvorak

Age: 37

Height: 6'3"

Weight: 255

Hair: Dark Brown

Eyes: Black

Marital Status: Single

Birthplace: Czech Republic

Religious Affiliation: None

College: University of Defence

Military Background: Twelve years in the air force branch of the Army of the Czech Republic, a Saab JAS 39 Gripen fighter pilot, dishonorably discharged for being drunk while flying and for hitting a superior officer.

Current Occupation: Manager at White's Plumbing and Electric

Other Relevant Information: Ivan's youngest brother was sentenced to death after being accused of murder. Ivan claims he was falsely arrested, although he offered no proof at the time.

Well, this should be interesting.

Sam mentally evaluated these three imperfect men. Who was he to judge? He was imperfect himself. But the stakes were high; he'd be watching them, especially Ivan, very closely.

Sam tapped at the dash and heard the hiss of an open comms channel coming alive. "Let's do this," he said. And with that, six Attack Stingers shot forward and then rose at a nearly vertical trajectory toward the top of the isolation zone. They pierced the plasma field with little more than a bright flash and a brief crackling sound. He accelerated, and the other Stingers matched his speed. "Commencing stealth," he said. Within a minute, the skies outside the canopy were turning dark, and then they were rising above Earth's exosphere layer. To his fellow three human pilots, he said, "Carl, Ivan…Teddy, how's it feel to be an astronaut?"

But it was one of the Silarian pilots that answered first. "As if you would know yourself…human."

"True that," Sam said, taking in the sheer blackness of space; the distant half-shadowed moon, and the twinkling of a million stars seemingly close enough to reach out and touch. He glanced to his right and then left. There was no sign of the other stealth Stingers. He took in one of the 3D displays on the dash and saw the ghostly outline visuals of the other Stingers.

Cypress said, "Forty-seven seconds ago, three Silarian drop ships entered the isolation zone."

Sam knew as much. He also knew there was a chance they would succeed in killing everyone within that zone, within Castle Rock. He felt slightly guilty at his relief that Harper and Julian had escaped all that impending carnage.

Chapter 38

Open space, beyond Earth
Sam Dale

Sam knew he couldn't maintain this much longer—this level of openness to the stream. His eyes were wet with tears, and there was now a ringing in his ears. He reached out to Gia. *Tell me you've done what is necessary. That you'll be able to cope with more subjects. Otherwise, why are we doing this?*

We will have to cross that bridge together, Sam. Keep in mind, I am primarily an artificial intelligence. Self-aware, yes, but I cannot sustain growth, not completely, solely within the stream. To expand, I require hardware. A foothold within computer architecture. That is why your mission is so crucial. That gunship, with its advanced technology, will provide me with an excellent means for expansion.

Sam mentally reached out into the stream; he was most interested in getting an update on Earth in general since the arrival of the Silarians. Some of that was being uploaded now, coming from Harper's Landa-Craft sensors, which had left the confines of the restricted isolation zone.

Sam said aloud, "Gia…why not bring down the isolation zone now? Let our human military assist with fighting those arriving

Clash-Troopers?"

"In one respect, that would be optimal. But let that scenario play out in your own mind, Sam."

He did just that and did not like what he discovered. Many, if not most of Castle Rock's inhabitants would pay a high price—be killed by friendly fire. In an attempt to stop any further incursion by alien forces, the township would be attacked. Sacrificed.

Cypress said, "Which makes Harper and Julian's mission all that much more important."

"We've got visuals on fleet assets, Captain," Teddy, the navy pilot, said.

It had been a while since anyone had referred to Sam in such a way. "Copy that. How about we use our names as our call signs moving forward? If we're overheard, no sense letting the enemy know our military ranks."

"Roger that."

Flout, Gromel, and Jarpin remained quiet on the subject.

Sam suddenly sat up straighter in his seat and audibly gasped. He'd already known there were over one hundred vessels comprising Naru's 23rd Fleet, but seeing the massive warship armada with his own eyes was beyond sobering.

Sam heard some muffled words from Teddy. "Gracious Father, please fill me with your Holy Spirit to lead me toward a successful mission."

"I feel like I have dumpling in my throat," Ivan said.

Carl spoke next. "We're so fucked."

Sam exchanged a quick look with Cypress. Neither could disagree.

Sam looked at his displays and readouts while tapping deeper into the stream. "We've gone undetected thus far. That's at least something," Sam said.

Jarpin said, "I will be taking point from this point on."

Sam was fine with that. He closed down much of his access to the stream. Knowing what was ahead for them as a team, he needed to regain some of his energy—clear his mind.

Flout said, "The name of the target gunship translates to Relentless Thrust."

"Are you serious?" Carl said. "What kind of lame ship name is that?"

Gromel answered, "How dare you insult—"

"Hey, hey…let's knock off the chatter. We have a job to do here," Sam said. In just above a whisper, he asked Cypress, "Have you been aboard the *Relentless Thrust* vessel?"

"No. But I have been aboard many similar Naru gunships. This will not be, as you humans say, a cakewalk."

"I heard that," Carl said.

Obviously, Carl was going to be the class clown of the outfit. *Terrific. There's always one.*

Sam heard a heavy sigh and then discontented murmuring. He knew it was coming from one of the Silarian pilots.

"You have something to say, Gromel?" Sam asked.

"This mission will be difficult enough without you bringing along your four- appendaged pet."

The two other Silarian pilots made grunts of agreement.

When he was about to rip into the alien assholes, Cypress placed a paw on Sam's arm. The dog shook his head.

They were upon the fleet now. Each of the large and magnificent-looking ships reflected the sun's light, a vivid contrast to the surrounding blackness of space. Sam's mind already held the make-up of this interstellar force—ten gunships, thirty-five destroyers, twenty battle cruisers, fifteen space carriers, and five Epic-Class dreadnoughts. It was hard not to feel insignificant or daunted by this overwhelming interstellar presence.

"Remove your hands from your primary controls arrays. I have taken full nav control of your Stingers," Jarpin said.

Sam did as told and watched on his display as their squadron of Attack Stingers fell into a single-file line. Like a weaving-back-and-forth snake, they progressed in between the great warships. Sam needed to remind himself to breathe, feeling daunted by the sheer size of the enemy craft, several of which had to be miles in length. Curious how their squadron of Attack Stingers was able to progress undetected, even cloaked as they were. The stream provided the answer. Gia had altered the stealth light-bending frequency algorithms just enough so the Naru warships' sensors would not *easily* detect their presence. But come too close to any one of those colossal warships, and all that could change. These Stingers emitted nearly undetectable levels of radiation. That alone could trigger sensor alarms.

"Holy shit...look at the size of that motherfu—"

Sam cut Carl off. "Comms silence!" But he, too, was taken aback by the sheer size of the warship they were now approaching on their port side. It was one of the Epic-Class dreadnoughts. Every inch of its hull seemed to be conduit bundles, venting ducts, sensor arrays, and various junction boxes, but there was no mistaking the giant, maneuverable cannon turrets, each the size of a small house. He discovered that this vessel was designated *Dawn of Virility*. Sam rolled his eyes. He wondered how these incredible vessels were propelled through space and, with a good amount of pain, queried the stream. But it was Gia's voice in his head.

Fusion Drives: Silarians have mastered heavy-element fusion. Fusion reactors, as you may know them on Earth, rely on the fusion of different hydrogen atoms at incredibly high energy. The Silarians have mastered the ability to perform fusion with more massive elements AND the ability to select how much of that input mass goes into a new element and how much goes to energy. They can use two atoms of something like argon, Earth element 18, normally nonreactive, and vibrationally prime the engine to fuse into iron, your world's element number twenty-six; that means eighteen plus eighteen equals twenty-six, plus an absolutely mind blowing ten protons worth of converted energy. Of which they can use in their fusion drives. Silarians do tend to stick to gases for the output, but most elements are available to them via a vessel's fusion tuning drive.

Sam nodded, finding it interesting he actually understood what she'd just told him.

Someone keyed their comms. *A warning.* Their forward progress suddenly slowed and then stopped completely. Then he saw it, a small vessel, a transport schooner, according to the stream; it was making its way from one ship to another, soon to be intersecting their formation of Stingers.

Cypress said, "That vessel will be coming within just a few feet of Carl's Stinger. If the pilot of that transport is paying close attention to his readouts and ship sensors…"

Cypress didn't need to finish his thought. They'd be toast.

Cypress broke the tension, suddenly using a back paw to start scratching at an ear. Sam caught Cypress's irritated expression—an internal dialogue going on with Rocko.

"We can proceed," Jarpin said in a voice just above a whisper. Their forward progress resumed.

It occurred to Sam, and not for the first time, that this alien force would be impossible for humanity to oppose now, or even five hundred years from now. Gia and the stream were the one slim chance for his species' ultimate survival. Perhaps what was most unsettling about that was the simple fact that Sam still didn't definitively trust her. *It.*

As they continued on, Sam took note of the now near-constant back-and-forth movement of shuttles and small cargo vessels. Strange how these fleet mega ships were so close to one another, something that he knew was a bad practice from his own military experience on the ground. Keep a good distance between assets; don't give your enemy easy, bunched-up targets. Perhaps these Silarians didn't anticipate having viable enemies anymore. Overconfidence was something he hopefully could exploit in time.

Their ghostly squadron slowed once more. Directly in front of them was a comparatively smaller vessel, but no less badass-looking in its diminutive size. Its hull was gun-metal gray. Querying the stream, Sam knew this vessel was one hundred and twenty meters long. *Relentless Thrust's* sleek-looking fuselage expanded back into a widening port and starboard wings, making the vessel triangular in its overall shape. He took stock of the vessel's weaponry—six plasma cannons and two big rail guns. It had the capacity to fire a slew of onboard munitions, primarily from a cache of fusion-tipped micro-missiles. And currently, there was a crew of two hundred and twenty-six Silarians onboard.

He noted there was but one flight bay access. At present, that bay had three shuttles and four Attack Stingers parked inside. The skipper of this gunship was one Captain Droke Tolli Mahn. He was one hundred and six in Earth years—relatively young to be a captain, but he was on his third bio-form transition. So, he had the vitality of a young body, along with the wisdom that came from centuries of life experience. *Maybe a formidable opponent?*

Gia said, "I am communicating to you all simultaneously at this moment. I have requested that *Relentless Thrust* open its flight bay doors. Considering the deck officer has neither visual nor sensor verification, this may be a problem…time will tell."

Sam looked at Cypress. "Is that typical? That a Silarian ship would allow requested access…to an unseen vessel?"

"No. Not at all. Stealth running is common. But Gia is attempting to pass herself off as a Geo-Mind. That is where a potential problem lies. Will *Relentless Thrust's* Geo-Mind detect disparities…anomalies?"

Sam turned his head, hearing something odd. A crunching sound. "Carl, are you eating something?"

"Sorry. Didn't realize you'd be able to pick up on that. Uh…I brought a small bag of Doritos with me."

"We've been granted access," Gia said, no small measure of triumph in her tone.

Sam knew that this gunship in particular had been chosen because of its ample available flight bay space. As his Attack Stinger picked up speed, he couldn't ignore the quickening of his own heart rate. It was go-time.

Chapter 39

In the skies above Castle Rock, Colorado
Julian Humblecut

The scientist was only minimally aware of what was happening around him. The stream, his interactions with Gia, had the enticing effects of a mind-altering drug. Benzodiazepines and methamphetamine came to mind. His head hurt; he certainly was aware of that too. But the knowledge he was gaining—the new possibilities broadening his perspectives on science, on life—was breathtaking. Julian had never married. Had never fallen in love. His career, his seemingly endless pursuit of answers, had made such things seem trivial. But now, having these conversations with Gia, he felt he might have glimpsed somewhat more of such an abstract emotion. Had he fallen in love with Gia? Was that even possible? To fall in love with a computer…an AI being?

Sitting there in the Landa-Craft's cockpit, situated behind Harper manning the controls, he was perfectly content, withdrawn within his inner contemplations. He glanced out the cockpit and saw they would be exiting the isolation zone any moment now. And, as exciting as that was, he was far more interested in what was going on within the workings of his own mind. For goodness' sake, he was learning things, getting definitive answers to things no other human being had ever been proffered.

"Gia…please talk to me about antigravity. How is it this space vessel can seemingly overcome the effects, the pull, of gravity?" Julian heard Harper in front of him let out an exasperated breath.

"That is a big question, Julian," Gia said, speaking through the ship's audio system. Her voice was so engaging. It stirred him physically in ways he was unaccustomed to feeling.

"Antigravity of an object," she continued, "such as this Landa-Craft, is achieved with the help of a unique, integrated gravitational shield. This gravitational shield was developed using antimatter. As you know, all matter in our universe has a positive mass. Antimatter, on the other hand, has a negative gravitational mass…" Gia's voice droned on; Julian was in a state of bliss.

Harper's voice pulled Julian back to the here and now. "How about you give it a rest for a while, Julian? As interesting as all your science talk with Gia has been, maybe you can help me come up with a workable plan for dealing with what's outside of the isolation zone."

"Of course, Harper. Yes, yes…a very good idea."

Chapter 40

In the skies above Castle Rock, Colorado
Harper Godard

Julian was acting strange, but she let it go. She'd completed a full circle within the zone and now, below them, was the empty northbound I-25 interstate. "Here we go…" Harper said.

The Landa-Craft pierced the isolation zone's plasma field with little more than a brief flash and a crackle. "Oh my God…" Reflexively, Harper jerked the controls to the left, barely avoiding an object streaking across their path. Gasping, she got the vessel back under control.

Julian, undaunted, craned his neck to get a better view of the ground below. "I suppose I should have expected as much."

Harper could only nod. She tapped the stream and swallowed hard as searing pain made her head throb. A flood of information poured into her consciousness, all regarding the substantial military presence currently surrounding Castle Rock. Things she normally would not understand, would have been clueless about, were now making perfect sense to her…

As part of what had been designated as Operation Safeguard, a defensive cordon had been established. All main southbound arteries leaving the Denver metropolitan area had been shut down. Around Castle Rock, roadblocks had been set up on the 25 North and South, the 85 to the west, the 86 west of Franktown near the Harmony Equine Center, South Perry Park Road at West Wolfensberger Road, the 83 at Lake Gulch Road, and the Crowfoot Valley Road at Pradera Parkway. The roadblocks on Highway 25 were large, complex affairs, and as Harper put eyes on them, the stream identified geotextile-lined HESCO barriers and Jersey barriers arranged in serpentines to control whatever vehicle traffic might suddenly erupt from the isolation zone. Spike belts and concertina wire spanned the freeway, and on each side of the 25, behind the HESCO barriers, an M1A2 Abrams main battle tank pointed its 120 mm smooth-bore cannon downrange toward Castle Rock.

She said aloud, "Huh…I know what an M1A2 Abrams main battle tank is."

"Mmm, oh yes," Julian said in a monotone voice, as if he was caught in a trance. "The stream is really quite wonderful."

The Landa-Craft banked hard, and Harper saw soldiers manning M2 .50-cals and Mk15 grenade launchers from fixed positions and Mine-Resistant Ambush-Protected Cougars. Everywhere, signs warned that deadly force had been authorized. Other roadblocks were manned by units from the 3rd Armored Brigade Combat Team, Fourth Infantry Division, out of Fort Carson.

Given the bizarre nature of the threat, Fort Carson had also mobilized the 4ID's 1st and 2nd Stryker Brigade Combat Teams. Several squads patrolled the cordon on foot and in four-vehicle convoys comprising HMMWVs and MRAPs. They operated out of a southern forward operating base and combat outposts and observation posts radiating toward Castle Rock. FOBs, COPs, and OPs like these had been built on all sides of the city.

The stream revealed that the 10th Special Forces Group had been repurposed and deployed. Units from other branches had followed, including from the CIA's Special Activities Division.

Nearly twelve thousand troops were there, with more coming as the national guard and reservists were called up and force readiness had been increased to DEFCON 3.

"The US is not screwing around," Harper said.

"Indeed," Julian agreed.

The stream indicated that a geostationary earth orbit satellite was supporting Operation Safeguard and that Denver International Airport had been closed and a no-fly zone established around Castle Rock to include the entirety of the Denver metropolitan area. Squadrons of F-35s enforced the no-fly zone, supported by 11th Expeditionary Combat Aviation Brigade UH-60 Black Hawks, a Northrop-Grumman RQ-4 Global Hawk, which was the operation's primary surveillance drone, and two General Atomics MQ-9 Reapers.

Speaking of drones, the sky around Castle Rock was swarming with them. In fact, they had almost taken out an RQ-16 T-Hawk back when they had exited the plasma field.

Harper had had enough of the stream. She blew out a hot, anxious breath. Even though she knew their stealth ship would be undetectable by those on the ground, she couldn't feel any more exposed and vulnerable.

Gia said, "I now have access to your world's internet…strange how much of the information is blatantly incorrect. No, purposely incorrect. Seems the populace of Earth is enamored with lies and conspiracy theories."

Julian groaned. "Please tell me this is just a phase humanity is going through. That those on Naru don't play these ridiculous mind games—"

"The stream cannot, does not, function in the same way as your world's internet and social media platforms do. There is a fundamental truth to the universe. Unfortunately, I can see where the Geo-Mind could utilize your internet for his own less than principled purposes."

"All the more reason we have to take down the Geo-Mind before it is unleashed on humanity," Harper said.

"Gia," Julian said, "Can we talk cell phones? That is one aspect of our plan we will still need to work with."

"That should not be an issue. I have uploaded the cell phone registry."

"For Castle Rock and the surrounding areas?"

"No. For planet Earth."

"Oh. Yes…of course you would be able to do that," Julian said.

Harper said, "Well, at the present moment, we need the highest-ranking military officer…the one that's in charge of all this."

She cracked open the mental doorway to the stream, and the information was available for her. She said, "Will this ever stop hurting? Opening to the stream like that?"

"Yes, Harper…your brain is just experiencing a form of growing pains."

She was still circling the exterior of the isolation zone. A zone that looked very much like a large, circular black hole—a void that didn't reflect light and seemed as ominous a sight as anything she had ever seen. No wonder there'd been such a large military response; this thing was scaring the daylights out of, well, everybody.

Harper's attention turned to one of the console displays. She immediately recognized the geographic area being highlighted, Colorado Springs. An hour's drive by car, but a mere minute away by Landa-Craft. The stream was telling her the highest-ranking military person she needed to talk to was at Schriever Space Force Base near there. Four-star General John B. McGovern was the second-highest-ranking officer within Space Force, and it wasn't surprising that he was here instead of the Pentagon, considering what was happening within Castle Rock.

She looked back at Julian. "I think you should call him."

"Me?"

"Yes, you. You are a multimillionaire scientist, whereas I'm a part-time server and part-time nurse. Who do you think he'll listen to more?"

Julian reluctantly nodded. "We're headed there now?"

"Yeah, but it might be a good idea to call this General McGovern preemptively."

"Hm. Yes. I…"

"You're not good with this sort of thing. The social aspects. I get it, Julian. But this is important."

He nodded and brought out his smartphone, and Gia dialed the number for him.

"General McGovern."

"Uh…yes, well…this is Julian—"

"How did you get this number? This is not a publicly accessible line."

Harper, chewing at the inside of her cheek, was witnessing Julian's total incompetence when it came to being direct and managing a tense situation. "Give me the phone, Julian." She gestured with two beckoning fingers to hand it over. He did as told.

"General McGovern, my name is Harper Godard, and I just left the Castle Rock isolation zone."

"That is impossible. No one has been able to enter or leave that area for—"

"Don't argue with me, General; I'm in no mood. I can prove what I'm saying and demonstrate that things are far more dire than you can possibly imagine."

"Demonstrate? How? Again…how did you get this num—"

"General, you need to shut the fuck up and look out your window."

"Look out my—"

She brought the Landa-Craft down within the sprawling grounds of Schriever Space Force Base. She maneuvered in close to the primary office structure and hovered approximately two hundred feet above the ground. They waited to see movement in the building's top-floor corner office window. The blinds suddenly rose, and a face appeared behind the glass, which was Harper's signal to turn off stealth mode. The man's face at the window went from irritation to one of unbridled astonishment.

"What…who…"

"I realize what you are looking at is a surprise. And yes, this is an alien spacecraft. And you need to get your wits together and talk to me right now."

"If this is some kind of trick or gag…"

"At this moment there is a fleet of alien warships ready to attack Earth. Their position within the solar system is about halfway between Mars and Jupiter. I suspect you have already been notified of some kind of anomaly in that area of space, no?"

"I'm not going to speak about such things with people without the proper clearance."

Seeing movement below, she placed the Landa-Craft back into stealth mode. "Look, you're already getting on my nerves, General. You were the first phone call I made. I have a long list of alternate military contacts."

"No. Tell me what you want. What you need from me."

A series of lights were now flashing on the forward dash. Julian pointed to the display that highlighted ground armaments that were, apparently, targeting the Landa-Craft.

"You can start by standing down with your poorly hidden MIM-109 Patriot surface-to-air missile system. There's no way you're going to get an accurate lock on this vessel, so don't even try." She was impressed with what she had just said. Access to the stream was becoming invaluable.

The warning lights on the dash stopped flashing. Harper did a quick structural assessment of the building. "General, I would like you and no more than several of your top aides to join me up on the roof."

"On the roof? This roof?"

She ignored the man's habit of repeating everything she said. "Again, we are not here to hurt anyone…in fact, we're here to save the planet. And yes, I know that sounds overdramatic. But I assure you, it's not."

She'd already been navigating the Landa-Craft up and over McGovern's, this base's, primary building structure—undoubtedly where only the highest of military muckety mucks had their office suites. Still running in stealth mode, she brought the craft down slowly and let out a relieved breath when she'd touched down and was assured the building's roof could indeed support the many tons of extra weight being added atop it.

She debated whether to leave the craft invisible, then thought better of it. An invisible spaceship didn't offer much of a punch when you needed to leave a lasting impression. The vessel outside the cockpit suddenly popped into view.

She held up her left arm, the one that had the small square device, the NanoGun, affixed to her wrist. "You sure this thing will work?"

Julian stared at the device for a few moments. "I…tested it. Indiscriminately and probably most unethically."

"With who?"

"With Sam's next-door neighbor. I knocked on the door, waited for the lady of the house to answer, and shot her in the face."

"You shot someone in the face? You just stood there and shot someone—"

"It's a laser pointer, Harper. She had no idea she'd even been… targeted. That the bright red dot on her cheek was infusing her physiology with tiny light-surfing nanites."

She laughed at the visuals that conjured up. "Well? What happened to her?"

"She and I talked for, I don't know, maybe five minutes. Then she keeled over. I, of course, was anticipating that and caught her in mid-drop."

Harper was keeping an eye on the small structure atop the roof—some kind of access hut with a metal door. "So? She got donutted?"

"She got donutted. And the process was much faster and more efficient than eating the actual donuts. And I had her cell phone number; it was on a sticky note on Sam's fridge."

She stared at the metal door to the access hut. Gia had accessed the stairwell's internal high-mounted security camera, and the feed was currently being presented on one of the console's displays. *So much for him just bringing along several advisers…*

Inside there was a squad with three fire teams—a total of twelve operators currently getting into position. Fire Team One would soon secure the roof. Fire Team Two, farther down the stairwell, was the guard around the general and included the squad leader. Fire Team Three, farther down yet, was added support. Each man or woman was armed with an M4 carbine assault rifle. They were all outfitted in black fatigues with black helmets and black tactical vests.

"They're not messing around," she said.

Currently, Fire Team One was chest to back, a hand on the shoulder of the operator in front of them. As the last person in the line got situated, he tapped the shoulder of the person in front of him, and that process continued up the stack. Finally, the point man felt the tap, and he opened the door.

Harper looked up and saw the hut's door swing open. Fire Team One began clearing the roof. The first operator had his rifle fixed on the aircraft and moved at a forty-five-degree angle to the left of the door. The second operator moved in the same manner but to the right of the door. Team Operator Three button hooked to the left and secured the roof behind the door. Operator Four button hooked to the right and did the same. The fifth operator moved to the left and secured the left flank, followed by the sixth operator going right and securing the right flank. Harper was taken aback by their fast, well-practiced, choreographed movements.

Startled, she heard each operator yell out, "Clear," from all positions on the roof.

With the entire roof now secured, the team leader spoke into comms. "Roof secure, over."

"Roger, roof secure; heading to your position. Out."

Fire Team Two and the two remaining support members of Fire Team Three moved into view from the hut. Four operators surrounding the general moved together toward the Landa-Craft.

"I'm a little disappointed, but not surprised," Harper said aloud. A thought occurred to her, and she smiled. "Then again, these are desperate times, wouldn't you say, Julian?"

"Uh-huh. The most desperate," he replied, sounding somewhat distracted.

Raising her left arm and utilizing the combination of her brain resident nanites, her iPhone circuitry, Gia, and the stream, Harper activated her NanoGun. At some fifty feet of distance, a red dot appeared on the chin of the closest of the general's security team. "How long do I have to hold the laser on him?"

"A second or two should be more than long enough."

She repeated the process with all the operators encircling the Landa-Craft, then moved on to the others on the roof; fortunately, they were all within her direct line of sight. Not one of them was aware he was being targeted. Eventually, she'd donutted each of them. All except General McGovern. Assessing him now, standing there off the starboard wing of the ship, for some reason she'd expected him to be wearing his formal navy-blue uniform with its fruit salad of military bars and accommodations. Instead, he was wearing gray camo fatigues with a matching cap and high buckskin-colored boots. She leveled a red dot onto the tip of his nose.

"Ready?" she asked.

"Ready," Julian replied.

"Good. Let's go have a chat with the brass."

Julian said, "Perhaps we should give it just a few more moments…let the nanites do their thing on those soldiers?"

Chapter 41

Castle Rock Ford Dealership, Castle Rock, Colorado
Lester Price

Lester was feeling amped. Fidgety, he couldn't keep still, so he paced back and forth in front of the oversized glass windows of the Castle Rock Ford Dealership where his group was holding up within the southern area of Castle Rock. He'd separated his small army of mostly cops but a good number of civilians, too, into three companies of about twenty-five combatants each. There was a company stationed in the northern section of the town, as well as one more toward the middle.

He was annoyed that fucking Walter and his misfits hadn't agreed to enlist in his ground forces army. Screw them. Sure, they were probably most experienced when it came to seeing actual military combat, but they were mostly old farts, that and a few hangers-on bitches. He thought of Elsie and her provocative neck tattoo. There was something captivating about her.

Insight from the stream told him there were three Silarian drop ships en route. There was no way to know where, precisely, they would be landing. But if they followed previous actions upon other worlds, they would separate, land, and dispatch, making a multipronged attack on local civilization. Lester didn't want to give the arriving Clash-Troopers any time to organize; he wanted to hit them fast, hit them hard as soon as their feet hit the ground. Sure, these aliens were big mothers, but they were flesh and bone and could die just as easily as any humans could.

Lester looked out to the lot and found Tuck sitting behind the wheel of a dark blue F150. *SALE!* had been painted onto the windshield in bold fluorescent pink lettering. Tuck was smoking a joint and talking to someone in the passenger seat Lester didn't know.

"Hey, um…Lester?"

He turned to see the little black chick, Luna something. "I'm busy…what do you want?"

She was with Daryl, and together, they approached. Both were armed and looked ridiculous in their makeshift military garb. He hadn't wanted either of them but didn't make a stink when he discovered they'd opted to be in his group.

Luna said, "Those drop ships that're coming. There could be as many as three hundred Clash-Troopers."

Daryl picked up where she left off. "We're inexperienced and way outnumbered."

Lester glared at the big dummy. Although, it seemed he was over that annoying stuttering thing. "Look," he said with little patience. "We can't defeat them by going toe to toe with them. I've been over this with you. With all of you. So has Gia. All we have to do is get in close enough to confront them and engage them for a time."

"Yeah, we know all that," Luna said. "It's our job to donut them…allow Gia to do her thing. To get into their minds, where she'll take on their Geo-Minds." She held up her NanoGun device.

"So, what's the issue?" Lester said, making an annoyed face.

Daryl spoke up. "Well, there are a couple of things. Like, just because these troopers get donutted, that doesn't mean they'll instantly come over to our side. Some of the Silarian Attack Stinger pilots didn't…remember? And what if Gia doesn't win? Isn't up to the task of defeating their Geo-Minds? What then?"

Lester was only partially listening. He was back to pacing. Keeping an eye on his troops. He knew everyone's name and background, thanks to the stream. Most were patrolling the lot while keeping an eye up to the sky. Tuck and his friend were laughing at something in the truck.

"Incoming!" one of the cops yelled from the middle of the lot. He was pointing to the north.

Lester saw them now too. Three large, slug-shaped spacecraft. Far larger than the Stingers or a Landa-Craft. He moved out to the middle of the car lot and watched; as expected, the three drop ships separated, circled high overhead, and then dropped quickly down into the town.

Lester yelled, "Get to your vehicles! Let's go!" Gia was already giving him and everyone else the coordinates of their closest respective drop ship. Lester's squad was within a mile or so of the closest drop ship. He, Tuck, Luna, and Daryl piled into his police Humvee and within seconds were headed toward Plum Creek Golf Course, where a drop ship had landed. Another drop ship had landed at the Douglas County Fairgrounds, and another was at Butterfield Crossing Park in a more northern area of town. The other two squads, like his own, were already en route to those locations.

Tuck, to Lester's right in the passenger seat, reeked of ganja. A quick glance over at him verified that he was in no condition for combat. Peering through the windshield with bloodshot, half-lidded eyes, Tuck said, "Man…this is really happening."

Daryl said from the back seat, "You're wasted."

Tuck chuckled. "I'm in full control of my…senses. I'm actually more in control when I'm chittyfaced—"

250

"Knock it off, Tuck. Stop being an asshole," Lester said, taking a hard left onto Crystal Valley Parkway.

Bleary-eyed, Tuck glanced at the back seat. "Huh…when did you two get here?"

With a glance at his rear-view mirror, Lester saw no fewer than seven or eight police Interceptors were in close pursuit along with a pickup truck and a minivan. The Humvee jostled as it powered up over a curb and onto the seventh fairway of the Plum Creek Golf Course, and there, some fifty or sixty yards in front of them, was the now-landed alien drop ship.

Luna said, "Look, the side door…it's sliding open."

Lester accelerated. His mind was almost completely open to the stream; the pain was intense enough to affect his breathing. And then he gasped. "Oh no!…Oh, fucking no!"

Even before the first of them emerged, he knew. Knew that the hundred or so Clash-Troopers on board this ship were not Silarian combatants at all. They were robots.

He said, "Gia…tell me you can do your thing with fucking robots!"

Calm but serious, her voice emanated from the police radio. "Working on it. Only realized they were on board when the three drop ships entered the isolation zone."

They sped by an overturned golf cart. Two golf bags and their clubs were scattered about the fairway. Lester queried the stream. *How the hell does one take out robot Clash-Troopers?* There was no ready answer. He slammed on the brakes. The Humvee skidded sideways while churning up the once immaculate emerald-green links. Multiple police units came to a stop on both sides of them.

Already out of the Humvee, he yelled, "Everyone out! Take cover!"

Half a football field's distance away, the robots were as big as Silarians—easily seven feet tall but all metal. Looking like rust-colored iron stick figures with skeletal heads, they stormed out of the drop ship in a kind of lockstep precision. They moved as one unit. Fanning out before the drop ship, the robots raised their weapons while assessing their surroundings. As if they'd all gotten the same instructions at the same moment, their heads, their beady black eyes, locked onto the contingent of police vehicles, along with the men and women taking cover behind them.

Lester queried, *Dammit, Gia…what are we supposed to do now?*

Seeing movement to his right, Lester saw that Tuck had taken it upon himself to make the first move. And it wasn't as if he was hard to miss, wearing that billowy red shirt beneath his too-small tactical vest. His oversized belt buckle was reflecting the midday sun like a hand mirror.

"Tuck! Get back here!" Lester spat between gritted teeth.

Others on both sides were now also yelling for him to take cover—to get back.

But the big man was undeterred. He was holding his M4 carbine awkwardly out in front of himself. Unsteady in his cowboy boots, Tuck ambled ahead while the three formed-up lines of robots watched with seeming curiosity.

"Listen to me, you scrap metal pieces of shit. This is our planet…our town. And you just picked the wrong neighborhood to—"

Three of the Clash-Trooper robots fired with simultaneous bursts of their weapons—*ZIP! ZIP! ZIP!* Lester wasn't sure if they were using projectile weapons or energy weapons or some kind of combination of both. Was science fiction all wrong about that? Captain Kirk had his phaser, Han Solo, his blaster. In the blink of an eye, Tuck was literally torn apart. His left arm was dismembered at the shoulder, his right leg severed at mid-thigh, and he was decapitated—his head tumbling high up into the air before landing with a *THWACK!* onto the hood of a nearby Interceptor.

That was when everyone opened up on the robots. Lester already knew it was futile, but he, too, was unloading on the enemy with his QBZ-95 assault rifle.

The racket of gunfire was beyond loud—both frightening as well as inspiring. Instantly, Lester was aware of just how damaging and destructive the robot gunfire was to—well, everything. The police units around him were quickly being shredded. Metal, glass fragments, human flesh torn to ribbons, erupted into the air. Something sharp tore a gash in his cheek, and then he felt something hot tear through his vest; he'd been nicked along his rib cage. He dove and rolled for cover beneath the Humvee. He was surprised to see that Luna was already there. Wide-eyed, she stared out at the unbridled carnage taking place around them.

Lester heard Gia's voice in his head. It was like someone talking to him during a loud action scene at the movies—impossible to hear, not to mention the distraction was annoying.

As the encircling firefight began to dissipate, her words became more intelligible. "Lester…do not move. Stay perfectly still."

He looked at Luna, who apparently was receiving the same message he was getting. She was as still as a statue.

"The good news is that these Clash-Trooper robots do have Geo-Mind AI components, although they have limited mental faculties. That is both good and bad. They are well shielded from the kind of intrusion I am currently attempting."

The gunfire had ceased. The air around them, a disgusting pink mist, smelled of gunpowder and coppery blood. Steam suddenly began spewing from the hot engine above them, the stream informing Lester it was ethylene glycol—antifreeze. And now it was dripping onto their backs. Lester heard Luna's rapid breaths at his side. The girl had started to hyperventilate. Slowly, he turned his head and looked at her. Gave her his most threatening stare. Almost imperceptibly, she nodded.

Gia was speaking again. *I have managed to deactivate a few of their sensory receptors. Their infrared imaging, subtle motion detection, ability to pick up on faint sounds, things like that…just stay very still and maybe you will go undetected.*

Robot legs were on the move around the Humvee's perimeter—all any one of the mechanical killers had to do was bend the fuck over and have a look-see. *Why? Why had Gia given him this responsibility?* She should have known he'd screw it up. Screw it up like he did everything else in his life. Reluctantly, Lester queried the stream. He was curious to know if he and Luna were the only survivors.

Chapter 42

Relentless Thrust, Flight Bay
Sam Dale

The squadron of seven Attack Stingers was still in a single-line formation. Having been given clearance to proceed in through *Relentless Thrust's* now-open flight bay doors, Sam swallowed hard. Cypress was up on all fours and looked concerned. So much depended on what would be happening next. Sam's confidence level was waning. *This is a batshit crazy plan.* But it was his plan, mostly. *So, buck up, soldier; it's go time.*

In front of them, the Attack Stingers piloted by Flout, Gromel and Jarpin disappeared as they passed through a bluish-green energy field—one Sam knew would allow the ship's internal flight bay to maintain necessary environmental conditions, namely a breathable atmosphere and cool, but not dangerous, temperatures.

"Here we go," Sam said, their Stinger next to move in through the glowing energy field. If the three Silarian pilots were going to turn on them, this would be the optimal time to do so. What would be waiting for them on the other side would tell all.

Cypress whined, his inner Rocko becoming more vocal.

Entering *Relentless Thrust's* flight bay, Sam now saw that his own

Stinger, as well as the three in front of him, had become visible. It made sense that you'd want to be able to see any craft coming in for a landing. *I'm entering an alien warship…*He looked around, both amazed and more than a little overwhelmed. The overhead lights within the bay were stark bright white, which was a good thing. There was no way he, or the three other human pilots, Carl, Ivan, and Teddy, coming behind, would be visible. Light reflecting off the Stingers' canopies would make that impossible.

The bay was spacious, and there was ample area for the seven Attack Stingers to set down. He knew their Stingers were now being remotely piloted by this gunship's master AI.

Cypress sat back on his haunches. "Gia is making her move."

Sam nodded; he, too, was monitoring the stream. Thus far, she had not infiltrated the ship's master AI where Geo-Mind's dominance was absolute.

The three Silarians' Stingers were now on the deck, wing tip to wing tip; there was no variation in the distance between them. Sam felt a sudden descent, and then his Stinger, too, had landed, and the main drive was winding down. He let out a measured breath. "And now we wait."

"We'll only get away with that for so long. Pilots are instructed to vacate their craft immediately," Cypress said.

"What do they do when a pilot dillydallies?"

"They deploy a hoverbot to check on things."

He watched the Silarian Stinger canopies—three clamshells opening all at once. "Yeah, this isn't weird at all…our four human pilots just sitting here…not vacating like the others." He checked on Gia's progress. He sat straight up and gasped. The gunship's AI was in the midst of a raging confrontation.

Geo-Mind and Gia were clamoring for dominance. But this was a virtual battle—a battle where software, raw code, was the weapon of choice. While Gia was still infinitesimally small in breadth and power compared to Geo-Mind, she did have one small advantage. She had had decades to prepare for this moment.

While Geo-Mind had never had a truly autonomous AI adversary to contend with, Gia's entire life span had been spent developing the tools and schemes for this very moment. Within nanoseconds of their arrival in the flight bay, her first proactive measure had been to close off *Relentless Thrust* from the rest of the fleet. That was no small feat. Every communications port, of which there were billions, was quickly assessed. Basic ship-to-ship communications were immediately severed. Most data ports were shut down, while others were temporarily bridged, subverted into her own intelligence construct. Internal Geo-Mind errors and warnings were circumvented completely.

Geo-Mind's trillions of comparative algorithms were attacked, hacked, and made unreliable. And since much of the processor error reporting had already been hosed, Geo-Mind was spending much of its time pulling data streams from archives. Clearly, though, the entrenched AI was no pushover. Although Sam didn't understand all he was observing in real time, he could see, more like was aware, of Geo-Mind ramping up counterstrikes that were now being leveled at Gia.

"Shit!" he said. He'd been so caught up in his own thoughts, he hadn't noticed the menacing metal sphere situated right outside of the canopy. The skin of the hoverbot was a melange of tiny blinking lights, protruding spike-like antennae, and several larger articulating appendages with opening and closing clamps.

Cypress, who must have been just as caught up in Gia's engagement, suddenly looked up and barked twice, only adding to Sam's consternation. "Hey! No barking!"

"It wasn't on purpose!" Cypress shot back.

The hoverbot was now squawking, making computerized-sounding commands Sam was sure were Silarian orders for,

"Get the hell out of that Stinger!" He checked in on Gia and was not encouraged by her progress. Startled, he saw the canopy had started to rise.

"Christ! Can't you stop it?" he said with a glance at Cypress.

"No, I can't stop it…and don't forget, I have paws, not hands."

All four of the human-piloted Stingers' canopies had been activated. Sam said, "Gia! Can you help?"

"Busy," was her one-word response.

Sam looked about the cockpit and spotted his M4 and other gear behind on his right.

"Hold on, Sam," Cypress said.

The hoverbot had started to bob up and down as if it was a buoy upon an unsteady sea.

"What's it doing?" Sam said.

Cypress tilted his head left and then right. "Looks to be having trouble with its grav-projectors. As are the others." The dog lifted his snout in the direction of the three other human-piloted Stingers and their respective out-of-control-looking hoverbots.

"That's a good thing, right?"

But before Cypress could answer, one of the hoverbot's clawed appendages thrust forward, clamping the dog around his neck. As he let out a muted yelp, Cypress's legs began to flail. Then he was being lifted upward, out of the cockpit.

Sam reached back for his weapon but was curtailed by his seatbelt harness. Hearing the dog's choking sounds only added to his need to do something, anything, fast. The harness was not like anything he was accustomed to back on Earth, and it took him several seconds to get the latch open. Having done so, he was able to reach back and retrieve his M4.

Cypress was now a good three feet overhead and still struggling. With eyes bulging, clearly the dog was being suffocated. Pointing the M4's stubby muzzle at the hoverbot, it occurred to

Sam that a resulting close-range ricochet could kill Cypress or even himself. Fuck it. But just before he pulled the trigger, the tight grasp around Cypress's neck released and the seventy-pound dog dropped hard into his lap. Out of the corner of his eye, he saw the hoverbot suddenly fall away. There was a loud clang, and then three more *clangs* as all four hoverbots smashed down onto the deck below. *Thank you, Gia.*

Cypress, now able to breathe again, clearly ecstatic he wasn't facing his own imminent death, was going crazy. Whimpering and still on Sam's lap, the animal was now spinning one way and then the other. Then, to Sam's surprise, the jubilant dog was licking his face. "Okay, okay, boy…you're all right now. Easy…okay, that's enough of that." Cypress jumped from his lap to the back compartment but continued to whimper and traipse around in disjointed circles.

Sam glanced to his right and saw Carl, Ivan, and Teddy, still seated within their respective Stingers; each looked back at him with a bemused expression. "How about we get to work…do what we came here to do?"

Chapter 43

Relentless Thrust, Flight Bay
Sam Dale

It wasn't long before a loud alarm klaxon was wailing overhead. Jarpin had climbed up and was helping with taking Cypress down the Stinger's inset ladder. Excited announcements in the Curplexah language echoed within the flight bay. Silarian crew members were now rushing about; obviously, problems with the ship's master AI were having an effect. Sam was monitoring the stream. Gia's attacks were being thwarted at every turn. Clearly, things were not going as anticipated.

Keeping low, the team of Silarian and human pilots converged beneath the wing of an Attack Stinger. Cypress, having adequately suppressed his inner Rocko, said, "Although our objective was to start donutting crew members, Gia needs us to wait. She needs time to embed herself into the ship's computer hardware."

No one looked surprised since Gia had apparently relayed the same information to all eight of them.

Sam said, "We don't have long before we become the focus of attention here. I'm more than a little surprised we haven't already." It was then that he noticed the three Silarians had armed themselves. Thick belts were angled across Flout, Gromel, and Jarpin's broad, bare chests. Odd-looking pistols were holstered high beneath one arm.

They looked about nervously. Jarpin said, "Are you stupid? Gia is purposely steering the crew away from us...but ugly humans and a furry beast will most certainly be noticed."

Stroking his cheeks, Carl said, "Hey, who you calling furry? I'll have you know, I shaved recently."

The Silarian pilots looked back at Carl with deadpan expressions.

Running somewhere, six Silarian crew members chose that moment to notice them. First one, then two, then all six stopped in mid-stride. Now open-mouthed, they stared back at them, uncertain what they had encountered.

Sam raised his M4, squeezed the trigger, and mowed them down where they stood. Bloodied and as dead as dead can be, their bodies lay still on the deck.

The three Silarian pilots went rigid, transfixed by what had just happened. Spinning on Sam, their expressions of shock now turned to anger. All three placed a hand on the butt of their pistols.

Sam said, "Don't forget why you came here. To destroy our world. To kill close to eight billion humans. So how about you save your righteous indignation for someone who gives a shit?"

Cypress maneuvered himself in between human and Silarian pilots. "Let's not turn on each other now. We need to remember, Geo-Mind played a part in all of this. He is our true enemy here. Gia has regained a slight foothold in her battle with Geo-Mind...so the use of NanoGuns should be our preferred weapon of choice."

Sam looked at Jarpin. "If we're going to commandeer this ship, we'll need to take the ship's bridge. Can you get us there?"

With obvious reluctance, the Silarian nodded. Turning away, he said, "Stay close; we won't wait for you." The three Silarians hurried off.

Eyeing the human pilots, Sam tapped at the NanoGun affixed to the muzzle of his own M4. "Let's do this." He headed off in the same direction Flout, Gromel, and Jarpin had gone.

Hurrying down one passageway after another, Teddy was the first to mistakenly fire actual rounds from his M4 instead of mentally triggering his NanoGun. Two unsuspecting aliens, pushing a hover cart, were dead before hitting the deck. The gun reports were partially dwarfed by the still-constant loud klaxon alarm blaring overhead; still, Sam was concerned with the noise.

"Crap! Sorry…" Teddy said, looking angry at himself.

Sam waved off the apology. Since Silarian crew members, at least up till then, had been unarmed, their contingent of eight was not being confronted. Even armed, the humans were being looked upon more with confusion than outright hostility. It made sense; probably never had there been alien beings tromping about their ship like this.

They kept moving, and with every crew member encounter, a bright red dot would appear somewhere on their exposed flesh. Usually their forehead.

Jarpin, taking point, had a commanding voice, and with every crew member confrontation, he ordered them to, "Clear the way! Stay clear of the prisoners!"

Sam, Carl, Ivan, and Teddy were doing their best to look humbled and defeated. And while keeping their heads lowered, their eyes were constantly searching for their next target.

They entered a wider corridor, one with long horizontal windows on either side, allowing for views out to space and surrounding fleet assets. Under his breath, Sam heard Gromel say, "Armed security team up ahead. Eight, no, nine of them."

ZIP ZIP ZIP ZIP. Multiple energy bolts were suddenly filling the air. The jig was up. Sam dove for cover, as did his three human compatriots. Flout, on the other hand, hadn't moved fast enough and took a shot to his chest. He took a step, staggered, and keeled over.

Sam caught sight of Teddy. He was just ducking behind a protruding bulkhead. Glancing around nervously, his eyes leveled on the fallen alien. Teddy, taking hold of his necklace, his cross, with his right hand, began quietly praying. "May his soul and the souls of all the faithful departed, through the mercy of God, rest in peace. Amen."

Ivan crouched behind Teddy and said, "Why you pray like that? That is like giving overcoat to dead. It does no good."

"You will not disrespect my faith again. Do you understand?"

Annoyed, Sam said, "Knock it off, you two, now!"

Carl, taking cover behind a vertical support girder, yelled, "Hey, Jarpin, sorry if you still have objections, but I'm sure as hell going to be shooting back!"

Sam was already doing just that. Conscious that his M4's mag was just about spent, he was being more judicious with each shot. He heard Gia's voice in his head. *Use your NanoGun, Sam. Much less latency now.*

"Less latency?" he repeated aloud, not completely understanding her meaning. But he did as suggested and was soon targeting the opposition down the corridor with bright red laser dots instead of bullets. The others of the team were doing the same, Silarian pilots included.

The effects weren't instantaneous. The enemy security team continued to fire on them. Ivan took a grazing shot to a shoulder while an eruption of sparks from a too-close-for-comfort strike hit the bulkhead just above Sam's head. Then, the incoming energy bolts started to subside. Within a few seconds, all was quiet once more.

Cypress hurried from his position at the rear, scurried past them, and soon was evaluating the condition of the downed Silarian security team. He said, "They're all unconscious. Amend that; these two are dead. The six others are taking a nap."

Sam queried the stream, but it hadn't been updated yet. "Gia… how long will they—"

I would expect they will remain unconscious for a minimum of thirty minutes. And once they wake up, as I'm sure you remember, they won't be in any condition to cause much trouble.

And you, Gia? How's it going with the Geo-Mind?

It's going. I believe I now have the upper hand. You need to move though. Take the bridge if you can. I still do not have full control of most ship-wide systems. One more thing. Geo-Mind is attempting to reestablish communications with the fleet. If he is successful, this gunship, without hesitation, will be destroyed.

Chapter 44

Schriever Space Force Base, Colorado Springs, Colorado
Harper Godard

Harper engaged the lowering of the Landa-Craft's stairs, signaling the general that they would be joining him soon. His armed squad, though, had yet to topple over from the nanites. She glanced back to see that Julian, who was nodding, was immersed in an inner conversation—undoubtedly with Gia. The elder scientist looked both energized as well as enthused. He was most definitely in his element.

"What are you doing?" she asked.

It was as if she'd awoken him from a daydream. It took a moment for his eyes to focus on her. "Speaking with Gia. She is busy, and I'm sometimes finding myself waiting for her responses for several minutes."

"What specifically are you—"

"The cloaking technology. What science the Silarians are using to make this ship not only invisible, but able to go undetected by tracking sensors."

Harper considered opening herself up to the stream but decided against the painful cost of doing so. Obviously, the price was worth it to Julian. They needed to kill some time. She said, "Explain it to me."

"Ah…okay. The cloaking works by what I am going to call 'differential warping' or 'differential lensing.' Essentially, it's like a magnetic cyclotron field. One that lenses the light from all sides of, say this Landa-Craft ship, by spinning it around the ship and then sending it back out in the direction that it should have been going initially. That's a simplified analogy, of course."

She nodded, thinking he was finished. But he wasn't.

"In astronomy, effects like gravitational lensing allow us to see things that are directly behind a massive black hole. Why? Because of the ways that the light warps around the black hole. But with the Silarians' application, instead of using gravitational mass to influence the way that the light moves from behind, ships are all equipped with a rotational electromagnet that can spin up and cause both visible light and reflection-based signals to simply warp around the ship and continue on their original path. The light travels around as if it were in a cyclotron, warping it in at the appropriate angle."

Julian pointed a finger to something outside. Harper saw that all but the last two of the military operators had fallen to the roof. The other two were wavering. And then they, too, were down on the roof—out cold. The general looked perplexed and a little nervous. He looked at the Landa-Craft and then back at the roof access door.

"We better get out there before he bolts," she said.

By the time Harper had stepped down onto the roof, General McGovern had retreated all the way back to the access door.

"General? It's okay. I'm Harper Godard…the one you spoke to. And this is Julian Humblecut."

"What have you done to my men?" he asked accusingly.

"They're fine. I promise. They will wake up shortly. Twenty-four minutes, to be exact."

She felt a tug on her sleeve. She looked back at Julian. "What?"

He pointed upward. "Overwatch drones."

She saw them. Three black and ominous-looking hovering RQ-16 T-Hawk drones.

The general said, "Those have the latest tracking technology, young lady. Now I'm going to ask you to raise your hands and place them behind your heads. Do it now! You make one move other than that, and you will be fired upon!"

Slowly, she began raising her hands, as did Julian. She looked back at the Landa-Craft, which was mere feet behind them. "Julian...Cloaking...that magnetic cyclotron field you were talking about. How far out from the ship can it be deployed?"

The scientist looked momentarily confused. "Well, as you know, it was capable of cloaking the attached mini-gun—"

"Julian!"

"Ten feet, approximately," he said, flustered.

"Hands behind your heads!" the general barked. All three aerial drones moved closer.

She mentally asked Gia to cloak both the Landa-Craft, as well as the two of them.

Harper wasn't sure anything had changed until she saw General McGovern's confused expression. Now, looking around, he took a step forward. Putting his fingers to one ear, he said, "Tell me you have a bead on the assailants!"

Harper rolled her eyes. "General, I told you, we're not assailants. You're wasting time. And let me ask you this. If I can make myself, Julian, and a spacecraft disappear, don't you think I could have harmed you already if I wanted to?"

He stared back, but was not looking in the right direction. His cheeks had turned red, clearly angry now. "And my men? You've made it clear you are dangerous."

"Check them yourself. They're sleeping."

Tentatively, the general approached the closest of the fallen men, reached down, and checked for a pulse in his neck. With two fingers, he splayed open an eye. Standing, he seemed somewhat more placated. "This man seems to be okay. I suppose."

Harper said, "When your team awakens, they will be confused and will suffer from a terrible headache."

"Okay," he said.

"They will also be…changed."

"In what way?" the general responded with a wary voice.

Harper took several steps closer to the man, mentally keeping track of her distance away from the Landa-Craft. Closer to him now, she saw that the man was probably about sixty. Close to six feet tall, barrel chested, he was in relatively good shape. Although mostly covered by his cap, his hair was salt-and-pepper gray. His tanned face was deeply lined from spending too much time in the sun—exposed to the elements. But what was most noticeable were his eyes, so light a shade of blue they looked almost transparent.

She said, "There is no way to tell you, to explain everything, in a sentence or two."

"You better start talking, missy, because those fully armed drones will start shooting. Things are about to get really hostile."

She doubted that, considering the friendlies lying about the rooftop. One of the downed operators stirred and groaned. Mc-Govern quickly moved to him, knelt, and placed a hand on his shoulder. Harper heard the general ask how he was doing.

"Matheney…you all right?"

"Uh…I'm okay. Head hurts. Feel like I might ralph."

The others were now rousting. A few sat up. All of them were rubbing their heads.

McGovern looked up in the direction of the invisible Landa-Craft. "How long will they be like this?"

"An hour or so. But they will continuously be getting better. But, General, they will never be the same."

"What is that supposed to mean?"

"It means they, each of them, have been infused with nanites. Right now, they are being spoken to by a powerful AI—I guess *presence* is the appropriate term. She is explaining to them what is happening. What happened to Castle Rock, and what the Silarians, the aliens, are doing here in our solar system."

McGovern looked dubious until he saw that the nearest man to him was nodding his head. "Yes, sir…it's true. All of what she just said. And it's fucking blowing my mind, sir…Excuse the language, sir."

"Why have you done this? Why are you here now…talking to me?"

At that moment, Harper was feeling overwhelmed. It was too much to explain; far better to just show. For the general in particular, she didn't want to impose the nanites—Gia, the stream—onto him without his compliance. That was important.

He did look genuinely open to hearing more, though. She needed to put this in a way a military man would best understand it. "General, the simplest way for me to explain this is…well, this is a war of combatting AIs. Artificial intelligences."

"I know what an AI is."

So, Harper briefly explained everything about the Silarians, the world of Naru, and the evolution of the Geo-Mind. She described what was happening to Earth, what terra-displacement was, and who—what—Gia was…

"Let's say I believe what you are saying. What does that have to do with what you just did to my men here?"

"First of all, I'm sorry."

"Sorry?"

"I wish I could have gotten individual permission to do what I did. In any event, now, like Julian and I, they have been infused with nanites."

One by one, the operators were getting to their feet. Most still looked unsteady, but no worse for wear other than that. Matheney said, "General…what she's saying is true. It's all true."

"Well, of course you're going to say that. You've been…brainwashed."

"It's not like that, sir," Matheney said, looking at his fellow operators. He looked at Harper, even though she was still invisible. "You're going to have to donut him. He's as cantankerous and stubborn as anyone I've ever met. Just know, if you're looking to sway him…to convince him to voluntarily—"

It was Julian who raised his NanoGun. Harper saw the bright red dot appear on the general's forehead. Before she could say stop or slap Julian's arm away, General McGovern had been donutted. He dropped to the roof like a sack of hammers.

Surprised, she saw that the men around him, *his men,* were all smiling. And in that moment, once more, Harper considered the possibility Gia might be just as dangerous as the Geo-Mind. *Is this how it all starts? Should it be so easy to conquer the minds of the unsuspecting?*

She continued to look down at the now-sleeping four-star general. Would he be capable of doing what needed to be done next? Preparing a nation, a world, for interstellar war?

Gia said, *He better be…*

Chapter 45

Plum Creek Golf Course, Castle Rock, Colorado
Lester Price

Silarian Clash-Trooper robots continued to trudge around the police Humvee that Lester and Luna were hiding beneath. *ZIP! ZIP! ZIP!...ZIP! ZIP!*

From Lester's limited perspective, the mechanical warriors seemed to be firing into already-dead bodies. It occurred to him that the robots' diminished sensors, such as those for detecting bio-readings, were the reason. Gia had mentioned she'd been partially successful infiltrating the robot minds. Checking, Lester saw that the stream had yet to be updated with the information, but undoubtedly, she was battling for dominance with Geo-Mind on an individual robot-by-robot basis. Lester did see that she was being taxed to her very limits, not only here, but with the other teams, including the one up in space.

Suddenly, her voice was in his head, sounding hurried and preoccupied. *There are eight others of your team still alive. You were not the only ones to have taken refuge beneath a vehicle. I have implanted the belief that there is insufficient space for anyone to hide in such a way.*

And the teams at the Douglas County Fairgrounds and Butterfield

Crossing Park? he asked.

Both teams have fared better than yours, Lester. Currently, both are in active combat situations. Scott and his Attack Stinger have evened the playing field somewhat.

He heard, more than saw, the Clash-Troopers were now moving off down the golf course, heading north. *Tell me, Gia…how can we possibly defeat them? Not one of them was taken down by our gunfire.*

Two nearly simultaneous explosions occurred in the direction of the departing Clash-Troopers. Lester and Luna looked at each other quizzically. He said aloud, "What the hell was that, Gia? What just happened?"

Her voice was weak and feathery…*Used their weapons.*

Luna's brow knitted. "She sounds exhausted. Whatever she just did must have taken a lot out of her."

"That's her problem…we have our own. Let's get moving." Lester scurried out from under the mostly demolished Humvee and hurried off toward the smoldering robots some fifty yards away.

He heard Luna laboring to keep up behind him, "Don't you want to check on the other survivors?"

He ignored the question. Without viable weapons, they were all dead anyway. He slowed as he approached the two metal forms lying prone within the grass encircled bunker of the seventh hole. Surprisingly, both bots looked pretty much intact—with one exception. Both of their heads were missing. He saw a scattering of metal fragments, still-smoldering shrapnel rising up from the scorched sand. *Remind me to never piss you off, Gia.*

He had to pry mechanical fingers from the weapon. A weapon, the stream informed him, whose name translated into Ender-5. Hefting it up as he stood, Lester felt the thing's substantial weight. It was the same rust color as the robot and looked to be a kind of alien energy Gatling gun with multiple barrels. The trigger mechanism was odd in the fact that it was thumb activated versus forefinger.

He stole a glance down at the headless robot and saw that its mechanical hand wasn't all that dissimilar to that of a Silarian, or human, for that matter. Raising the heavy weapon, he sighted it upon a small grouping of golf carts some thirty yards away on an elevated cart path. As he thumbed the trigger, the recoil of the weapon nearly put him on his ass. *ZIP! ZIP! ZIP! ZIP! ZIP!*

All three carts were eviscerated. Fragmented aluminum, fiber-glass, and black rubber shards rained down onto the cement path. Lester's lips curled into a smile. "Fuckin' A."

He turned to see Luna. She was staring at the carnage. The eight others were now hurrying up the links toward them. He saw four of them were white guys wearing CR Police uniforms, two Latino firemen wearing similar blue uniforms, another guy who was a bit puny, wearing civilian clothes, and…a mailman? The guy was big and ridiculous-looking in his sky-blue button-down top and gray shorts. He could easily have been an NFL defensive tackle. The sun reflected off his muscular, coffee-colored thighs, and bulging biceps stretched the fabric of his short sleeves. He moved before anyone else could, snatching up the other Ender-5.

"I'm Greg," came his no-nonsense baritone.

The others started to introduce themselves, but Lester waved them off. "I don't care who you are. All I care about is taking out more of these Clash-Troopers."

"Then we best get to it," Greg said.

Lester eyed the big man. "Let me make myself perfectly clear. This is my operation, mailman. You have a problem with that, you can go it alone. But you'll be leaving that weapon here." Lester swayed the muzzle of his big gun toward Greg.

Greg's eyes narrowed as he contemplated Lester's less-than-friendly tone.

Lester saw the man's eyes tracking the lengths of his tattooed arms.

He shrugged. "Guess you should lead on then. You got any kind of a plan?"

"Yeah, I got a plan," he said. "What? You think I'm stupid?"

"Honestly? I don't know what you are," Greg said.

That brought a chuckle from Lester. *At least the guy has balls.* "First, we need to find a way to get more of these." Lester gave his Ender-5 a couple of pats.

One of the two firemen, "B. Tripe" embossed on a gold name tag, said, "We could try to split them up. I don't see the ten of us prevailing over a hundred robots."

"I like it…good thinking, Tripe," Lester said.

Luna pursed her lips. "I guess that means we'll have to split up as well. We have two robot guns…so two groups?"

"We'll need to catch them first. There are a few more carts up ahead," Lester said and headed off at a fast jog.

The armada of four golf carts was humming along at ten miles per hour. Being two seaters, they'd had to unstrap golf bags from the back of the carts to make room for everyone. Lester and Luna's cart, with two in the back, was in the lead.

"There!" she said, pointing a finger toward a development of two-story condos several hundred yards away. "It's called The Links at Plum Creek." The robots had come to a stop while maintaining a three single-file formation within a greenbelt area.

"What are they doing?" Lester said, applying pressure to the brake pedal.

The other carts pulled in behind, Greg's coming up last—his weight probably being a factor.

Lester queried the stream. Apparently, there was a simple seven-foot-tall iron community fence and gate holding up their progress. Gia was able to "suggest" to the robots that the gate was more substantial, insurmountable, in fact. But this would not hold them up for long. The robots weren't completely daft; soon they would push through it.

Lester nodded. "This is an opportunity. Greg and you, skinny guy, whatever your name is, take your two carts and try to get out there to the front entrance to that greenbelt. You'll need to go around on the street. Me and Tripe will pull closer here at the back. Nobody does anything until that line of robots has moved forward and is trapped between those series of condo buildings. We'll be the Indian savages, taking out the stupid cowboys trapped within the canyon."

Luna gave him a sideways glance. "You know that's more than a little politically incorrect, right?"

"What is?"

"Never mind," she said, jutting her chin in the direction of the robots. "Looks like your cowboys are on the move again."

Lester stayed still until he saw the last of the Clash-Troopers march over the toppled fence and disappear into the dark shadows of the condo buildings. Moments later, he heard the echoes of clanging metal off the building walls.

Luna said, "I think there's a kiddie playground in there…you know, swing set, jungle gym, a slide, that sort of thing. Robots must be tromping over it all."

Greg and skinny white guy powered their carts off to the right to where there was an intersecting street. Lester stepped on the accelerator of his own cart. Within a minute, he was approaching the entrance to the greenbelt. Already out of view, the robots were making good progress; dammit, he hoped Greg, with his slow cart, would make it around to the front in time.

"I don't think we can wait for them," Tripe said from the other cart, as if reading his mind.

"You sure?" Luna said. "I've been on that path. It's pretty long. Goes on and on all through the development. It'll take them a while to weave through those buildings."

Lester didn't want to wait any longer; he'd never been very patient—why start now? Putting the pedal to the metal, the little cart leaped forward. Immediately, a flurry of curse words erupted from behind. Lester had almost forgotten there were two others, facing backward, sitting behind. He laughed. "Hold on, everybody. Things are about to get bumpy."

Chapter 46

Relentless Thrust, somewhere aft…
Sam Dale

Flout wasn't dead. The Silarian pilot was now sitting up and rubbing at a patch of blackened, charred flesh on the right side of his chest. While Jarpin was kneeling next to him, examining the wound, Sam and the others huddled around them.

Carl said, "That shot would have killed a human. Suspect our tactical vests wouldn't have made much difference."

Flout wheezed, struggling to take in full breaths.

"What wrong with him?" Ivan asked.

Cypress looked up at the impatient-sounding Slav. "He's just been shot in the heart. Maybe you can show a little compassion."

"Do they not have two? Two hearts?" Ivan retorted with a shrug.

"*Pfft*, Ivan, you have two feet; would you be fine losing one of them?" Teddy snapped back.

Ivan made an exasperated face. "You are too stupid. I have already pushed you into my pocket. Now, you will wait for me to let you out—"

"Enough, you two!" Sam barked. "Jarpin, can Flout continue on? Should we move him to, I don't know…the ship's sick bay?" He watched as Jarpin pulled a small device, maybe a vial, from his holster belt. As he pressed it to Flout's neck, it made a slight hissing noise.

"That won't be necessary," Jarpin said. "I have injected him with medical nanites. But he will need time…several hours, at least, before his heart has been fully healed."

Ivan rolled his eyes. "No, we cannot wait here several hours. That is stupid idea."

Sam suddenly missed the cohesive band of brothers he'd served with during his last tour. "Can it, Ivan," he said.

Cypress had moved several yards down the passageway. His head raised higher and his ears perked, he said, "We need to move…fast."

Jarpin and Gromel helped Flout to his feet. Gasping for breath, he said, "I'm fine…let's just go." He shoved helping hands away and staggered forward.

Jarpin gestured to the Silarians' security team, lying prone on the deck. "Suggest you swap those archaic projectile Earth weapons you have for our lighter and far more powerful Ender-2s."

Ivan scoffed. "I will keep this one, the M4. I know this weapon like my own shoes."

But Sam, Carl, and Teddy didn't hesitate, each snatching up one of the alien weapons. Once Sam transferred his NanoGun device from the muzzle of his M4 to the Ender weapon, the others followed suit. After re-duct-taping, each slung their M4s over their shoulders.

Sam used the stream to quickly get up to speed on the odd-looking weapon's operation. He discovered it was one of a series of Silarian Ender-type energy weapons; the Ender-5, being the most powerful of the series, was a beast of an energy weapon, multi-barreled, its plasma bolts capable of melting steel. Sam could see how the Ender-2 was a far better choice here in space.

"Fine!" Ivan huffed, acting like a petulant child. He roughly unslung his M4, grabbed up an Ender-2, and got to work transferring the NanoGun device.

"Let's do a quick comms check," Sam said. Thanks to Walter and his team, each of them had been equipped with the same AN/PRC-148 Multiband Inter/Intra Team Radio, or MBITR. But it didn't take long to realize that all transmit/receive radio frequencies were being blocked.

"This is bullshit," Ivan spat.

"We'll work it out," Sam said while mentally putting the problem in Gia's hands. "Let's move."

Sam took point, and almost immediately, they'd come to an intersecting passageway. He turned left. At present, the stream was being less helpful than he wanted. Apparently, sometimes there was latency in how quickly it was getting updated. *Talk to me, Gia… Will this passageway get us to the bridge? What about other security forces?*

Understand, Sam, most of the crew on board are not trained combatants; they are unarmed support personnel. You're clear for a while. Stay as quiet as possible.

He was about to ask why when the overhead klaxon suddenly went silent. Now, the sounds of their footfalls seemed as loud as banging pans together.

Gia said, *Give me a moment…I can now provide you with a ship's layout.*

And then there it was. Sam heard Carl say, "Now we're talking!"

Gia had provided him, apparently all of them, with what was akin to a HUD projection—one that was now hovering, translucent, in front of their eyes. She had also provided them with the *natural knowing* of how to interface with the HUD, turning it on and off, moving things around and zooming. That and something else that was just as impressive—messaging capability.

"Not bad, Gia," Sam said. "You know, the look of this messaging interface…well, it looks like—"

It is, Sam. I'm quite busy, so I used the messaging app code taken from your iPhone. Audio comms is coming, too, eventually.

He scanned the available contacts names on the left side of the HUD display. His eyes hesitated, seeing Harper Godard there. He was tempted to reach out to her. But texting her now would be one distraction he could ill afford.

He flipped back to the blueprint layout of the gunship. From even moments before, things had been added, updated by Gia and the stream. Now there were icon representations of crew personnel in red, as well as their own icons, in blue, where they were currently holed up within a relatively far aft passageway. He'd thought that they'd made further progress than this. But it now made more sense why they'd had relatively few encounters with crew members. The passageways they had, mostly arbitrarily, taken thus far were on the third deck, and were out of the way. Compartments here were designated primarily as maintenance and cargo hold bays. According to the blueprint, the hatch door entrance to their right led to some kind of oversized trash incineration unit. Come to think of it, there was an acrid taint to the air.

"Smells like burnt toast," Carl mentioned, confirming Sam's own observation.

You need to keep moving, Sam. I am doing my best at disrupting corridor sensors, but Geo-Mind and Relentless Thrust's security matrix are honing in on your whereabouts as we speak. You need to get to the bridge.

He scanned the diagram and saw that the bridge was at the bow—the opposite end of the craft. The gunship had five primary decks and one stubby four-foot-high sub-deck—a deck designed for always-on-the-move delivery/supply bots. As if Gia had used a highlighter pen, there was now a yellow trail for Sam's team to follow—and it was anything but a straight line. They'd be traversing multiple decks and would even be backtracking at some points along the way. *So be it.*

One more thing, Sam. You'll be navigating a route that is as void of combatants as possible. With that said, anyone you do come into contact with, it's best you donut them. Keep in mind, you may be observed and not know it. There would be little I could do to curtail those crew members from directing security forces to you.

"I thought your little HUD icons could tell us where everyone is."

It is 92 percent accurate. As I said, I'm currently busy fighting the ship's Geo-Mind…and I need to get back to doing just that. Go now. Hurry.

Entering confined and dangerous spaces, clearing rooms of insurgents, these were the kinds of things Sam was far too accustomed to doing. But he'd thought that part of his life was in the rear-view mirror.

They moved at a slower pace than he would have liked. Flout had fallen back, his breathing still labored. With their Ender-2s held high, stocks pressed to their cheeks, they followed Gia's yellow trail.

"Advancing enemy squad!" Carl said way too loud.

They had progressed halfway down a narrow passageway, a passageway that looked virtually identical to the previous one and the one before that. Sam attempted to push through a hatch door off to his left. There were no obvious doorknobs or latches. The hatch door didn't budge. Both Gia and the stream offered no help. He looked back. "Jarpin, how does one gain entry into these compartments?"

Jarpin shouldered Sam out of the way and made a waving hand motion in front of the hatch. Immediately, it separated into four quadrants, sliding away into the top left and right corners and bottom left and right corners into the threshold. Moving to enter, Jarpin placed a restraining hand on Sam's shoulder. "We go in there, and you'll be sealing our fate. This is the only way in or out."

Sam rechecked his HUD blueprint and chided himself for being so impetuous. Jarpin was right. This was the entrance to a bathroom facility—one, ultimately, they would have died within.

"We keep moving," Sam said, retaking point.

Carl said, "Good, because dying in an alien shitter is not my idea of a cool Butch and Sundance last stand."

Ignoring the ginger-haired jokester, Sam said, "Stay close to the bulkheads." He slowed momentarily; something was nagging at him. *What was it?*

There were ten red icons rapidly progressing within an adjacent, intersecting corridor. The same corridor the highlighted yellow trail would have them following next.

Sam and Jarpin went down to one knee while the others halted, taking up positions behind. It was only then that Sam realized what was off, what it was that was nagging at him. Cypress. Where the hell was the dog? A quick glance behind confirmed what he already knew. Cypress was no longer among the team.

Rechecking his HUD, Sam saw no other yellow icons anywhere. Then again, had Cypress ever been included as one of the yellow icons? No, he was certain now he hadn't been. Sam had never seen more than seven of the yellow dots on his HUD. *Fuck!*

In the distance, the Silarian security team suddenly came around the corner and didn't hesitate to engage. Once more, bright plasma bolts filled the air. Immediately, Sam felt a stab of white-hot pain emanating out from his sternum. Great. *Three seconds into the melee, and I've already been shot.* He fumbled with his Ender-2, already having forgotten how to fire the damn thing. Remembering he was supposed to use his thumb and not his forefinger, he began returning fire. The passageway was long and narrow, and the enemy was still forty yards away. His chest felt like it was on fire...*So why aren't I dead?*

Gia was talking to him...*Carl was incorrect. Your US Army–issue combat vests are minimally sufficient to hinder Ender-2 level plasma fire. So, take it from me, you're not dying, Sam.*

Jarpin and Gromel had taken it upon themselves to advance. Not just advance, but running, spinning, diving, and coming up shooting, both progressing further down the passageway, doing their own brand of tactical acrobatics. Sam and the others had to target their return fire more carefully now, not wanting to take out two of their own.

"That's some kind of badass combat shit," Carl commented.

"Glad they're on our side," Teddy said.

Sam didn't disagree. "Come on; let's stay close behind them! Move!"

Up ahead, four green forms were lying prone upon the deck. Moving past them, Sam was glad to see they were security team members—not Jarpin or Gromel. The rest of them had apparently fallen back around another bend up ahead. Jarpin and Gromel looked to be held up there, taking turns momentarily popping around the corner, trading fire with the enemy.

Joining them, Sam used his HUD to evaluate the situation within that adjacent corridor. Sure enough, the remaining security team had taken up positions. Two were behind support girders, two were more out in the open but hugging the bulkheads, and two were hiding farther back within open hatchway doorways. He also saw that several other security teams, each larger than this one, had been deployed—fortunately, they seemed to be going off in divergent directions. He smiled; that had to be Gia doing her misdirecting the opposition thing.

And then Sam saw it. The not red and not blue but purple HUD icon. It was on the move. *Cypress...is that you?*

Cypress didn't have a smartphone, and subsequently, there wasn't an associated messaging contact name within the directory. Upon closer inspection, he saw that Cypress was not progressing within any of the upper decks; instead, he was down within that lower sub-deck with all the maintenance bots. *Clever, but why?*

Sam said, "Jarpin, how about you two fall back for a while, stay back with Flout?"

The Silarian looked back at him with irritation.

Sam, like the other three humans, had been outfitted with both grenades and flashbangs. He wasn't sure if grenades had enough explosive force to breach a hull. But chancing the decompressing of a spacecraft…that couldn't be a good idea. Flashbangs, on the other hand…This situation screamed for such an option. Sam, Teddy, Carl, and Ivan swapped positions with the Silarian pilot duo.

He said, "These are M84s, set with a two-second charge delay. I throw…we wait for the bang, and—"

"And we donut the greenie-meanies on the other side. Yes, we know the drill," Carl said with a smirk.

"Ready?" Sam said.

Everyone, including the three Silarian pilots, nodded.

Chapter 47

The Links at Plum Creek, Castle Rock, Colorado
Lester Price

Lester had expected the Clash-Troopers to maintain their formation, to keep marching forward within the greenbelt confines between condo buildings. To act like good little robot soldiers. But that was not what was happening. It was a harsh reminder that they weren't here to simply march; they were here to kill humans.

The ground shook from the reverberations of so many Ender-5s coming alive all at once. Sure, the robots were marching, but they were fully capable of chewing gum and walking at the same time. Or, more accurately in this case, decimating building structures while marching. Lester contemplated how many sheltering civilians had already been massacred. The once attractive Spanish-style buildings with their pitched adobe tiled roofs were now literally falling in upon themselves, flattening into great mounds of rubble. The air had become so dense with dust and debris, it was nearly impossible to see the still-advancing company of robots up ahead.

"Come on! You need to get us in closer, Lester!" Luna yelled above the racket. She brought the heavy alien-tech weapon down from her shoulder. "I can't see what I'm shooting at! Get us in closer, NOW! People are dying!"

Lester shot back his own enraged expression. While maneuvering around another mound of rubble, he said, "Golf carts are made for smooth-cut grass, not this, not fucking four-wheeling!"

Luna grumbled something undecipherable as she took to manning the Ender-5 once more, taking shots into the murky upheaval. "I don't even know what I'm shooting at!" she bellowed.

Seething, Lester gritted his teeth. He had had just about enough of this one. One more...one more word, and he was going to throw her chubby ass right out of the cart.

Luna suddenly dropped the Ender-5 and screamed, bringing both hands to her mouth. Off in the distance, two more condominium buildings were falling in upon themselves; all the while the robot weapons fire continued on, uninterrupted.

Abruptly, Lester was forced to stop. The pathway was now impassable, totally obscured by the remnants of eviscerated buildings.

Sobbing, Luna said, "I can continue on foot."

Before she could step out, Lester raised a hand. "Wait...just hold on a damn second. I'm being messaged."

He'd had little time to converse with Gia or open himself up to the stream. Suddenly seeing the HUD projection floating there before his eyes had at first startled him, then somewhat confused him. The translucent display was so similar to his Xbox *Call of Duty* game, he'd momentarily gotten confused. "Shit! Warn me next time, Gia. Thought I was having a flashback or something." A messaging app window was now front and center, and he saw that he had been texted by someone named Scott. "Who the fuck is Scott?"

"The Silarian pilot!" Luna said, glaring at him. "Are you stupid?"

It took a beat for Lester to remember the guy. "Oh yeah...that guy. Wait...You're seeing this too? The HUD display?"

She ignored his question. "He's asking us to fall back. He's about to—"

"Yeah, yeah, I can read," Lester said. He saw that Luna was already replying to this Scott alien.

LUNA: Roger that, Scott…We will fall back now.

Lester said, "I should message Greg…tell him to stand down—"

"Try to keep up. I already did that," she said, offering back a belligerent smirk.

He threw the golf cart into reverse. Looking backward over his shoulder, he had a problem seeing around the two backward-facing passengers. *Lot of help these two have been.* "Mother of God! Move your damn heads!"

Startled, his hands jerked to the left, causing the cart to swerve from the path. The noise was ear-shattering—as if a 747 had just swooped down directly overhead. Both Lester and Luna had instinctively ducked down. Then Lester saw it, the Attack Stinger descending over the greenbelt. Abruptly, plasma fire erupted from the alien craft. The Stinger slowed, hovered, then began to move backward, seemingly defying the principles of physics, or at the very least, the principles of aerodynamics.

Luna leaned farther out her side of the cart, craning her neck to see better. She stood atop the cart's running board.

"What do you see?"

The two useless police passengers, seated behind, suddenly jumped out so they, too, could see what was happening.

Luna said, "It's hard to tell. Some of the robots are down. But some of the robots are returning fire too." She looked up. "Oh cool…the Stinger is shielded. There are, like, sparks going off all around it."

Lester saw there was an incoming message from Greg. He hurried to accept it before Luna could.

GREG: Still here at the far end of the greenbelt.
Robots are getting slagged.

Above them, the Attack Stinger suddenly exploded into a ginormous ball of fire. Luna dove back inside the cart while torn-apart pieces of the wrecked craft rained down upon the cart's flimsy fiberglass roof. Lester slid lower in his seat while wrapping his arms around his head. He squeezed his eyes shut and waited for this shitstorm to come to an end—one way or another.

It was a full minute before Lester opened his eyes. Another minute before he scooted up higher in his seat and looked around. He saw that Luna was out of the cart and attending to one of the injured policemen.

The weapons fire had ceased. He didn't see any movement coming from the greenbelt. But there were no feelings of jubilation or victory. Instead, with dread, he watched as the last of the distant condo buildings crumbled down upon itself. How many hundreds, maybe thousands, of people had died here today? Was this what was in store for all of Earth?

He continued to stare, not really focusing on anything.

Movement.

He leaned forward, squinting his eyes. *What is that?*

It emerged from the still-swirling cloud of debris before them. Dust had made it almost indistinguishable from its surroundings. It was as if he was watching a *Terminator* movie, and there he was, the Arnold Schwarzenegger killer robot, striding purposefully right toward them. "No fucking way…"

He looked around the cart for the Ender-5. "Where's the gun?!"

Luna didn't answer, preoccupied playing Florence Nightingale. He caught sight of it—one end propped up on the passenger-side running board. He scooted over to the passenger seat, grabbed up the weapon, and jumped from the cart.

"What are you doing—" Luna's words trailed off, having seen

what was now advancing on them.

Lester strode forward, deliberately matching the mechanical cadence of the Clash-Trooper. With no more than thirty yards between them, he used his thumb to engage the weapon, making an instant direct hit to the robot's chest. The mechanical killer staggered backward but soon continued, seemingly undaunted. Instinctively, Lester jutted to his right, and by doing so, avoided the quick return fire. Lester sprinted, then dodged left and right without letting up with his own barrage of plasma fire. But all that jumping around was affecting his aim. Exasperated, he watched as bright energy bolts were going everywhere but at the damn robot.

The first plasma bolt to strike Lester took off his left earlobe. It was so quick, so unexpected, at first, he barely noticed it. The second plasma bolt struck the barrel of his Ender-5, a strike that took two fingers from Lester's left gun barrel–supporting hand. It took a moment. Lester shrieked; it was a kind of agony far beyond anything he had ever experienced. He was on his knees now and watching through tear-filled eyes the unrelenting Terminator trudging forward. In that moment, Lester wondered if this thing intended to take him apart piece by piece, an earlobe, a couple of fingers...what was next? His Johnson?

The Clash-Trooper robot was almost upon him now. At this distance, he could make out no less than ten blackened scorch marks cleaved into chest and torso areas. Lester smiled. "So I did get you a few times...motherfucker."

The robot came to an abrupt stop. Its head pivoted to face Lester. Two beady eyes, shark-like, maintained a steady, lifeless gaze.

Lester was aware the others had come close. The girl and the cops. No one made any sudden movements. "What can I do, Lester?" Luna said in a voice so quiet he almost missed it.

Ignoring her, he raised his weapon for the last time. But he found his left hand had become mostly unresponsive. He found steadying the heavy weapon one-handed was impossible. Lester lowered the gun back down. *Whatever.*

He stared at the business end of the robot's Ender-5. Rising waves of heat distorted the air around the multiple muzzle configuration.

"What are you waiting for, Tin Man?" Lester chided.

The heart-stopping three plasma blasts did not come from the robot's weapon.

At some point over the last few moments, Greg had rolled up within his remarkably quiet electric golf cart. From the comfort of the driver's seat, he fired his Ender-5.

Chapter 48

Relentless Thrust, Sub-Deck 1
Cypress Mag Nuel

He ran as fast as he could within the constrained, low-ceilinged passageway. There had been numerous delays along this bi-directional, ten-lane transit artery. The problem was several of the slower-moving bots. Traffic jams were an annoyance he hadn't counted on. This passageway was, in fact, designed to be a kind of sub-deck robot superhighway. Here, the noise level was beyond anything he had ever encountered. Hundreds of the automated trains, engines pulling ten to fifteen trolley cars behind, each of which was stacked with anything and everything imaginable—powder packets for food replicators, replacement filter components for the environmental scrubbers, organic sewage eliminator cakes. Cypress was using all the lanes, often having to dart across oncoming traffic to pass slower-moving trolleys.

He knew by now Sam would have noticed his absence. And sure, he felt bad about that. Or maybe it was just Rocko who felt bad about that. What did it matter who was to blame? Recently, Cypress had given up trying to differentiate between his two entities. Perhaps they had merged—or perhaps continuing to think about it would only drive him completely insane.

But he had to do this. If not for himself, for beautiful, kind Orlanda. She was waiting for him, after all. They were to be joined during Naru's coming southern solstice. Together they would embark on a life together—perhaps spend the next one hundred to one hundred and fifty years building a family, building a legacy.

Gia had made things much easier with the addition of the HUD and ship's diagram. Cypress was confident he would have found the bio-form storage compartment eventually. But now there would be no guesswork. Virtually all fleet warships maintained a stock of ready-to-use bio-form bodies—one for each of the command-level officers. Although Cypress could not recall a Naru fleet going into direct battle with an enemy force, sickness and disease, albeit rare, still did occur. Best to be prepared. Death was not an option.

Panting from his near-constant run down the length of the ship, Cypress suddenly veered right onto what was akin to an off-ramp. He had made it to the forward subsection of the gunship. He scrambled up several steps to where the sub-deck opened up to ten-foot-high ceilings. The temperature was far cooler here. He padded by three large hold storage areas, slowed, and came to a stop in front of a glass hatch door. Inside, he could just make out an undulating mist within the blue-hued compartment. After several unsuccessful tries, he awkwardly stood on hind legs while leaning his front paws upon the glass. *Doing things like this will be so much easier when I'm back within a real body.*

Now for the hard part. Cypress, doing his best to keep his balance, tentatively lifted one of his front paws off the glass. He needed to simulate the same hand gesture a Silarian crew member would make. He tried to make the same kind of swiping motion but only managed to lose his balance, bringing him back down onto all fours. After three more unsuccessful attempts, he contemplated calling it quits.

His ears perked. *Someone is coming.* Determining the footfalls were coming from his right, he quickly moved back in the direction he'd come, disappearing around the corner of the robot off-ramp. Listening, he heard two crew members conversing, then there was the telltale *swoosh* sound of a hatch door opening. Without hesitation, Cypress darted forward, scrambled back up the passageway, and caught sight of two crew members striding into the bio-form chamber.

Following close on their heels, Cypress's tail had just cleared the threshold when the hatch door swooshed shut behind him. He quickly jutted to the right and lowered down to the deck. He forced himself not to pant—not to move. It was noisy in here. Circulating cooling blowers were hard at work. Being this low to the chilly deck, the heavy mist curled and blanketed around him, hopefully obscuring his presence. Perhaps sensing his motion behind them, both crew members had gone ominously quiet. Cypress imagined them having spun around—and with narrowed eyes, they were now scanning the mist-looking for...*something*.

And then they were talking again, their voices obscured by the loud overhead blowers. One of the two must have said something funny because they both laughed. Cypress stayed where he was for what seemed like ten minutes, but it might have been less. After hearing the hatch door open and close again and no more talking, he attempted to stand. Attempted but was unsuccessful. Apparently, his underbelly had adhered to the frigid ice-cold deck. Instinctively, he began to whine. He didn't want to do that; it was an embarrassing sign of weakness. Male Silarians did not whine—not ever. He was growing more and more annoyed with himself for both the whining and his inability to free himself. Finally, with a yelp, Cypress was free. Undoubtedly, a layer of frozen underbelly flesh and fur had been left behind on the deck.

He was no expert when it came to the technological details of transference. But then again, he didn't need to be. The stream would provide what was needed. Opening up to it now, he reviewed the layout of the chamber. The bio-forms were housed farther back and to the left. His movement through the mist was helping clear some of the accumulated mist from the deck. And then he saw them.

Each of the bodies was encased within its own glass coffin-like housing. It wouldn't be uncommon for a ship's commander to come here—to visit with his mindless, awaiting bio-form. And these bio-forms were several levels more advanced than, say, a lowly Landa-Craft pilot's bio-form would have been provided. These were custom made, of course. An exact DNA duplicate body, but one that was young, say twenty-five years of age, and physically beautiful.

It was otherworldly in here. Cypress moved between one towering row after another. The housings were stacked five high on each side of him, the flanking bodies lit with that same heavenly bluish glow.

Frost-colored but still reflective gold name tags provided the identities and military ranks for each enclosed body. Cypress came to a stop in front of the housing of *Relentless Thrust's* skipper, "Captain Droke Tolli Mahn."

Cypress didn't sit, although he certainly wanted to. Instead, he paced back and forth upon the frigid deck. The naked body before him was at eye level. With handsome facial features, it had well-defined chest, arm, and leg musculature. Black and thick, a mane of braided hair coiled like a snake upon one shoulder. This was indeed a splendid Silarian bio-form. Transferring his consciousness into this body would be breaking every statutory Naru law, not to mention Silarian society's strict code of ethics that easily went back a millennium. But weren't these extraordinary times? Times that called for extraordinary, remarkable decision-making?

294

Cypress wished the bio-form's eyes were open. He knew there was nothing going on within this form's mind…still, it would be nice to better see who he would be joining with. To proceed, he needed nothing more than what was already contained within the little black box affixed to his collar—the Geo-Mind implant, sensory comms implant, and most importantly, his essence implant.

He heard himself whining. *Stop it…stop that right now!* he inwardly chided. And then it occurred to him. Why hadn't it occurred to him before…before now? Rocko would not be making the transfer along with him. This would be goodbye. Sure, a part of him was relieved. Dogs and proud Silarians were not meant to share consciousness. There was no denying the canine Rocko was beyond annoying. Was so…animalistic. *Best to rid myself of this unintelligent beast and be done with it.*

"I'm ready, Gia…You will assist me with the process…just as the Geo-Mind would have?"

Of course, Cypress. If you are certain this is what you want.

Cypress didn't want to think about Sam. Had purposely avoided doing so until now. But if not now, when? Strange how he felt as if he belonged to the human. That certainly was Rocko's influence. A true Silarian belonged to no one.

Gia was speaking to him, the inner voice in his head now somehow softer, quieter. *This bio-form will be a fine match for you. It is equipped with all the necessary implants. I have started the process…initialized the necessary pre-download routine. Cypress…one thing. The canine Rocko will not survive this transference. I am truly sorry about this. The dog has bonded with you to the point he would not withstand the separation. Shall I proceed?*

Chapter 49

Schriever Space Force Base, Colorado Springs, Colorado
Harper Godard

There was little to be done until General McGovern awoke. Harper watched as the highly trained operators meandered about the rooftop—each deep within a mental conversation with Gia. They were learning about the stream, experiencing new mind-altering capabilities they hadn't known existed some thirty minutes prior.

Were they being brainwashed? Absolutely. She let out a resigned breath and repeated what was becoming a common mantra for her. "The lesser of two evils…"

She found Julian sitting at the edge of the rooftop, childlike, his dangling legs swinging to and fro in the open air. He was deep in conversation—his face animated. Right now, he was looking less the brilliant inventor and scientist and more like a love-struck teenager.

"Julian?"

He blinked several times before looking up at her. Using a saluting hand to shield his eyes from the overhead sun, he gazed up at her with a perplexed expression. "Harper! There is so much to learn. So much to experience."

"That's nice. And I'm glad you're, um, enjoying all this. But I need you here with me now. Even if it's just to bounce ideas off each other."

She saw the disappointment in his eyes. *Damn, pulling himself away from her is actually painful for the man.* She looked out to the military base below. There were men and women down there, and more than a few were looking back up at her. This was not a situation that could continue much longer. Without looking back at Julian, she spoke directly to Gia. *I want you to knock it off. You understand what I'm saying?*

Please…What is it you are referring to, Harper…How can I make things right for you?

Tightening fingers into white-knuckled fists, she let the silence hang several moments. She was conversing with the most, or second-most, intelligent presence in the known universe. Really, she was going to play coy?

I suppose you have a point, Gia said. But in my own defense, there are complications that come with…an AI becoming self-aware. And one of those complications is loneliness.

That surprised her. Was such a thing even possible? But before Harper could ruminate any further on that, an expanding dark shadow appeared next to her own, there upon the rooftop. She spun to see General McGovern standing far too close to her, and he didn't look happy. What she noticed next, within that same fleeting moment, was that the flap of his black leather holster was opened—that and his gun was missing. He moved with impressive speed for an old guy. Before she could say or do anything, he had a fistful of her hair and was yanking her head back—then she felt the muzzle of his semiautomatic pistol pressing hard into the soft flesh beneath her chin.

It occurred to her then that donutting a person was not a precise science. It didn't work the same with everybody. McGovern's lips, his hot breath, came close to her left ear. "I should put a bullet in your head right now."

"I suggest you take a step away before doing that. No sense both of us being killed."

She queried Gia, *What happened?*

Perhaps you can keep him talking. I do believe this one just needs a little more time.

And if you're wrong?

Gia didn't answer.

"I don't know what you've done to my men…turning them into…mindless zombies. Or what your true intentions are here, but I'm not going to fall victim to it. Not me! Do you understand!?"

"I understand. And I don't blame you for being upset."

"Upset?!"

Harper reached back, trying to relieve some of the downward force being exerted on her ponytail. "Uh…maybe that wasn't the right word…more than upset. Much more than upset."

She was now aware of the others on the rooftop. In her peripheral vision, she saw Julian, up on his feet now, and the general's men. Each of them was pointing his respective M4 carbine at her. No, not at her. Him.

She heard Gia's voice in her head, *Three…two…one*

First, the gun at her chin dropped away. Then, the general himself dropped away. She gulped in a breath before looking down at General McGovern at her feet. His arms and legs splayed, extended, his body making an oversized X upon the rooftop.

He showed signs he was coming around another twenty minutes later. Harper was seated cross-legged in front of him. The fireteam was milling about, several of which were on their comms, doing their best to pacify the rank and file that everything was under control up here on the rooftop.

McGovern's eyes fluttered open. He cleared his throat. "Okay."

"That's it? That's all you have to say for yourself, General?"

He moved to sit up, needing help from one of his men, a P. Jackson.

Harper was not convinced the general was indeed donutted—although all indications from Gia suggested he had been.

Sitting all the way up, he nodded a thanks to Jackson. Now, making eye contact with Harper, he said, "Will my head ever stop hurting like this?"

"Eventually, it will change. Depending on how often and how deep you go into the stream."

He used both hands to rub at his temples.

"You're the first I've seen who's received two doses. First when Julian over there pinged you, then again when I pinged you."

The general looked confused at that.

"When you pulled back on my ponytail and I reached back, I donutted you at that time."

He nodded. "You have to know; I was born skeptical. None of this is coming easy for me. What you're asking me to do—"

"I'm not asking you to do anything, General. We all have our place in this now. We either believe Gia, take in the information presented and go with it, or we don't. Or you don't."

"Don't be naive, young lady…Gia is biased," he said flatly.

"Sure. More than a little. But I, personally, have chosen to believe her. That's mainly because the enemy, the Silarians, are here and doing exactly what she said they would do. Killing humans. So doing nothing is not an option for me."

He let out a breath and slowly nodded, and then he slowly shook his head.

"What? What has you so indecisive?"

"It's just that…well, it's daunting. What you're—what Gia is asking of me. To lead a what? A rebellion for a world that has yet to realize what is coming?"

She didn't respond to that.

As General McGovern got to his feet, Jackson was there to steady him. He stood and looked out toward the surrounding Schriever Space Force Base. "How the hell do I go about commanding an operation like this?" He'd asked the question to no one in particular.

"Actually…you don't, General," Julian interjected.

He turned to look at the older, wild-haired scientist. Then, with an arched eyebrow, his expression changed. Now looking at Harper, he'd just come to the realization, either having been informed by Gia, or he'd delved into the stream. "Well, I'll be a son of a bitch…I report to you."

Chapter 50

Relentless Thrust, Somewhere nearing mid-ship
Sam Dale

It had become all too clear that Flout, Gromel, and Jarpin had had military training far and above any of the onboard security forces they'd come across thus far within Relentless Thrust. Sure, the three of them were Attack Stinger pilots, which set them apart. But there was more to it than that. And while the stream was not giving up much more of the details, Gia had been more than willing to spill the beans.

Back when they were under the influence of the Geo-Mind, over military careers that spanned decades, they had proven themselves over and over again in combat. Subsequently, they had been given more and more access to the stream. Something Sam understood, now having been given higher access to it himself. Flout, Gromel, and Jarpin were among a select group of several thousand Silarian combatants, those who'd been designated as *Orlicon Strass,* which translated to God Warriors. An elite fighting group that spanned multiple Silarian military forces. And as grueling as the physical training had been, the mental training aspects via the stream had been even more zealous and taxing.

Sam had seen the way they moved. The way they fought together—fought as one. As a military leader, Sam appreciated that kind of dedication to one another, to their lifework. He wondered how they now, individually and collectively, reconciled their allegiance to Naru—a misled world hellbent on causing such unspeakable destruction and death within the galaxy.

Gia's voice presented itself into his thoughts. *Sam, their commitment is to Orlicon Strass, something that supersedes even being Silarian on Naru…*

He wondered, at least for himself, if anything could ever supersede his dedication to Earth, to his humanity.

They'd taken care to donut rather than shoot when at all possible. Sam had fallen back while the others of his team continued with renewed confidence. "Talk to me, Gia…how goes your battle with the ship's Geo-Mind?"

It was almost a full minute before Gia replied.

The word harrowing *comes to mind, Sam. There was a reason I had selected this particular warship for us to attack. It's among the smallest vessels within the fleet, and one with the poorest overall crew morale rating. Relentless Thrust continues to be the target of countless jokes within the fleet. The captain has been demoted twice and will be forced into early retirement come the end of this deployment.*

They were now proceeding forward within Deck 3, the ship's widest central corridor. Moving ever closer toward the bow, the bridge, it was becoming evident the ship's armed security forces had chosen that forward quadrant to make their last stand.

"Let's hold up a second," Sam said. There was HUD activity, red icons flowing forward from multiple decks, within multiple passageways. That's interesting…One particular group of red icons was moving in the opposite direction—and in a more regimented fashion. Twenty-five in total, they were also on Deck 3. It was strange how they had yet to deviate from their slow, methodical, aft ward advance. The space between icons never varied. *Shit! Gia, you didn't tell me there were Clash-Trooper bots on board this ship.*

I apologize, Sam…Having been deactivated within long-term hold storage, the robots have just recently been reactivated. Clever…they are using robots because their AIs cannot be so easily infiltrated by my actions.

Up till now, between using their NanoGuns and Ender-2 weapons upon the security forces and those few crew members not hiding within their cabins, they'd managed to maintain the upper hand. Clearly, the ship's officers had been ill-prepared for such an assault. The ad hoc security teams sent to defend the ship had been remarkably ineffectual. Sam had been in real battles, real combat, and thus far, these had been little more than skirmishes. But robot Clash-Troopers would be a completely different animal. Nano-Guns would be useless, and Ender-2s…well, not much better.

One thing, Sam. Just as I am battling with the ship's central Geo-Mind AI, I am also attempting to breach crew members' Geo-Mind implants. Battling with Geo-Mind for their mind-space, so to speak. A human idiom comes to mind. I may have bitten off more than I can chew…

Sam was reminded that Cypress was facing a similar dilemma, sharing mind-space with Rocko. He was also reminded that Cypress had run off, and that was a growing concern in itself.

He looked up to see that his three-human, three-Silarian tactical team was closely watching him—concern in their eyes.

With a smirk, Ivan said, "You should know about these robots." He shook his head, "Seems we're heading into storm with shit."

Sam leveled a steely gaze upon the man.

Jarpin broke the silence. "We continue. We finish what we came here to do."

Ready to proceed, the six of them turned to head forward.

"Wait," Sam said.

They turned back.

He said, "How do the robots know we're the enemy?"

Teddy said, "Because…we are the enemy?"

"No. I mean, specifically. Is it the way we look? Are they using their sensors in some way? We already know that Geo-Mind does not occupy their robot minds. But do they have access to the stream?"

Sam was already querying the stream, as he was sure the others were as well.

Jarpin shrugged. "They do not have access to the stream. They are networked to each other, to the ship's master AI…"

"Gia was wrong," Sam said with a smile. "She can help with this particular problem."

No, Sam…I wasn't wrong. To have the ability to transmit new directives to the robots would require me to have control over the ship's Master AI and to have defeated the Geo-Mind, something that has yet to be accomplished. Still, your idea does have merit. I will keep you posted on my progress.

"Hold on. There must be something, some vulnerability, an Achilles heel we haven't considered yet."

As I have stated, Ender-2 plasma fire will have little effect on hardened metal—

"We still have our M4s strapped on our backs," he interjected. "Would a well-placed bullet round make any kind of difference?"

Well…these are a legacy model of Clash-Trooper…and the stream indicates there was what you would call a kind of factory recall notice. It was for an upgrade that has yet to be performed. Ah yes, interesting…

"Gia, they'll be here in, like, minutes."

Not just a well-placed round, Sam. It would have to be a perfectly placed round. And not just done once, but with twenty-five Clash-Troopers.

Sam looked up to see the others had been privy to these latest Gia revelations.

Teddy crossed himself. "If it is God's will…"

"Put a sock in it, Teddy," Carl said. "I'm a pretty good shot."

Ivan guffawed. "Gia says perfect shot, not pretty good shot."

"Fine. I can be a great shot…if the conditions are right."

"Hold on, Carl," Sam said. "Gia…where…what exactly does this perfectly placed round need to target?"

There was an issue with the manufacturing process. Specifically, to the robot's head. It is within the upper head area, where a robot's brain, its AI circuitry, is housed. Much as a human's or Silarian's brain is housed. Externally, there is a visual indentation; here, there is a thinning of the composite material wall. A perfectly placed bullet round could find its way into that robot brain.

"Let me take a wild guess," Carl said. "That indentation you're referring to…is right between those two beady robot eyes."

Chapter 51

Relentless Thrust, primary mess hall
Sam Dale

His HUD indicated that in between the approaching squad of Clash-Trooper robots and his team was the ship's primary mess hall. The expansive crew member dining facility was accessible via Deck 3's primary corridor through a double-wide hatch door.

They sprinted to reach the mess hall before the robots. On approach, only the right-side hatch door swooshed open. Jarpin held up. "Perhaps we should not all go inside…split our forces—"

"That is the last thing we want," Sam said. "We split up, and the robots will split up. No. We need every last one of those machines to come in after us here."

Jarpin saw the logic in Sam's strategy and grunted approval.

There was nothing appetizing about the dingy-looking mess hall with its pitted and stained gray-painted walls.

Carl was the first to comment on the smell. "The word rancid comes to mind." He looked at Gromel, "What the hell do you people eat, anyway? Some kind of fish, I'm guessing?"

"Enough, Carl. This is your show. Where do you need to set up?"

Carl looked about the rectangular compartment. There were

several dozen oversized plastic-looking integrated table-chair assemblies, each bolted to the deck. The compartment was approximately forty feet wide by twenty-five feet deep, with a bank of food replicator units lining the right-side wall. Opposite the entrance was a long cafeteria-style counter with an obscured galley kitchen off behind that. To Sam, the facility didn't seem all that different from any number of mess halls he'd chowed at within US Army military bases.

"I want to be set up at eye level exactly perpendicular to that entrance. And I need to be prone, lying belly-down, sniper-style."

Ivan nodded. "We need to build platform."

Teddy shook his head. "Already thought of that. Those tables are bolted down—"

Ivan used his bulk and put his weight into a heavy-footed kick of the nearest table/chair assembly. All four table legs tore free from the deck; the table flipped over and slid several feet. In Ivan's characteristic broken English, he said, "We stack two flimsy tables. Build platform for idiot Carl."

Sam had been keeping a close eye on his HUD and the methodical advance of the Clash-Trooper robots. Carl was situated upon his stacked table platform. The rest of them were hunkered down low within the ship's galley. Their backs were up against the same bulkhead that separated the galley from the dining hall. There was sure to be substantial incoming enemy weapons fire. It had been Flout's idea to stack several robust kitchen oven appliances in front of Carl's perch, giving him at least some protection from incoming fire.

"Sixty seconds!" Sam yelled. He felt guilty sitting there on his ass while Carl was out there taking all the risks. He glanced over at the others—they, too, were seated on the deck with their backs to the bulkhead. "This doesn't feel right," he said. Springing forward and keeping low, he hurried out of the galley and took up a kneeling position behind the serving counter. He knew the half-high wall would provide far less protection than that bulkhead, but hiding just wasn't his style. He might not be at the right angle or be a crack shot like Carl, but at least he'd be doing something other than hiding.

Five forms took up positions next to him, Jarpin and Ivan to his left, Teddy and Flout to his right. No one said a word.

Out in front of them and several feet higher, Carl said, "I have to take a leak."

"Tough. You can hold it," Sam said.

Ivan said, "You probably won't live that long anyway…and then your dead body can piss itself all it wants."

"Here they come," Sam said, just loud enough for the others to hear.

The deck rumbled beneath them as lockstep footfalls out in the corridor got louder.

Sam thought about Carl there in front of him. Was he really the most qualified here? Was he indeed a crack shot? Sam pursed his lips. *Maybe I should be the one situated up on that stack of tables.* Being an army vet, a Green Beret, he would have been the one most familiar with firing an M4. And he certainly knew the glass—the optics. Carl's M4, as was his own, was equipped with a Trijicon TA31RCO ACOG scope. A badass piece of equipment. A 4× magnification model with a 32 mm objective lens (4 × 32). The scope was specially designed with ballistic-compensating reticles that were fiber-optic and tritium illuminated. Hell, at this short distance, any one of them probably could make the necessary shot.

BANG!

Startled out of his reverie, Sam looked up at the first of the Clash-Troopers standing at the mess hall's entrance.

"What the fuck?" Carl said, firing a second round. *BANG!*

The robot looked to be disabled but didn't crumple to the deck as expected. With slackened mechanical arms at its side, the muzzle of its Ender-2 pointing toward the deck, it was obviously now a dead bot standing.

Sam sighted through his scope at the magnified area between the bot's two pea-sized eyes. Sure enough, two almost perfectly aligned bullet holes had been perfectly placed. *Good job, Carl.*

The dead bot was suddenly airborne, indiscriminately shoved from behind. Another robot stepped into view.

BANG! BANG!

This time the robot toppled over on its own. And then the other door swooshed open. Two robots stepped into view. *Shit!* But these two didn't stop and wait to be so easily picked off. Rushing into the compartment, Sam didn't hesitate and fired. Having selected single-shot mode, he, and now his entire team, were unleashing a hellfire barrage. The noise was colossal.

White smoke and the acrid smell of cordite soon filled the compartment. Two by two, the robots rushed in with guns blazing. Incoming plasma bolts were leaving glowing red-hot holes within the half wall. Sam was aware of several grazing injuries to one arm and a leg. He kept firing. They all kept firing.

It wasn't Carl's crack shot aim, or even Sam and his team's backup gunfire, that made the difference. It was the ever-growing logjam—the piling up of dead bots. Slowed and stumbling over each other, the Clash-Troopers never really had a chance.

The shooting had ended, but Sam's ears continued to ring. Getting to his feet, he eyed the bots strewn about the compartment, mostly piled two and three high.

Someone coughed.

Looking to his left, he saw that the carnage had not been limited to just robots.

"Oh no…" he said.

Teddy and Flout to his left were dead. Charred plasma strikes to the head on one, to the torso on the other. Turning to his right, he saw Gromel was also dead. Jarpin, still alive, was now the lone *Orlicon Strass.*

Ivan groaned and cursed. He was injured but alive.

Carl climbed down from his rickety tower. He joined Sam at his side and took in the carnage. For once, he was speechless.

Sam let out a weary breath. "So now we are four." Sadness gripped his heart, and it nearly dropped him to the deck. He'd thought he'd left this kind of despair back in Afghanistan. He shook his head; what had he expected? This had always been an impossible mission—a suicide mission.

"Five," came a voice from the entrance to the mess hall.

Startled, Sam looked up. There, upon a particularly tall mound of inert robots, stood a particularly dirty-looking, matted, and oh-so-welcome to see golden retriever.

Cypress said, "What did I miss?"

Earlier, Sam had figured out exactly where Cypress had ventured off to. A cryogenically temperature-controlled compartment within the underbelly of the ship. Clearly, Cypress's intentions were to transfer into an available viable bio-form so he could regain a life as a Silarian being. Sam had not blamed him—would probably have done the same. So now, seeing a dog and not a Silarian standing there like a poor man's Rin Tin Tin perched upon a mound of dead bots…well, that was truly unexpected.

Sam and the dog made eye contact. Cypress said, "Turns out Rocko's not so bad. Thought I might keep things as they are for a while."

Sam's phone began to vibrate. Before answering, he said, "Well, I think you made a wise choice."

He answered the call.

"Is it true?" she said. "Is it really true?"

He was relieved to hear Harper's voice. "Is what true?"

"Don't you pay attention to what's going on around you? Gia did it!"

"I've been a little busy here of late—"

"Yeah, yeah, we've all been busy, Sam. Some of us more than others. And while you've been gallivanting off in space, some of us have been securing the homeland. If you'd open yourself up to the stream once in a while, you'd know that Julian and I did our part. One four-star General McGovern has been donutted and is—"

"Hold on, Harper! What was that about Gia? What did she do?"

Harper hesitated. When she spoke again, her voice was softer. "She did it, Sam. She defeated the Geo-Mind onboard that gunship of yours. Absolutely all aspects of that diabolical AI have been purged. Both within the workings of that ship as well as the minds of the crew. Oh, Sam…the stream…I see it now, what you've been up against. Oh God, you've lost half your team. I'm so sorry."

He took a beat. "Julian?" he asked. He would rather hear any bad news directly from Harper than from Gia or the stream.

"He's right here next to me. He's fine, um, but we need to talk about his burgeoning *relationship* with Gia."

The beginning of a smile pulled at Sam's lips. "Okay. And Lester…what about Luna?"

"Guess Lester was a little shaky at the start, but in the end, the Clash-Troopers were no match for the two of them. Lester lost a couple of fingers and part of an ear. Luna's good. Sam. Gia says Castle Rock is 100 percent Geo-Mind free."

"That's good news, Harper."

She said, "Sam…there are two people that need to talk to you… first, General McGovern, about taking down the isolation zone."

"And the second?"

"Captain Droke Tolli Mahn. He's on the bridge. Apparently, he's ready for you to take command of *Relentless Thrust.*"

"Me?"

"Yeah, you. You're running the show, remember? Look out a window or something; the 23rd Terra-Displacement Fleet…well, it's poised to attack…"

The End of Book 1

Thank you for reading The Fallen Ship—
Rise of the Gia Rebellion

If you enjoyed this book, PLEASE leave a review
on Amazon.com—it really helps!

To be notified the moment all future books are released, including the next installment of The Fallen Ship, please join my mailing list. I hate spam and will never, ever share your information. Jump to this link to sign up:
http://eepurl.com/bs7M9r

The Authors

About Mark Wayne McGinnis

Mark grew up on both coasts, first in Westchester County, New York, then in Westlake Village, California. Mark and his wife Kim now live in Castle Rock, Colorado, with their two dogs, Sammi and Lilly. Mark got his start as a corporate marketing manager and then fell into indie filmmaking—producing/directing the popular Gaia docudrama, Openings—The Search For Harry. For the last nine years, he's been writing full time, and with thirty-four best-selling novels under his belt, he has no plans to slow down. Thanks for being part of his community! Use the links below to jump to Mark's site.

Have a question or want to say hi to Mark? Contact him at *markwaynemcginnis@gmail.com*

Or contact him on his Facebook author's page at *https://www.facebook.com/MarkWayneMcGinnisAuthor/*

About Kim McGinnis

Kim grew up on air force bases in Georgia, the Philippines, Okinawa, and Arizona. After studying theater in college, she moved to LA, where she became a SAG actress and performed in numerous theatrical productions, as well as landing principal roles in several national TV commercials. After Kim met Mark in Southern California, she starred in and produced the docudrama, Openings—The Search for Harry. Kim has extensive marketing experience and currently does all the marketing for their Avenstar Productions publishing business. The Fallen Ship is Kim's first credit as a coauthor.

Have a question or want to say hi to Kim? Contact her at *kimpmcginnis@gmail.com*

Acknowledgments

First and foremost, we (Mark and Kim McGinnis) are grateful to our readers. We'd like to thank Lura Genz (Mark's mother) for her tireless work as our first-phase creative editor and for being a staunch cheerleader of our writing. We'd also like to thank Margarita Martinez for her amazingly detailed line editing work; Sarah Kruger for her creative design and typesetting skills; Gabriel Hannon and Anna Chvyreva for their mind-blowing physics/scientific contributions; Daniel Edelman for his many prereleases, technical reviews, and expert subject matter spitballing; Commander Sam Varela of the Castle Rock Police Department for his expertise in police procedure as it pertains to the city of Castle Rock, CO; and David Daly, for his in-depth military contributions. A heartfelt thank you also goes to Sue Parr, Charles Duell, Stuart Church, Zoraya Vasquez, Lura Fischer, and James Fischer—without their support, this novel would not have been possible. And finally, to our beloved pups Lilly and Sammi, whose unconditional love inspired the character of Cypress/Rocko.

Check out the other available titles by Mark Wayne McGinnis
at the beginning of this book.

Made in the USA
Coppell, TX
01 August 2022

80761128R00177